MW01063134

Montana MYSTERY

JOSIE JADE

MONTANA MYSTERY: RESTING WARRIOR RANCH

Chapter 1

Kate Tilbeck

I played the voicemail again on speaker as I pulled into the parking lot. Because I got what it was saying, and yet I still couldn't wrap my head around it. It was a nurse, calling to tell me that my brother had been brought in to the ER, was alone, and was going into surgery.

This was the last thing I'd expected today. But then again, no one ever really expects to get that phone call, do they?

Terror gripped my chest. The last time I'd gotten a call like this, I'd been too young. It had changed my life, and Brandon's life, forever.

Silently, I begged the universe not to turn my life upside down again today. Please. I couldn't handle it.

Parking took too long. Why were there so many people at the hospital? Shouldn't there be like, emergency parking for people who were in a hurry? *There.* A space near the back. At this point I didn't care, I just needed to get inside.

Thankfully, I was wearing the right shoes to sprint.

The automatic doors weren't opening fast enough for me. Amazing how something so trivial on a good day took an eternity on a bad one.

I shoved the thought to the side. But this time, it didn't want to leave. Part of me had been waiting for this particular call. The fear had been lurking in the shadows for a while. But its arrival didn't bring me relief. Dread was the only thing left.

The emergency room nurse looked up as I ran in, eyebrows raised. This wasn't a town full of running-worthy emergencies. Except for me. Today.

"Brandon Tilbeck," I managed, trying to catch my breath. "I'm his sister."

"Sure. Can I see some ID?" She was already looking him up, though from the call I'd gotten, I was shocked she didn't know who he was. Fumbling with my wallet, I managed to get my driver's license out, though my hands were still shaking with adrenaline.

The nurse nodded. "Down the hall and to the left. He's in room three, and the doctor will meet you there in a few minutes."

"Thanks."

I tried not to run, but I wasn't doing a very good job of it. "Oh my God." The words tumbled out under my breath as I pushed into the room.

Brandon was still as death, and if I hadn't *known* that it was him, there was a chance I wouldn't have recognized him. His face was swollen and bruised. Lip cut, one eye black and puffy. He looked like someone had held him down and used a meat tenderizer on him.

What I could see of his arms wasn't in better condition. Darkening bruises and blood that was dried and not yet cleaned. Were those . . . *bite marks*? Nausea rose in my gut.

"Miss Tilbeck?" I jumped. A doctor stood behind me. He held up a hand. "I apologize. I didn't mean to startle you."

"That's okay." I pressed my hand to my chest, willing my heart to slow down. "Just a bit jumpy and wrapping my head around this."

He nodded. "I can understand that. It's never easy to see a relative in his condition."

"What . . . happened? The message said that he was in surgery?"

"Dr. Godin." He held out his hand, and I shook it. "You mean what caused it? That I can't tell you. He was dropped off outside the emergency room and was barely conscious. There was some internal bleeding that we addressed in surgery. Currently, he's sedated, and I'm afraid that he needs to stay that way. For now."

I sat down, rubbing my hands over my face, trying to take it all in. "Why?"

"He has a concussion. A bad one. His brain might be swelling, and there's no telling what effect that will have. But for now, we need to keep him under so his body—and brain—can rest and heal."

"So he'll be okay?"

The doctor made a face that he quickly covered. "I'd say the chances of a full physical recovery are good. Whatever happened, he got lucky. No broken bones, and with the bleeding addressed, he's out of danger in that way. But like I said, until we can safely wake him, we won't know the state of his mind."

"What's the worst that could happen?" I took a shaky breath.

The doctor looked away, probably deciding whether or not to sugarcoat it. Thankfully, the drop in his shoulders and sigh convinced me he was telling me the truth. All of it. "At the absolute worst? Brain damage, though I'm sorry I can't tell you what form that could take. It could be accompanied by memory loss. There's also a chance for memory loss without cognitive impairment. But," his eyes softened in sympathy, "there isn't a way to predict which way it will go. Brains are funny that way."

"Yeah." I knew all about that, at least. It wasn't the first time I'd been told that someone I cared about might not be themselves when they woke up. "But he will wake up?"

Dr. Godin nodded, folding his hands behind his back. "Yes. Of course I wouldn't be doing my job if I promised you one hundred percent. But right now, I'm confident that he's out of the woods."

Good. That was good.

"Once he's settled a bit more, we'll move him out of the emergency room. And of course, we'll keep you updated."

"Thank you."

"Do you have any questions?" He checked the chart at the end of the bed, glancing through notes. "Anything else I can answer?"

There were a hundred questions running through my mind. Unfortunately, Dr. Godin wasn't the one who could answer them. Only Brandon could do that, and it looked like I wasn't going to be able to talk to him for a while.

He wasn't going to die, at least not yet, and the rest we needed to wait on. "Just one. For the physical injuries, how long do you think he'll have to stay?"

"That I don't know," he said. "Conservatively? A week. Easily more if he doesn't heal quickly."

"Then no, I don't have any more questions."

He slipped the chart back into its place at the end of the bed. "All right. If you have any more, feel free to ask."

"Thank you."

There was no fanfare with his exit. Just a return to the filled silence that defined hospitals. Brandon's heart monitor beeped, low and even. Outside there was the squeak of shoes on floors and the occasional call or overhead announcement. In here, it was way too quiet.

Now that I was over the shock, I noticed more details. The tubes coming out of Brandon's mouth and the ones in his nose, adding oxygen. The drips into his arms and a few other wires that were attached to him in places covered by gown and blankets.

"Brandon, what the hell did you do?" I asked more to the air than my brother, who clearly wasn't talking.

A nurse appeared with a new IV bag and quickly switched it out, flashing a smile at me. "You're his sister?"

"Yeah."

"I'm glad they got ahold of you."

The sentiment made sense, but it didn't *feel* right. Glad you're here to see your baby brother look like he was run over by a semi thirty-seven times. Congrats!

"What's in there?" I asked hesitantly.

"It's keeping him sedated," she said. "We need to—"

"The doctor told me." I cut her off. I couldn't hear someone else say that out loud right now.

She smiled again, but this time it was tighter. "Let us know if you need anything."

Once I was alone again, I melted into the chair and stared at the ceiling.

Was this really happening? Maybe this was the worst stress dream of all time.

I hated the feeling of inevitability to all this. This shadow had been haunting him ever since he'd come back from overseas. The brightness in his eyes was missing and the old habits he'd left to avoid were back in full force.

But he'd been getting better. He'd told me he'd gotten a

job, and there'd been no signs that he was in trouble. Most nights he was home at a decent hour. He was paying his portion of the rent on time. I'd even seen him smile occasionally.

So why this? Why now? What could I have missed and what had Brandon obviously been hiding? The way he looked was too brutal—too vicious—to be some random act of violence.

Still, even with his struggling after deployment, I hadn't expected *this*.

Across the room, a plastic bag sat on another chair. Clothes. I doubted I'd find anything in there, but maybe I could get some idea of what he'd been doing when all of this happened.

I took a deep, steadying breath before I opened the bag. These were not washed clothes. They were stiff with dried blood and tattered from either injuries or perhaps the bites on his arms.

There wasn't much. Nothing that could tell me anything. A wallet. No money, but then Brandon wasn't one to carry cash. Cash got him into trouble, and we'd agreed that he wouldn't. If money was out of sight, it was out of mind.

Nothing in his pants pockets, and I even checked his shoes, though that was unlikely. The jacket was last. His phone was long dead, the screen cracked. And there wasn't much else. Except . . . my fingers brushed a piece of paper in the inside pocket. Nothing fancy, just a torn piece of notebook paper with Brandon's scrawled handwriting.

Noah Scott. And a phone number.

That name sounded familiar. Why? I was sure I'd heard it before.

I grabbed my phone from my pocket and went to Google. With his name and number, it was the first result.

And now I knew why I remembered. He worked at Resting Warrior Ranch. They specialized in helping veterans with PTSD, and when I'd found them, it had seemed like a sign from the universe.

Brandon had been there less than a week when he came back, darker and surlier than ever, claiming it was a joke and that they would never be able to help him. That had been a couple of months ago now.

But then why would he still be carrying around Noah's number? Unless he hadn't really quit. Unless maybe the people at Resting Warrior weren't who they said they were, and that's where Brandon had gotten himself into trouble.

I'd never met them. But if the military men I'd met through Brandon were any indication, then they probably weren't the squeaky-clean men their website claimed they were.

From an image on the ranch's website, Noah looked straight at me. Jet-black hair and blue eyes so dark that they pierced through the screen. It was easy to see how eyes like that could be entrancing . . . or threatening.

Well, I could handle that. And if my brother couldn't be conscious to tell me what the hell happened? Then I was going to talk to someone who could. Maybe that person was Noah Scott. Either way, I was going to find out.

The address for the ranch was a bit of a drive, but it was better than sitting here listening to Brandon breathe. "I'm going to figure this out," I said to his unconscious form. "You're going to be okay."

I shoved his clothes back into the bag, grabbed my keys, and braced myself for war.

Chapter 2

Noah Scott

I braced myself against the sharp gust of wind and the memories that came with it. Along with that surge of emotion and adrenaline, I shoved my hand a little deeper into the fleece of the alpaca in front of me.

"Little cold out here, right, bud?"

He hummed, looking back past my shoulder toward the rest of the ranch. Probably saw one of the horses.

"Noah Scott is standing in the cold with an alpaca" was never a sentence I'd thought I'd say, but here I was, forcing anxiety through my fingertips and keeping my feet planted on the ground instead of heading inside.

Strictly speaking, I didn't need to force myself to be out here, but I wanted to try it for a bit longer. The days I had appointments with Dr. Rayne, Resting Warrior's therapist of choice, always left me raw. And she would probably tell me to take it easy. But when I was the rawest, it felt like an opportunity to face things head-on.

Winter was always harder for me, with the cold and the blowing wind that threw me back into darkness and pain. But this year it was hitting me harder than it had in a long time. Why? It took a lot for me to admit that I was struggling, but I was.

Being with the animals helped though. Even if it meant that I had to brave standing in the cold. I loved all the alpacas here, but this one and I had formed a special bond. Part of it was that intangible thing that happened with animals. Sometimes you just connected.

The other part of it was that he was named Al Pacacino, and no matter how many times I heard it, that made me smile.

Resting Warrior Ranch was the only place I could imagine being in to help with everything I was going through. After all, it's what this place was designed for. A peaceful place for people who struggled with PTSD of all types, though retired military members were our most common client. The seven of us that ran the ranch were all former SEALs, all with our own trauma. We'd created the place that *we* needed first, with a goal to help others as well.

The animals, like the one in front me, were here to help our clients, and to be trained as therapy animals. Once they were trained, if they were deemed ready, we placed horses, dogs, and alpacas with therapy facilities and practices all over the country.

A gust of wind came down from the north, and I grit my teeth. Phantom pains rippled across my chest and legs. Closing my eyes, I forced my hand to move, stroking down Al's neck. I wasn't there. The memory was a long time ago. I was safe.

My mind flipped to the grounding exercises. What could I hear? The wind and the shuffle of animals. Far away, the slamming of a car door. What could I smell? The distinctive cold, snowy smell of Montana in the winter. Straw. The less fun smells associated with caring for animals.

It was enough to root me in the present. For now.

"As much as I'd like to stand here all day," I said, patting Al's neck, "got to take care of everyone else too."

He hummed again as I turned to leave, hauling in a large, cleansing breath. Especially with the cold, there was even more than usual to do. On top of regular feeding and cleaning, cold weather in Montana meant double-checking the heaters in all the animals' spaces and making sure that the water wasn't frozen over.

I dragged a hand over my face. Then there were the kittens. Salem and Garfield. They were probably tearing down every curtain in my house right this very second.

Generally, we didn't take on cats at Resting Warrior. It wasn't that cats couldn't be trained, but the training was much more individualized and dependent on the long-term owner of the animal. But the rescue had been full of cats, and I couldn't bear to let the pair go to the county shelter. They wouldn't have lasted.

If I could end the practice of kill shelters, I would. But I was only one man. Instead, I now had a pair of adorable little monsters wrecking my house for the next couple of months. At least.

Snow crunched under my boots on the way to the stables. I focused on the sound to keep myself in the present. Things were jumping at the edges of my vision, and that was never a good sign.

Wait . . .

It wasn't in my mind. There was someone on my periphery. Someone I didn't recognize. A woman. Even from this distance it was clear she was stunning. Hair such a pale blond that it rivaled the color of the snow. She was moving with fervent energy, clearly searching for something.

Frankly, she looked a little like a hectic whirlwind in the way she was storming down the road.

Someone we didn't know on the property was usually a cause for concern. But this wasn't. Not because women couldn't be dangerous, but because I felt nothing. Like the other men that lived and worked here, I'd learned over time to sense danger.

Those instincts had saved my life more than once. They were the reason that I was standing here at all. And this woman, whoever she was, wasn't a danger. Not physically, at least. But why was she here?

I was nearly at the stables, so I moved quickly, hiding behind a corner of the building where I could observe her. It must have been her car door I'd heard slamming earlier.

The real question was, why hadn't she gone straight into the main lodge? Most people new to the property stopped there automatically. Big building, the first thing you encountered. It often triggered that instinctual authority that made everyone assume it was where you went for answers. They weren't wrong.

So either this woman wasn't the typical person who came to Resting Warrior, or she was already familiar with us and was looking for something specific. I was betting on the latter.

As she explored, I moved with her, keeping myself hidden. Another reason I didn't think she was a threat. If she had some kind of underhanded agenda, she ought to have more awareness of her surroundings and who could be watching.

She was still a fair ways away, walking past the resident cabins. Not knocking on any doors yet, but with the determination in her step, I wasn't putting anything past her. Something about the way she was moving, kicking up snow behind her with the force of her steps, made me smile.

When she made her way toward the stables, it was time to stop hiding. As amusing as it was, she was farther into the ranch than someone should be before we knew their reason for being here. Resting Warrior was a sanctuary for both humans and animals, and that meant that we had to keep it sacred.

I stepped out from my hiding place and held up a hand in greeting. "Hi there. Can I help you?"

She froze, startled. For a second I thought she might bolt like a rabbit, but she caught herself and stilled. She pulled herself together and found her courage. The closer I got, the easier she was to read. Her beauty became that much clearer as well.

Her gaze took in all of me as she stood her ground. "You're Noah Scott?"

"I am." I wasn't afraid to reveal my identity. All of ours were public. At least our faces were. Jude kept the majority of our details private. If someone went looking for me, a name and a face were all they got. "You have me at a disadvantage."

"My name is Kate Tilbeck," she said. There was rage in her face now. "You should know who I am now."

Tilbeck. A couple of months back we'd had someone staying on the property named Tilbeck. "Brandon," I said. "He's your . . ."

"He's my brother." Her face was both livid and expectant. But right now, even instincts like mine couldn't put together what it was she wanted.

When I didn't immediately respond, she seemed even angrier. "Do you know what happened?"

I paused. "I'm sorry, Miss Tilbeck, but I haven't seen

your brother since he stayed here a couple of months ago. Did he say otherwise?"

Her face fell for a second before the anger and strength returned. "Call me Kate. And no, he's not exactly capable of speaking right now." She pulled out a worn scrap of paper. "I found this in his things."

I recognized the piece of paper once she handed it to me. Brandon had written down my name and number—at my insistence—on the day that he'd left. He'd never used it. "Is he all right?"

Kate just glared. What did she think I should know? "No," she said finally. "No, he's not all right. He's in the hospital, beaten all to hell. Unconscious because they have to let the swelling go down in his brain before he can even have a *chance* to wake up, and your number is the only thing that was in his clothes that points in any direction."

My eyebrows rose up into my hair. That wasn't what I'd expected. "I'm sorry to hear that."

"So you had nothing to do with it?"

I shook my head. "I'm sorry. The last time I saw Brandon was the morning he left the property. When I gave him my number." I held up the piece of paper. "He only wrote my number down because I insisted. Honestly, I kind of expected him to throw it out the window as soon as he passed through the gate because he seemed less than interested."

Kate covered her face with her hands. A shudder ran through her, and I didn't think it had anything to do with the fact that we were standing outside in late winter.

"You didn't go to the lodge looking for me." It wasn't a question.

"There weren't any cars," she said with a shrug. "Didn't feel like spending time banging on a door if no one was home."

I laughed softly. Not at her or her predicament, but her tenacity. I had no doubt that she was going to find out what happened to her brother. That fact alone made me want to help her.

"Despite the lack of cars, I'm sure someone is there. Would you be okay with going there to talk? It's warmer, and you can tell me more in detail what you know."

"Well, if you're not the reason he's in trouble, I'm not even sure why I'm here."

So that was what happened. She'd found my number, and her adrenaline and fear had driven her toward the only possible target she could see: us. Now that all of the adrenaline had run out, she was lost. We'd helped people for less. At the very least we could get her warm and listen to her story. Sometimes that was all a person needed.

"Well, we have a kitchen with the best baked goods you'll ever find and some really good coffee. Come sit for a bit and get warm."

"Yeah, okay."

She was still vibrating with energy, nervous and angry and desperate. And yet she seemed fragile, wrapping her arms around herself as we walked. I pulled out my phone and dialed Daniel.

He picked up immediately. "Yeah?"

"Who's at the lodge?"

"Right now? Liam and I."

"Whoever else is on site, get them over there right now."

"Why?" His voice sharpened. "What's going on?"

I glanced at Kate, who was walking a little faster than me, eyes intent on the ground. "Not sure yet, but we have a visitor, and there's something we need to talk about."

"That's vague."

"Intentionally."

14

Daniel made a sound. "Oh. They're right there. Okay. I think a few others are around. I'll bring them in."

"We'll be there shortly." I ended the call and lengthened my stride to catch up with her. "Long drive for you?" I asked.

"It's not so bad. I'm used to driving. And if I'm honest, I don't remember most of it."

Made sense, given why she was here.

We were walking up the steps of the lodge when she stopped and turned to me. "I know that you don't have anything to do with this. But will you help me? I don't know what to do here."

I smiled. "Tell me what you know, and I'll see what I can do."

Kate nodded once, stoic. Like she understood that it was the most I could promise right now. "Okay."

Chapter 3

Noah

Daniel never ceased to surprise me. He saw Kate and brought everyone through the back into the security office instead of surrounding her with a bunch of men. That was who he was—always anticipating the needs of others before they knew it. It was one of the reasons that we looked to him.

Instead, I got her story and then left her with a steaming cup of tea by the fire while we were meant to discuss it.

Liam was the last to arrive. As usual. He burst in like a bomb. "Winter is supposed to be the slow season. What the hell is with all the urgency?"

About two seconds after he stopped speaking, he absorbed the tone of the room. "Okay, so I'm guessing this wasn't a joke."

"Do I ever call you in on an emergency and have it be a joke?" Daniel sighed.

Where Daniel was calm and anticipated needs, Liam was chaos and often saw the needs after he plowed straight through them.

Liam held up his hands in surrender. "I'm here. What's going on?"

"Brandon Tilbeck," I said.

"The kid who bolted after a few days?"

I nodded. "That's the one."

"What about him? Did he come back?"

This was the part that they'd been waiting for. "Not exactly. His sister is here and wants to know if we had anything to do with the fact that he's currently in the hospital, beaten to within an inch of his life."

"What?" Grant sucked in a breath. "Why would she think that?"

"She's grasping," I said. "Desperate. He also had my name and number in his pocket. Scribbled on a paper I sent with him before he left here."

Daniel was sharp and focused now. "What's his condition?"

"No broken bones. There was some internal bleeding and he underwent surgery for it. According to the doctor, he'll make a full physical recovery. But his head got battered up good, so they're not sure what's going on with his brain yet."

Silence followed. We'd all had our share of hospital stays, and the pain Brandon was experiencing wasn't unfamiliar to us.

"So, he's unconscious," I said. "They don't know when they'll be able to fully wake him up."

"Well, shit," Liam said, after I'd told them everything. "That's not ideal."

"You don't say?" I rolled my eyes.

Daniel leaned forward, elbows on his knees. "It's

certainly not great from an optics perspective. To be clear, that's not what I'm concerned with right now, but it's worth mentioning."

It was. People's lives were always more valuable than optics. But no one would come here if they thought they were going to end up at the hospital and in a coma. "Yeah."

Lucas was leaning against the wall, arms crossed. "I didn't interact with the kid much. He wasn't here long enough."

"No." I shook my head. "I think he was here for four days. He left the day after his first meeting with Rayne. Probably would have left without us knowing if I hadn't gone to check on him. That, ultimately, is why Kate is here. I made him write down my name and number, assuming he'd throw it away. It was in his jacket."

Jude turned in his chair. "Think he was saving it for something?"

"More likely he stuck it in his pocket and forgot about it," I countered.

Grant sighed, leaning on the table. "Well, it's not like we were going to lock him on the property. He didn't want to be here, so he left. Simple enough."

"Of course," Daniel said. "We can't help people who don't want it. But I can't help but feel—"

"Responsible?" I huffed a laugh. "You and me both."

"What would you have done?" Lucas pinned me with a stare, but it was an honest question. "You didn't put him in the hospital."

I shook my head. "I don't know. Maybe I could have reached out and seen if he was really okay. I had his contact information."

"We all had it," Jude said. "If you're guilty, then so are the rest of us."

"I know. But he'd seen some shit. He didn't have to tell me that. I could see it in his eyes. Brandon looked like—" I cut myself off before I could fully let the thought out. On top of struggling with my flashbacks, this was icing on the bullshit cake I was going to have to eat today. Finally I found the words. "He looked like me after I came back."

No one commented on that. Thankfully.

"Do you think he was held?" Jude asked.

"I don't know. I never asked. It didn't feel like it was my business." We didn't ask those who came to Resting Warrior to share their stories. If they shared, we would listen. But trauma was personal, and prying it out of someone caused more harm than good. There was no getting around that.

If Brandon had been taken by the enemy while deployed, I understood the pain in his mind more than most.

"If Rayne thought he'd been a danger to himself or someone else, she would have said something to Charlie. As far as I know, she didn't," Jude continued.

That was a good point, and it made me feel more confident Brandon was a victim in all of this, but if we were going to look into this, we had no choice but to look at it from every angle.

Letting my head droop for a moment, I took a breath. "There's one more thing. I don't like to think about the possibility, but there is one. And this is not something we mention in front of Kate, got it?"

They all nodded their agreement.

"Kate said Brandon had what looked like bite marks on his arms."

I felt the cool shift that flowed through the room as they all processed the information. Over the last few months, rumors had popped up about fights. Nothing to really go on, but consistently enough that we believed there was some truth to it, even if it was exaggerated.

"What are you thinking?" Daniel asked.

With a sigh, I sank into a chair. "I hate that I am, but if they were dog bites, and with him leaving so quickly, I have to wonder if he was only here to scope out the dogs. Or maybe someone forced him to come here to do just that."

Grant winced. "I hope not."

"I hope not too," I said. "But it's a possibility."

"There's not much that we can do if it's all happening in Missoula," Daniel pointed out.

He was right. Missoula wasn't far. A couple hours. Better when the weather was good and there wasn't any snow. But even that was too far to conduct a true investigation. Things like this were often underground and required a flexibility and freedom of movement that distance wouldn't allow.

"No, I agree," I said. "But I can't let it go without at least doing some checking."

Daniel nodded. "I'd feel better if you did."

"Watch out though," Liam said.

"Why?"

He grinned. "The last time a woman stumbled into the lodge in trouble, she moved in and never left."

All of us looked at Lucas and he laughed. "You're not wrong. No regrets though."

No, I didn't imagine he would have any. Watching Lucas and Evelyn fall in love had been like watching everything I'd ever wanted, but never had. They fit together perfectly, and whether that was because of a bond through shared trauma or they'd just gotten lucky, it didn't matter. They were happy, and it was great to see.

Almost everyone was happier now. My brothers-in-arms had been falling one by one. And they . . . weren't wrong. There were some similarities here that made me chuckle.

Not at Kate, just at the situation. I wasn't blind. Kate was beautiful. When we'd come inside and she'd told me about everything more in depth, I'd gotten a chance to look at her. *Really* look. Her eyes were a blue that was unique, almost violet. With her pale hair, she was striking.

It wasn't a factor in my wanting to help her and, through her, Brandon. I would have done it anyway. But it wasn't like I was going to be able to ignore the fact that the woman was gorgeous.

"So," Liam continued. "Are we getting a new member of the family?"

"I've known her for a grand total of thirty minutes. So maybe you're skipping a few steps there."

He shrugged. "I think Lucas was in love with Evelyn in five minutes, so stranger things have happened."

We all laughed again. "I'm just going to see what I can do to help her," I said. "That's all."

"Whatever you say."

Another side effect of all the love that had been going around: everyone thought they were a matchmaker. I wasn't going to say no to the potential of something. But neither was I going to be the asshole that pushed myself on someone. Especially in her current situation. The last thing I wanted was for anyone to feel like they owed me anything.

All I wanted was to help her.

Granted, I wasn't sure what I was helping with yet. The information we had clearly wasn't the whole story. She was right. The odds that this had been a random attack were slim. So if the kid was in trouble, maybe that trouble could help us root out the rumors in our backyard. And even if we found nothing, I would feel a lot better making sure he was all right.

"So, now that you know everything, we can go see her. And try not to overwhelm her? Obviously, this hasn't been an easy day."

No one joked about that. We all knew what these kinds of days were like too intimately to make light of them.

Kate was curled up in one of the armchairs by the fire when I stepped out of the security office. She didn't see me immediately, and it was clear she'd been crying while we'd been discussing things. Her eyes were red and she was sniffling. I grabbed a box of tissues from the kitchen counter on my way over.

"Kate."

She didn't quite jump at the sound of my voice, but she'd obviously been in her own small world. "Sorry. Yes."

She took in the group of us. Thankfully she didn't seem afraid. But she *did* seem miserable. Sitting in the armchair across from her, I leaned forward on my knees. "Are you all right?"

"Not really. But then again, am I supposed to be?"

"No," I said softly. "I suppose not."

Daniel stepped forward and sat on the couch in the space nearest her chair. The twinge of jealousy I felt surprised me. I'd already told myself there was nothing more to this. Clearly, the subconscious part of my mind wasn't on board with that yet.

"Kate, my name is Daniel Clark. I'm very sorry to hear about your brother. For the short time I knew him, he seemed like a nice young man."

There was a brief flash of a smile. "He is. Most of the time."

"I just wanted to reassure you. No one at Resting

Warrior had anything to do with your brother's condition. Nor would we ever condone something like that."

"Yeah." Her whisper was choked. "I think I knew it was a long shot even while I was driving up here. But I had to try, you know?"

"Of course."

I cleared my throat. "We can't promise anything, because we know so little, but we're going to look into it and see what we find. If there's anything we can tell you, we will. If there's some kind of connection to us in what happened to him, we want to know about it."

"Will you help find who did this to him?"

Daniel spoke before I could answer. That didn't surprise me, because the words on the tip of my tongue were "of course." But I couldn't make that promise. None of us could. Because it wasn't one we could keep, and we did our best not to break promises.

"Let's see what we find first, and we'll go from there, okay?"

Kate looked at Daniel for a long moment, and whatever she found there wasn't the answer that she was looking for. Suddenly the bravery was gone from her face. Her shoulders drooped, and she looked . . . smaller.

I felt eyes on me. Liam was looking at me with barely concealed glee. I shot him a glare that told him the next time we were in the gym together, I was going to pound his ass into the floor.

Lovingly, of course.

"Thank you," she finally said before looking at me. "I guess I should be getting back. Long drive."

I stood. "I'll walk you out."

She grabbed her coat, and I pointed at Liam, making sure he was controlling himself before I followed her to the door.

"You're going to be cold," she said when I closed the doors behind us without my own coat.

"I'll be all right."

Her car was parked haphazardly in front of the lodge. It was almost strange not to see a truck sitting there. Most people up here preferred them for their utility. But this was a smaller car. "Will you be okay with the snow?"

The day was getting late, and it would be full dark before she made it back to Missoula.

"The roads weren't bad on the way up. I'm sure I'll be fine."

I tucked my hands into my pockets. "Good. You have my number now if you end up having trouble."

Her smile was still fleeting, and I couldn't help but compare this woman in front of me with the fiery whirl-wind that I'd run into in front of the stables. I didn't like the stark contrast. Where was the person filled with unrivaled determination?

The person shrinking in front of me didn't compute. And after seeing a glimpse of what she was capable of, I wanted to see that other side of her again.

She turned at the door to her car. "I'm sorry, by the way. For assuming you had something to do with it."

"You followed what you found in order to protect your family. That's not a bad thing."

"Yeah, but I'm still sorry. It feels awkward now."

I smiled. "Please don't. My feelings aren't hurt, I promise."

Kate fiddled with her keys. "Can I ask you something?"

"Of course."

"My brother . . ." She hesitated. "You met him. Talked with him. Do you think this is his fault? Like he got into something he shouldn't have?"

Choosing my words carefully, I gave her a small shrug.

"I don't think I'm in a position to say. You probably know more."

She frowned. "It's just that I thought he was doing better. There weren't any signs. But I know he can hide things. He has before. I don't know what to think."

"I'll find out what I can."

Kate shrank again. "I appreciate it."

Without more, she got into her car and pulled away. I watched her until she disappeared out of the gate.

Chapter 4

Kate

Well . . . that had gone well.

I pushed my head back into the headrest as I drove, focusing on the road to try to block out my racing thoughts.

Now that it was over, I could acknowledge how desperate I'd been to find answers at Resting Warrior. The fact that I hadn't, and instead found kindness, understanding, and maybe help, made me frustrated. Irrationally angry.

I should be happy—grateful—the people who had tried to help Brandon with his PTSD weren't part of this. But it told me nothing. Unless they were lying?

The thought was dismissed as soon as I had it. There was no doubting the sincerity of the men at Resting Warrior. You could feel it, like it was a part of their very being. They hadn't done this to him, and they didn't know who had.

Hopefully they would find something helpful, but I wasn't expecting much. I knew when I was being spun. They were going to look into it to find any connections to themselves and to cover their asses. But other than that, they didn't seem up for playing detective.

Not that I could blame them. Brandon had left the ranch in a hurry, and now I wondered why. He'd made it seem like the place was hellish. I'd always thought he was exaggerating. But now that I'd seen the place myself and talked to them, I had no idea where his description came from. Resting Warrior was beautiful, and what I'd seen of it had felt serene.

I sighed. Brandon was all I had left now. After our parents died . . . it had been really hard. The thought that someone would do this to him and I could lose the only family I had left? These thoughts sent me into a spiral of panic.

Spiral was the only way to describe the way my thoughts crossed and crisscrossed back over the little information I had, trying to put the pieces together in a different way that made more sense.

It wasn't possible. I didn't know enough. And I wouldn't until Brandon woke.

The winter sun had long since set when I pulled back into the city. I wanted to get back to the hospital, but if Brandon wasn't going to be awake for a while, I needed some things for me and for Brandon.

My apartment was small, and a lot smaller now that I was sharing it with Brandon. But walking into it now, it was unbearably empty. Like the space itself felt Brandon's absence.

"You're being ridiculous," I told myself out loud. "Spaces don't have feelings."

I grabbed a bag and packed a change of clothes and

my laptop. A water bottle, my toothbrush, and toothpaste. After considering a moment, I grabbed a set of Brandon's clothes too.

There was no way to know when he would wake up, but when he did, I wanted him to have clothes that weren't soaked with blood. Or a one-size-fits-nobody hospital gown.

Everything I needed, I gathered. Chargers and a couple of snacks. My wallet. It all went into the bag. The nurses at the hospital were going to think that I was moving in.

But I needed to be there. Even with him sedated, I *needed* to be at his side in case something happened. Weirder things had happened than someone waking up from sedation. I'd been too late to say goodbye to my parents. There wasn't a chance in hell I was going to risk missing that with Brandon. Nor would I let him wake up thinking he was all alone.

Now late, the hospital parking lot was much more empty than it had been. I was able to park close to the entrance. The new nurse at the desk didn't stop me once I told her why I was there. If they told me I couldn't stay because of visiting hours, I was prepared to sit in the middle of the floor and not move until they changed their mind.

Nothing was different when I reached his room. Brandon hadn't moved. His breath still pushed slow and even thanks to the tube in his throat, and the heart monitor kept beeping steadily. The lights in his room were dim, but that suited me just fine. I was exhausted from the driving and emotions and adrenaline.

I should probably catch up on the work I'd missed today because of all of this, but I couldn't muster the energy to pull the laptop out of my bag. That was okay. I could work on it tomorrow. Clearly, I wasn't going anywhere.

When I unlocked my phone, it was still on the browser with Noah's photograph. The photo Resting Warrior had used didn't do him justice. At all. Up close, he was like every person's dream of a cowboy. All he'd been missing was the cowboy hat.

While my brother was lying broken and battered, the last thing I should be thinking about was the way Noah Scott filled out his shirt and jeans. But I couldn't stop myself. He was gorgeous. And more than that, he hadn't treated me like I was overreacting. Or crazy.

None of them had. But for some reason Noah stuck out to me. Maybe because it was his face I'd been focused on my whole drive north. Maybe I'd attached my hopes for my brother to him. Maybe it was simply that I found him incredibly attractive despite the shitty circumstances. Either way, he was in my thoughts and I was too tired to push him out.

I drifted off to the image of dark blue eyes.

The beeping of the heart monitor became too much after a while, so I drifted from place to place in the hospital to work, always near enough that I could be called back to Brandon's room, but far enough for a change of scenery.

Thankfully, things at work had been running smoothly since I'd gone off the rails yesterday. Owning a business, I couldn't always guarantee that.

It started in the summers during college when a friend's family went on an extended trip and asked me to house-sit for them. While I was there, I realized that they weren't the only ones on vacation. A lot of their neighborhood was.

The lightbulb that went off in my head at the idea felt pretty literal for me that day. The number of vacation homes in Montana was high, and even with security systems, there was no replacement for the deterrent of seeing lights and movement in a house.

So I built it up. A network of people who needed money and had the freedom to travel. They monitored houses all across Montana. Either for people who used their home only for part of the year, or for people who were on a brief vacation but were concerned about their house being obviously vacant.

We'd grown enough that I usually didn't have to monitor houses myself anymore, which made it easier to do things like take off and go to a ranch, or work from a hospital waiting room.

I would never be a millionaire with this business, but I didn't care about that. I made enough to be comfortable, and nothing else I'd ever done had come close to the satisfaction of running my own business.

The itch to move settled in after another hour of arranging appointments and finding people to cover shifts at a house on the east side of the state. I packed my bag and went back to Brandon's room. It was almost the end of the work day anyway and my brain was beginning to feel scrambled.

After leaving it for a while, the rhythmic sound of the heart monitor was soothing. Almost like a metronome, it had gone beyond irritation and finally just faded into the background.

A soft knock at the door had me looking up. Dr. Godin stood there, clipboard in hand. "May I come in?"

I straightened in my seat. "Of course."

"How are you holding up?"

"I don't really think that I'm the one that matters right now."

He smiled grimly. "Things like this are always hard on the family. Just making sure you're taking care of yourself too."

"Noted." It wasn't something I wanted to talk about right now.

Dr. Godin sighed. "Things are looking good. I'd like to give him another day of sedation and then we'll try waking him up. See if he tolerates it. If not, we can increase the sedation again."

"Okay." I tried not to show my eagerness too much. Brandon awake was the only thing that I wanted. I *needed* to know what had happened to him. "I'd like that."

"So for the next day, you can feel free to go home and get some rest. There won't be anything happening here."

My own smile was forced. "I'll think about it, thanks."

Clearly aware that I wasn't interested in that idea, the doctor took his leave. I couldn't leave Brandon here. As much as sleeping in my own bed sounded nice, I knew that as soon as I went home and tried to sleep, all I would do was worry about what *could* happen while I was gone.

It would be as equally exhausting and uncomfortable as just staying the night here. I could catch up on good sleep later when Brandon was out of the coma and we knew more about what had caused this in the first place.

Time passed slowly in the hospital.

The next day, the nurse slowly decreased the drip that was keeping him sedated. Finally, she was able to turn it off completely. I was relieved. I'd been trying to convince myself it was all an accident. No matter how unlikely it seemed, that was what Brandon was going to wake up and tell me.

Wrong place, wrong time, and nothing more.

I was knee-deep in emails when I heard the rustle of fabric, followed by a groan. The sound was only pain.

Brandon moved for the first time since I'd seen him in the hospital. "Brandon?"

He opened one eye. The other was still swollen enough that he couldn't open it even if he'd wanted to. "Kate?"

Shoving my laptop onto the chair next to me, I was on my feet immediately. "Hi. Oh my God, Brandon. You have no idea how glad I am to see you awake."

Another soft groan. "Probably not as glad as I am to be awake. How long has it been?"

"Two days."

"Fuck." The word was soft under his breath. "That's not good."

Dread seeped through my gut. "Why? What the hell is going on? Who did this to you?"

He was pale from the pain. Whatever they were using to sedate him must have been keeping that at bay too. "It doesn't matter."

"The hell it doesn't. After Mom and Dad, you don't get to say that to me. I don't want another call that you've been dropped off at the emergency room beaten nearly to death. What happened?"

Anger and shame burned in his eye. He didn't want to tell me, but I didn't care. I wasn't going to give an inch on this. "I was gambling."

I swore quietly. "I thought you were doing okay with that."

"I was," he said. "It was a one time thing. Should have been a one time thing. You don't understand, Katie. It was a *sure bet*."

"Don't call me Katie. And you should know by now that there's no such thing as a sure bet."

"It was."

"Brandon—" I cut myself off. I was so happy to see him up. But now that he was, I was having a hard time keeping my own anger in check. "How much did you lose?"

"Enough."

"Enough? Obviously it wasn't enough if *this* is what they did to you for it. Who did this?"

He pressed his lips together. I knew him well enough to know it meant he didn't want to tell me and was going to try his best not to.

"Do you have any idea how out of my mind I've been? I went through your clothes and the only thing I found in there was Noah Scott's number, so I went out to Resting Warrior to find out what the hell was going on. But they didn't do this to you. So who did?"

"You did *what?*" The visceral anger in his tone made me take a step back. "Why would you do that?"

"What would you have done?" I asked. "If it were me and the only thing you could hold on to was a scrap of paper with a phone number? I did what I had to."

Grunting with pain, he pushed himself higher up the bed. "Those people need to mind their own business," he snarled. "They have nothing to do with this, and I don't want them anywhere near you or me."

"Brandon—"

"*No.* They need to stay out of this. I mean it."

That was far from the impression I'd gotten when they'd sat down and spoken to me. But the sounds screeching from Brandon's machines as he started to panic didn't make it worth the argument. "Okay. But I still want to know who you owe money to, and how much."

My brother slumped back down and was silent for a long time, looking away from me. So long that I wondered

JOSIE JADE & JANIE CROUCH

if the outburst was too much and he'd fallen asleep again. But finally, he looked back at me. "The Riders."

"I don't know who they are."

"Good."

"How's our patient?" Dr. Godin's entry startled me and I backed away from the bed. I tried to gather myself.

"He's awake."

"Certainly seems that way," the doctor said with a laugh. "How do you feel?"

"Like I've been put through a meat grinder," Brandon grunted through clenched teeth.

Dr. Godin nodded and wrote something on the chart. "We'll get you some pain killers here quickly." Then he looked at me. "Would you mind giving us a minute?"

I paused. I was family. Why would he ask me to leave? My mind went to these mysterious Riders. Would they have a doctor on call to kill? Shaking my head, I stepped back.

If this doctor wanted Brandon dead, he'd had the opportunity before I'd ever arrived at the hospital. I needed to breathe. "Of course."

I stepped out of the room and covered my face with my hands. *Way to go, Kate. He nearly dies and you yell at him within seconds of him waking up.* Guilt followed the anger. I was full of both.

"Kate?"

What? That voice made my hair stand on end, and not in a bad way. But it also didn't belong here.

Noah Scott was standing in the waiting room, looking straight at me. I couldn't help but take in the way that he stood, easy, confident, with a leather jacket that showed off his form. Even seeing him right here, it took me a moment to process that he was here. At the hospital. Not at the ranch.

"Noah. What are you doing here?"

A faint smile disappeared as quickly as it had appeared. "I didn't get your number before you left, so I had no way to update you. I figured with your brother's condition, you'd likely be here."

He'd driven all the way here just to tell me what he'd found? My stomach did a tiny flip that I did my best to ignore. "Did you find anything?"

Noah slipped his hands into the pockets of his jeans and closed the distance between us. He shook his head. "No, I'm sorry. I talked to Charlie—the sheriff—and he doesn't know anyone who would do this. At least up in our neck of the woods. We've been hearing rumors for a little while about a dog-fighting ring, which could explain why Brandon has bite marks. But I don't have any proof."

"Thank you for checking." I didn't know what to do here. Honestly, I'd been sure they'd look into it and then leave it alone. Not come all the way down here just to tell me they'd found nothing.

Everyone I'd met at Resting Warrior was nice, but I still wasn't used to military guys giving a shit about anyone but their unit. Their "brothers." And the ones I'd met both before and after Brandon's deployment were arrogant, loud, and careless.

Noah was anything but. He was gentle, kind, and handsome. Handsome was frankly an insult for how good-looking this man was. I liked him. And in another world where all of this wasn't going on, I might be bold enough to ask him if he wanted to get coffee.

But this wasn't a different world, and my brother was still lying beaten in the hospital. This wasn't the time or the place for me to be having less-than-platonic thoughts about anyone.

Brandon couldn't be right about the ranch, right?

Everything I'd seen, heard, and felt while I'd been there spoke of how much those people cared- for each other and those they helped. Even when they didn't have a reason to. But Brandon's visceral reaction to them was still clinging to me, and I couldn't quite shake it.

What did it say about me that I was attracted to a man who could be hiding something like that? What did it say about me that I still felt like I could trust him? Trusting Noah felt as easy as breathing. But then again, I'd trusted Brandon when he'd said that he was doing okay. Look where that had gotten us.

I realized too late that we'd been standing in silence for far too long. Clearing my throat, I straightened. "Thank you for looking into it. It's become clear now that this has nothing to do with Resting Warrior Ranch. Thank you for your concern."

Noah hesitated, and his body swayed forward like he was going to take another step toward me, and then he stopped.

"Really," I said. "It was nice of you to come all this way, but it's not necessary anymore. We have this handled."

There was a flash of hurt in his gaze. Just one flash, quickly hidden. Then he nodded once. "All right. I hope that Brandon's recovery is going well."

He turned and left, not looking back even for a second.

As he disappeared around the corner, I tried to ignore the feeling that I was making a huge mistake.

Chapter 5

Kate

The next day I was even stiffer than before. This hospital really should invest in some kind of reclining chair for patients' families when they were staying. At least we'd moved out of the emergency wing and into the regular hospital. To me, it was a sign that Brandon was on the mend.

But being on the mend didn't fix things.

"So," I said, "I heard a rumor you might be able to help me with."

He only glanced at me.

"There was something about a dog-fighting ring going around. Does that ring any bells?"

No response.

I tried other ways too. Gently asking. Pleading. But nothing was moving him to give me more information, whether or not it would make him safer.

This was a Brandon that I recognized, unfortunately.

When he'd come back from Afghanistan, he'd been like this. He'd sat on the couch for hours, just falling into the screen of his phone, like he was doing right now. One-word answers. Surly, dark . . . and broken.

It was never a word I would use when speaking to him. But I saw it, especially knowing what he'd been like before he'd left. Brandon had his problems, but he was still light and joyful, even in the middle of falling apart. Now it felt like I couldn't reach him at all. And every hour that passed, it seemed like he wanted me there less.

Dinner came and went, and he said nothing to me.

I saw Dr. Godin in the hall and quickly followed him. "Doctor?"

He turned. "Miss Tilbeck. What can I do for you?"

"I just wanted to see how long you thought my brother would be here. I was thinking of heading home overnight, but I didn't want to leave if his release was like . . . tomorrow morning or something."

To his credit, he didn't laugh at me. "No, Brandon will be here for at least three more days, and that's a conservative estimate. But he's not in danger anymore. You should go home and get some sleep in a real bed."

"Thanks." I smiled at him. "I'm think I'm going to try."

"Have a good night."

Stepping back into Brandon's room, he didn't even look up. "I'm going to go home for a bit, okay? Take a shower and get some sleep. I'll be back in the morning. Do you need anything from home?"

He shrugged. "No."

"Okay. Get some sleep, okay?"

"Sure."

I stared at him a moment longer. It hurt my heart to see him like this again. The progress he'd made was real.

Or at least I wanted to believe it had been. For him to slide this far backward after nearly a year? I felt for him.

At the same time, I knew better than most that grief wasn't a straight line. Brandon was dealing with things I'd never have to, but some of the steps were the same.

I slumped into the seat of my car. Tired. That's what I was. So freaking tired. The doctor was right, I needed better sleep. One night would be okay.

Our apartment wasn't too far away from the hospital. Nothing in Missoula was very far from anything. The small city was very compact, and right now that was a relief. I couldn't imagine doing this if we'd lived in a place where traffic made even a short commute an hour long.

Climbing the stairs, I got out my keys, only to see light pouring out of my doorway. My very *open* doorway. "Oh my God."

I raced forward, and everything in me sank. The apartment was in ruins. Things were shattered on the floor and pillows were torn apart. I thought scenes like this only happened in movies. Right now, this was very real.

Not only was it real, but I wasn't alone. Crashing came from the back of our apartment where the bedrooms were. They were still here. My heart kicked into high gear and I ducked into the small closet right beside the front door. The folding door on it was stuck, falling off its rails after whatever they'd done. Hopefully that meant that they'd already looked here and wouldn't look again as long as I was quiet.

I covered my mouth and nose with my hands, trying to slow my breathing and not give myself away. Were these the Riders? They had to be, right? What could they be looking for here?

Horror sank through me. They knew where we lived. That was obvious, but the knowledge *hitting* me was a completely different thing. These people were here to retrieve something, and given what they'd already done, I doubted they were going to leave without it.

"Nothing," a voice called. "I don't see why we're looking for cash here, man. Place is already a dump. There are plenty of nicer apartments we can hit if you want cash."

"Do me a favor." The second, more authoritative voice spoke. "Shut the fuck up when you don't know what you're talking about."

"How about you just tell me why the hell we're in a shithole apartment looking for nothing instead of busting my ass?"

"Brandon owes twenty grand. He told us he had it, and he didn't. So we made a deal for two grand a week before we made it clear that there would be no other offers."

The first man laughed. I wasn't laughing.

"Would have thought an army vet fresh off the plane could hold his own better, but he'll live. This week is going fast, and every week he doesn't pay, I'll put him back in with the dogs and raise the interest. I don't care if I have to pull him out of the hospital to do it."

"Still don't know why we're here though. If he doesn't have it at all, it's not going to be here."

"Just making sure," the second man said. Something shattered, and I made sure I was excruciatingly still. These were the kind of men who wouldn't think twice about hurting me if they knew I was here. "Maybe he has some. Even if he doesn't, I want him to know that we mean fucking business. Now check the rest."

"Fine."

There was more crashing and breaking. I closed my eyes. They were in my office. The small room was barely bigger than a closet, and it was where I'd stashed money in case of an emergency.

After Brandon's troubles before deployment, I'd learned the hard way that it was good to have money on hand just in case. Right now I wasn't sure if I hoped they found it, or hoped they didn't.

"Hey, here we go."

My stomach sank.

"Looks like you were right after all." I heard the quiet sounds of bills being flipped between fingers. "Hell, there's almost three grand here."

"Perfect."

"That going to lower his debt by three grand?"

The sinister laugh crawled across my skin. "Of course not. It's just interest on this week's payment. Looks like the little asshole gets a break. He's going to need it."

Footsteps were approaching the front door, and I shrank back into the shadows, sending up a prayer to whatever powers existed that they didn't look. Didn't see me.

"What are you going to do next week?"

"Don't know. Hopefully this will get his head on straight and I won't have to do anything. Otherwise . . . you know we keep the dogs hungry."

They passed out the door. "Glad I'm not on your bad side."

"Don't push your luck."

Their voices faded as they walked away from the apartment. I sank down, my knees no longer able to hold me up. Holy shit. Holy *shit*. If they'd known I was here, who knows what they would have done?

They had dogs. And they'd been here for Brandon. That seemed like enough to make the connection between the gang that Noah had mentioned and what had happened to my brother. He was in deeper shit than he realized.

Or maybe he realized exactly and was just refusing to tell me.

My heart pounded out of my chest, and there wasn't enough air to breathe. The apartment wasn't safe. Not only was the lock broken now, but they could come back at any time. They'd said next week, but it wasn't something I was going to count on.

I couldn't go back to the hospital. Brandon didn't want me there, and now that I knew how deep he really was, I was as angry as I was afraid. A hotel was an easy option, but I didn't want that either. The need to know the truth burned in my chest. Who were these people? Where were they? How could they do something like this and expect to get away with it?

Dark blue eyes filled my mind.

Noah was the only one who knew what was really going on now. He'd come all the way here to update me, and he hadn't had to. He'd come all this way and I'd dismissed him like it was nothing.

Would he still help me? I hoped he would. Because right now, he felt like the only option.

Pushing out of the closet, I shut the front door as best I could and found my suitcase among the wreckage. It would have to do. Whatever clothes had survived? I would take them.

It didn't take long. I didn't look back at the mess as I closed the door behind me. If I did, I would start crying, and I couldn't afford to do that right now. The mess could be dealt with later.

Instead, I tossed my suitcase in the back seat and pulled out, already retracing the route to Resting Warrior in my mind.

Chapter 6

Noah

Staring at a fire was always a therapeutic act for me. There was nothing to do but lose myself in the colors and movement.

Now interrupted by kittens, of course.

The tiny orange one—Garfield—threw himself off the back of the couch and into my chest in the process of trying to catch his own tail, terrorizing the sleeping black kitten—Salem—on my lap. The little one was tired enough to curl up and fall back asleep immediately.

Brother and sister, they certainly were a handful, but I didn't mind the company in the evenings. There was always something to smile about with them around. Plus, I didn't have to be in the cold to have some animal company, as much as I loved Al Pacacino.

My phone vibrated in my pocket, and I dug it out while trying not to disturb the sleeping kitten. It was starting to get late. Who was calling me right now?

Not a number I recognized. That could be either good or bad. I thought about sending it to voicemail, but my gut stopped me. I needed to answer.

"Hello?"

"Noah?"

That voice had me fully alert in an instant. "Kate." After her reaction in the hospital, I hadn't expected to hear her voice ever again. I'd tried to put it out of my mind since yesterday and ignore the tug in my gut that was bothered by it.

But now she'd called me. Far too late. "Are you all right?"

"I'm outside the lodge."

I wasn't sure what that meant exactly, but it couldn't be good. "I'll be right there."

"Okay."

I hung up and gently moved the kittens off my lap. Quickly, I banked the fire and put up the guard so those same kittens wouldn't hurt themselves, then I grabbed my keys and coat.

The air was crisp outside, but not as cold as it could be for this time of year. If I had more time I'd walk over to the lodge. But I didn't want to wait, not when Kate was waiting there. She was already hesitant and skittish—I didn't want to leave her there alone longer than necessary.

She was still in her car when I pulled up to the lodge. There was someone in the security office—there usually was until at least midnight—but if she'd knocked, I doubt they would have heard her in there.

But . . . if that were the case, wouldn't they also have seen her enter?

As I swung down out of the truck, she stepped out and shut her door. Her stance sent all my instincts spiraling to the edge before I even took in her face. Kate was scared.

This posture wasn't deflated the way she'd been when she'd left the ranch the first time. This was pure terror.

It settled in the body in different ways, and I knew what it looked like.

Calm and normal. That was what she needed if she was going to tell me what was going on. Calm and normal was something I could give her. "Hey." I smiled. "I'm surprised to see you. Seems like showing up unexpectedly is going to be our thing."

Kate didn't smile. She wasn't even looking at me, instead focusing on the ground right in front of my feet. Okay, different approach. "You know, it's dark, but it's still nice. Do you want a tour? I could show you a little more of what you were poking around the first time you were here."

Animals helped. They helped loosen tongues and made people feel safe. I knew more than anyone the power of companion healing. Maybe they could help her right now too.

"Sure." The word was quiet, but she fell into step behind me as we walked in the direction of the stables.

"Will you be cold?"

"I'm fine."

Maybe physically. Mentally, she was a million miles away. Up close, she was pale. Her skin nearly matched the extraordinary blond of her hair. Something had happened, and she didn't know what to do.

Well, Noah, treat her like anyone else who's coming here for the first time.

"I know you're a little familiar with us because Brandon came, but Resting Warrior is a place that's meant for healing. We use animals to treat trauma and face down things like PTSD—no matter the source. We also train therapy animals. Some of the animals come with a history

45

of abuse, which, if they can overcome it, makes them uniquely suited to be a therapeutic companion.

"But some animals aren't meant for that. So the ones that don't take to the training are adopted out through a network of local shelters." It was something I was responsible for. Originally, we'd tried to find the homes ourselves, but as we grew, it became impossible. Now the animals went to happy homes found by volunteers who knew exactly what to look for.

"Mostly dogs and horses. We have some alpacas, and I'm currently fostering a pair of kittens. They're wild."

That got me the tiniest twitch of a smile from her.

The stables were quiet when I opened the door, but a few horses whuffed in response. "Someone's awake." I led Kate over to one of the stalls where the horse had his head over the door already, waiting to be petted. "This is Penny. When he arrived, he was so wild that no one could get through to him. Until our friend Evelyn figured out that he was afraid of men. We worked with him on the fear, and now he loves pretty much everyone."

Kate reached out a hand and Penny lifted his nose up into it. It startled her, but she recovered quickly, stroking down his nose.

"Do you like animals?"

"I honestly haven't been around them much. We never had pets, and I'm not exactly a rancher. But . . . I think I like them, yeah."

The easing of tension in her body was clear, and that was enough for me.

She petted Penny for a few minutes, and I stepped away to give the other horses some attention. Kate seemed more than content to stay with him.

"Would you like to see the dogs? I can also show you the cabins where our clients stay."

"Have you heard anything more about that group you mentioned?" she asked. "The dog-fighting one."

She was still stroking Penny's nose. Too focused on it. The tension was back in her body. "No. They're slippery right now. All we have is whispers. This might be a group that is running drugs or weapons, but no hard proof."

Anger surged in me, and I had to steady my breath.

The fact that we knew so little was beginning to get under my skin. I hated it. Someone making animals fight for entertainment at *all* was horrifying. But it was more than that for me.

"The one concrete thing that came to our attention is the possibility that one of the dogs we trained here landed with the group. The sheriff got an anonymous tip, and he checked with animal control. But by all accounts the dog is fine."

Kate was quiet, but for the first time since she'd arrived, she looked at me. I'd forgotten how powerful her gaze was. Those eyes punched me in the gut, and they made me want to promise her everything.

"If someone is torturing an animal that I trained? That I helped to heal and feel safe? Then we are going to bring those fuckers down, no matter how long it takes. And if these assholes have anything to do with your brother and it will help you both? So much the better."

"Thank you." Another pause.

It felt like she had something to say, so I waited, but she stayed silent. "There are hot drinks in the lodge if you want something."

No answer yes or no, but she fell in beside me again as I shut the barn door. We didn't make it all the way to the stairs of the lodge. She veered toward her car. "I should go."

"Wait." I reached out to catch her by the arm but

stopped myself at the last second. She hadn't given me permission to touch her. "Are you going back to the hospital?"

"Yeah." The answer was too quick and too flat. "Brandon is awake now. So I should get back there."

"You're welcome to stay here," I said. "It's a long drive, and it's already late."

She was back to not looking at me again. No wonder, since I'd seen children craft better lies. "I'll be fine. Thank you. And thank you for the information. I hope you find them soon."

The silence spun out between us. She'd driven all the way here again. Was terrified of something that she couldn't make herself talk about. Whatever it was, it hadn't disappeared because she'd driven up here and petted a horse.

"Kate," I said quietly. "If you need help, I want you to know that you're free to come back here at any time. Even if you don't need help and you just need a friend."

Her eyes locked with mine, and I swore electricity crackled in the air, just like those moments they talked about in movies. Kate stared at me so long I wondered if we'd frozen time.

Then she unlocked the door to her car and got in. But she stared until she absolutely had to turn away.

Kate

I'd lied.

Noah knew it too. There's no way he didn't. Telling me

I could come back for help was too pointed. He absolutely knew something was wrong, and I was exhausted.

The little motel on the edge of Garnet Bend was good enough for the night. It was cheap, and most importantly, it was far away from my destroyed apartment. There was no way they knew where I was now, right?

The thought had me shivering even as I took the keys from the bored man at the front desk.

This was one of those motels where the rooms opened directly to the outside. Not exactly the bastion of safety my mind craved right now, but it would have to do.

I showered quickly, the feeling of clean clothes a small comfort. But I put on regular clothes. Not pajamas. What if I had to move quickly?

I wasn't built for this kind of thing.

I stared at the ceiling, trapped in some kind of nightmare. How had they known where we lived? Gambling was one thing, but I hadn't thought Brandon would just give out our address to people like that. Especially since he lived with me.

Had he told them I lived there too? Anything about me? God, I hoped not. I didn't want them looking for me.

But if Brandon hadn't told them where we lived, that meant that they'd found our address. Of course it wasn't very hard to dig for personal information if you knew how to do it. I just never imagined I'd be on this side of it.

Stop being ridiculous, Kate.

I was being dramatic. There was no way they knew where I was. They hadn't known I was in the apartment, so they hadn't followed me here. But if they were watching Brandon, they could know I existed. If they were watching him, they could be watching me. They could have seen that I'd charged my credit card here.

Stop. It.

Turning away from the light, I closed my eyes. My body was exhausted, sinking down into the bed. But every few minutes my eyes opened and took in the shadows. They jumped out at me, making me question whether I was seeing things or not.

Shapes formed and jumped and I rolled over onto my back again. Frustrated. Exhausted. I couldn't do this. There was no way I could sleep here when I felt like I had to keep one eye open.

My mind kept telling me it was nothing while every part of my subconscious disagreed.

Noah had said to come back to the ranch if I needed help. Was this help? Would it count? At the very least, I needed to try.

I pulled on my shoes and grabbed my suitcase, locking the door behind me. I would keep the key just in case I couldn't get into Resting Warrior. Worst-case scenario, I would come back here and barricade myself in the bathroom.

The moon over the mountains painted everything silver. Without the light pollution of the city, you could see so many stars it was hard to fathom. There was something beautiful about being out here with nothing around, if also a little terrifying. I wasn't used to the *completeness* of the silence that was a part of the rural countryside. But I didn't question why this was a place people chose to recover in.

Ahead, the gate was open. I took a breath in relief. Resting Warrior had walls like I'd never seen at any other ranch. Most of them had the bare minimum, just to keep the cattle from escaping. Resting Warrior had walls that were nearly ten feet tall, and I didn't doubt that they had other hidden security measures.

It made sense, given who their clients were and their own background. And because of that, I'd assumed that the gate to the ranch—equally intimidating—would be closed. I didn't know why it wasn't or if Noah left it open on purpose, but either way, I was grateful.

I parked in front of the lodge again. Noah's truck was gone. Even if I had to sleep in my car here, I felt safer than in the hotel room.

The incredible quiet enveloped me as I stepped out of the car. It was cold enough to see my breath. For a minute I stood and looked back at the stars. Absolutely incredible. This was something you forgot existed when you were in the city and the lights flattened out the sky.

The city sky was still beautiful—nearly everything in Montana was—but out here the deep blue couldn't be masked. The sky looked like velvet sparkling with diamonds. I must be more exhausted than I'd thought, thinking like that.

Nerves suddenly gripped my gut. Would they really be okay with me here?

If they weren't, I would deal with it in the morning. Easier to ask forgiveness than permission, I rationalized. There was a single porch light on over the door, and I held my breath as I tried the handle . . . and released that breath when it opened.

Inside it was warm and still, with a fire burning behind a screen. "Hello?"

No one answered or stormed in asking why the hell I was here. I called out one more time, and then relaxed. It didn't seem like anyone was here, but that was okay with me. Quickly, I locked the door behind me. Anyone supposed to be here would have a key, so I wasn't risking locking anyone out.

The faint smell of coffee hung in the air, and there was still some in the pot. So someone had been here recently. And the fire looked like it was ready to go all night. This was so much better than a hotel room. My mind was already more at ease.

I shed my coat and went to the kitchen. It had been hours since I'd eaten, and even now my stomach didn't love the idea of putting food in it. Tea though . . . tea sounded perfect.

I used a little electric kettle to heat the water, but even as I brewed the drink, I was fading. There were no shadows jumping out at me from the corners here. No violent men who could break in at any moment. If something happened here, at least there was a chance I would be heard.

I sank into the couch. There was a blanket over the back of it. I kicked off my boots and left them near the fire before stretching out and breathing in the comfortable silence. My tea sat on the coffee table, still hot.

The curls of the steam, limned with firelight, lulled me into long-needed sleep.

Chapter 7

Noah

I had a feeling.

One of those I couldn't run away from. My instincts told me Kate needed help, and I was going to make sure she got it.

Quickly, I drove the truck back to my place, made sure the kittens were okay, and jogged back to the lodge. Grant was just finishing up his shift in the security office and shutting things down for the night. "Closing the gate?" I asked.

"Yeah, I was about to."

I took a breath. "Leave it open."

"Why?"

Ever since Evelyn's stalker had gotten access to the ranch and terrorized her, we took no chances. The gate didn't stay open unattended. Especially at night. "I'll stay with it," I promised. "Can't sleep anyway."

Grant stood, stretching. "That's not an answer to the question."

"I just have a hunch."

"Wouldn't have anything to do with that car that came and left again a little while ago, right?" He smirked.

I dropped my coat on the couch. "You know, being a nosy bastard doesn't suit you."

"Maybe not, but it does make for excellent entertainment." He stretched again.

"Why didn't you let her in?"

Grant shrugged. "She never knocked. Never even got out of the car until you drove up.

Well, that answered that question. I took his place at the station with all the monitors. "How are you feeling?"

A couple of months ago, Grant'd finally had surgery on an old injury—shrapnel that had compressed his spinal cord. It had become an emergency when he'd saved his fiancée Cori from a fire. But he'd still come out the other side smiling.

"I'm good," he said. "Sometimes I still push too far too fast. But I'm finally almost at one hundred percent."

"I'm glad to hear it." I really was. Whenever one of us had some kind of victory over our past, it was cause for celebration. "Say hello to Cori for me."

Grant smiled. "I will."

His smile told me he was going to give her the kind of greeting I wanted no part of. He left out the back door.

I watched his car pull out of the gate, and then I sat back to wait. Maybe I was wrong. Maybe nothing would happen and this would just be another sleepless night.

But I didn't think I was wrong.

I pulled up the app Jude had synced to all of our phones, allowing us to watch the security feeds remotely, and went to make coffee. I would probably need it, but I wasn't missing a second of footage on that gate while I waited for our coffee maker to spit it out.

My instincts were the only reason I was still here and breathing. So I'd learned to listen to them. Even if they hadn't been screaming at me, seeing Kate so afraid would have made me do this. I wanted her to feel safe, and it was clear that she didn't.

I just hoped that the offer I'd given her stayed in her mind. And that she would take it if she needed to.

Nothing on the video while I brewed the coffee. And nothing for a couple hours after that. But lights suddenly flashed across the screen in front of me, and I sat up, staring at the image.

Relief and satisfaction flew through my entire body. It was Kate's car. She was back. I followed her on the cameras all the way to the lodge.

Nearly the entire outdoor property was covered in cameras, including the entrances to the lodge. We didn't keep them inside for obvious privacy reasons. But I watched her as she decided whether she wanted to do this. Whatever she was wrestling with, it made her nervous enough to come here in the middle of the night.

It hadn't been long enough for a round trip to Missoula and back, so where had she gone?

Finally, she walked up the stairs and tried the door. It was as far as I could see with the cameras, and I closed the gate remotely. There was a manual button on this side if she wanted to leave. But now I didn't have to keep my eyes glued to the screen.

Kate's voice sounded muffled as she called out, but I didn't answer. She was safe and had a place where she didn't have to worry about whatever she thought was haunting her. Surprising her right now didn't feel like the right thing to do. I would hear her if something went wrong. Other than that, I could at least try to get some sleep too. It probably wouldn't happen, but the itch under my skin was gone.

Sometimes, that was half the battle.

I threw back what was left of my cold coffee and stretched out on the security room couch. The best napping couch around, there was a reason we kept it here, a place where we sometimes had to stay over.

Still, sleep didn't come right away. My mind was filled with thoughts of Kate and her brother. He was young still. Just a kid who'd seen some bad shit on deployment.

Hell, the way I barely slept because of my own bullshit? I sympathized. Guilt crept up into my throat again. Realistically, I knew that none of this was my fault. Could I have reached out to Brandon? Maybe. But there was no telling whether he would have been receptive.

He hadn't been ready to accept help while he'd been here. So it was unlikely he would have wanted anything from me. All the same, I could have done more for him.

Another rational voice in my head asked if I was only feeling guilty now because I knew Kate and I desperately wanted to help her. I hoped that it was both.

I finally began the breathing exercises that sometimes helped get me to sleep, and let my eyes close.

They opened again later.

My phone told me that it was early—right around dawn. I'd never been able to kick the habit of rising early, even if I wanted to sleep in sometimes. My body simply snapped awake, no matter how little sleep I'd gotten.

One glance at the cameras told me Kate was still here. Her car was parked outside, and the rest of the cameras confirmed everything was clear.

Coffee. I needed more coffee.

Quietly, I unlocked the door to the security office and moved into the main room. The fire was low now. Still going, but it would need more wood soon. One tiny bit of Kate's platinum hair was visible over the couch. She was asleep.

I wouldn't disturb her. My boots were in the security office, allowing me to move silently in socked feet around the kitchen. Quietly, I made a new pot of coffee and set it to brew.

The temperature was dropping in here as the fire died. She was covered in blankets from the couch, but I didn't want the temperature to be the reason that she woke. I half expected me adding wood to the fire to be the thing that did it, even if I was careful, but Kate remained peaceful.

Didn't even stir.

The way she was lying, half her face was covered with the blanket, but I couldn't help noticing that she was relaxed. In a way completely opposite of the night before.

I made myself walk back across to the kitchen and sit at the table while I waited for the coffee to brew. The urge to study her, take her in, was strong. But I wasn't going to be the guy that watched her sleep. Not today anyway.

Once the coffee was ready, I texted the guys to make sure no one came bounding through the door at full speed, which would probably terrify her. She was obviously exhausted.

The hours moved slowly, but she still didn't stir. I took care of some things on my phone and took the morning shift on security to keep an eye on her. Liam took care of the animals for me. The guys all understood, and if they wanted to make jokes, they thankfully kept them to themselves.

It was just before noon when she woke, the second time I was rekindling the fire. At her small gasp, I turned to find those eyes trained on me. She wasn't fully awake, still in the space where everything felt like danger.

I raised my hands, stepping back so she'd know I wasn't coming at her. "Good morning." One glance at the clock told me that it *was* still morning. Barely.

"Morning," she murmured.

"Coffee?" I asked.

"Yes, please." Kate sat up and ran her hands through her hair. I poured her a cup of the caffeine that she needed.

She took it from me, a tinge of pink in her cheeks as she did. So was she embarrassed I'd seen her sleeping? Or embarrassed about being caught sleeping here? Either way, there was nothing to be embarrassed about in my eyes.

"There wasn't time for you to make a round trip to Missoula last night," I said, sitting in one of the chairs farther away from her. "Where did you go?"

"A hotel on the edge of town."

I wasn't trying to interrogate her, but I was curious. "You said you were going back to the hospital, so why didn't you? Or why didn't you go home?"

Kate didn't look at me. In fact, it seemed like she was trying to look at everything *but* me.

"Kate, please tell me what the hell is going on. I'm not upset you're here. I'm glad, because it was clear that you were scared, but I'd like to know what happened to make you look that terrified."

One slow sip of coffee later, she looked up at me and repeated herself. "I went to a hotel on the edge of town. I couldn't go home."

Talking, even barely, was good. "Why?" My only goal now was to keep her talking, and in a way that wouldn't make her afraid again.

"Brandon is awake. He woke up not long before you saw me at the hospital."

"Is he all right?"

She shrugged. "They say that he will be. But he's still being . . . cagey about what happened. I went home yesterday to get some real sleep, shower, take a break since I knew he'd be okay, and—" She took a shaky breath. "There were people in our apartment."

"*What?*"

"The door was open, everything was trashed, and they were still there. I hid in a closet that they'd already gone through until they left. They gave me a little more clarity on what's going on, but . . . I grabbed everything I could from inside once they were gone and drove straight here."

Well, that explained why she'd been so pale last night. That would terrify anyone. "What did they say?"

Kate swallowed more coffee. She was trying to hide it, but the way she was holding on to the mug betrayed how shaken she was. "Brandon owes these guys a lot of money. Twenty thousand. They were there to find something for their weekly payment, and they found it. I have—*had* an emergency stash. If he doesn't pay them two grand every week, they'll put him in with the dogs again. That's what they said."

Fuck. No wonder she'd asked me about the dog gang last night. She already knew they were one and the same. "Did you get a name for them?"

"Brandon said they were called the Riders. Anyway, when I went to the motel, I freaked myself out. I don't know how they found my apartment, and I'm not sure they won't follow me if they are tracking my credit card or whatever, and I just . . . you'd said I could come back."

Her face shifted to anger, and she put down the coffee cup. Standing, she shoved the blankets aside. Like she felt too much to be sitting still.

"How can they just do stuff like this and get away with it? They're going to keep coming after him until they get what they want. They might come after me too. I'll probably have to move, but I can't even think about doing that until they go away 'cause they'll just destroy wherever I go too. Obviously, I can't stay there now. Everything is ruined and the door barely works.

"On top of that, there's the money. I could maybe cover the payment next week. If I scrape, it could be two. But twenty thousand dollars? I don't have that kind of money. And how could Brandon be such an idiot? He knows better. A lot better."

I smiled at that, but it wasn't funny. "I'm sure he does."

Kate looked at me then quickly turned away. Not before I saw the tears in her eyes. She was trying to hide them, but she didn't need to. This was an impossible situation that was in no way her fault.

I gave her a moment, letting her breathe before I spoke. My voice was quiet. "Will you let me help you?"

Chapter 8

Noah

Kate was quiet in the seat next to me as we drove. I was glad she was letting me help her, but also worried this might be beyond me. Us.

This gang was bad news. Not only because of the animal cruelty, but because of the other scraps of information we had. There was every possibility they were deep into other illegal activity. Trafficking guns or drugs. Maybe both. And if they were throwing people in with the dogs, it added a whole other component we hadn't even thought of.

On the way out of town, we stopped at the motel so she could check out of the room she'd never used. I wished she'd told me last night. The guest houses were unoccupied currently, and she wouldn't have had to spend any time in a panic.

Most of the drive passed in easy silence, with nothing but the radio playing. Kate seemed lost in her thoughts, and I didn't want to interrupt them. It was only once we pulled into the hospital parking lot that she came out of her stupor.

"Holy shit," she said. "I'm so sorry."

"Why?"

She looked over at me. "I just . . . didn't talk that entire time. That was rude of me."

Chuckling, I put my truck in park. "You're anything but rude, Kate. You have a lot on your mind, and I live on a ranch. I'm used to quiet."

"Yeah . . ." She shook her head. "It's almost scarily quiet out there."

"At first."

"You get used to it?"

I jumped out of the truck and was around to her door before she'd had the chance to open it. "You do get used to it." I helped her down from the cab, very aware of how close it put us. Kate seemed to notice too. "At first it's unnerving because your brain is still listening for the background noise. But eventually it quiets down, and it feels like you can finally hear yourself think for the first time."

"That sounds nice," she whispered.

We walked toward the hospital, and when we got to the doors, Kate put her hand on my arm. "There's something I forgot to tell you. When Brandon woke up, I told him that I'd seen you. He reacted . . . badly. Told me none of you could be trusted and you were only in it for the money. That you had to be kept out of things at all costs. It happened right before I saw you in the waiting room, and it shook me. All of that is to say that I don't think Brandon is going to take kindly to seeing you. He's not himself."

I nodded and gestured toward the doors. "I've seen plenty of men at their lowest. Everyone recovering from something like this has to go through that place. I'll be fine."

"Okay." She didn't sound convinced.

The elevator ticked up slowly. "How much does he know right now?"

"I haven't seen him since yesterday. He doesn't know about the apartment, or that I know how much money he owes."

I slipped my hands into the pockets of my jeans. "Can I ask you a favor?"

"Yeah."

Following her out of the elevator, I slowed down, not sure how close to his room we were. "I'd like you to let me go in first."

Kate's eyes widened. Such a unique color, intense, nearly violet blue . . .

I snapped back to reality. Looking at her eyes was trouble. I wanted to stare at her, and I couldn't do that right now.

"Why?" she asked.

"Because you're right. He's not going to be happy to see me. And I'd rather him let the anger out at me than you."

Her spine straightened, gaze turning sharp. "I can handle my brother."

"I never said you couldn't. But you don't *have* to. Let him take out whatever anger he has at me instead of blaming you for going against his wishes."

Kate wrapped her arms around herself, barely conscious of the movement. "You think it will help?"

"I don't know," I said honestly. "But I don't think it will hurt."

Finally, she looked back up at me again. "All right."

"Feel free to listen. Come in whenever you feel you need to."

She led me down the hall and pointed to a room with an open door. It didn't sound like Brandon was in the physical shape to hurt anyone, but I would never underestimate the power of anger in a mind struggling the way his was.

I hadn't lied to Kate. I didn't want his anger directed at her. What I didn't mention was that I was worried that he'd lose himself so much that he'd try to hurt her. Not likely, but still possible.

"Hey, Brandon."

He looked up from his phone, and I watched him absorb who I was and the fact that I was here. He'd been worked over. The way his eye looked, he was lucky that he hadn't lost it entirely. Those *were* bite marks on his arms. But nowhere else that I could see. So he hadn't fought.

That was smart, at least.

"What the fuck are you doing here?" Brandon asked. A snarl might have been a more accurate description.

"Heard you were in the hospital, and I wanted to come see how you were."

"Clearly I'm great," he rolled his eyes, "ready to walk right out of here."

I kept my hands in my pockets and my body open and easy. Low key, nonthreatening. "I'd like you to tell me what happened."

"Why do you care?"

"Aside from the fact that beating people into a coma is unacceptable? We have several reasons we'd like to find these guys. The Riders."

Brandon's gaze narrowed. "Who told you that name?"

"It doesn't matter."

"Of course it does. It was Kate, wasn't it? I *told her* I didn't want any of you near me."

"Well," I said, "since you're well enough to walk, you can always leave the room and get away from me."

The only answer was a glare.

I walked to the end of the bed and leaned on it. "Listen. I don't know what happened while you were at Resting Warrior that made you want to leave. If you weren't ready, we respect that. If it was something we did, we want to correct it. But more than any of those things, we protect the people in our community.

"Your sister was desperate to know what happened, and she went to bat for you. But you already know nothing can happen unless you tell the truth, and we both know you know more about the Riders than you're saying."

"Fuck off, Noah. This isn't any of your business."

"I made it his business." Kate's voice came from behind me. She was standing in the door, the very image of sororal fury.

Brandon's hand tightened on his phone until his knuckles were white. "What the fuck, Kate? Why would you do that after what I told you?"

"First, because I make my own decisions, and nothing at Resting Warrior has made me feel they're untrustworthy. Second, because when I went home last night, there were two men destroying our apartment looking for the money *you* owe. They found my emergency cash, and it's the only reason they're not about to drag you out of this bed to do God knows what to you." Her cheeks were flushed, eyes on fire. "So drop the high and mighty act. You owe a gang twenty thousand dollars, and if I'd been home when those guys had broken in? I don't know if I'd be standing here right now."

To his credit, Brandon went pale. "They were at our home?"

"Hard to call it home now." She wrapped her arms around herself again. "Everything was destroyed."

"*Shit*." The word was low under his breath. He rubbed his hands over his face, revealing the true extent of the bruising and biting. They hadn't gone easy on him.

"Let us help," I said. "Tell us what you know."

Shoving his head back, he looked at the ceiling. "It wasn't supposed to get this bad. I swear."

I held up a hand low so only Kate could see it. Let him talk. He was going to, but at this point, we just needed to listen. She moved to one of the chairs and sat, waiting.

"It was just a party I got invited to," he said. "I'd been hanging with these guys and they said there was a cool place where we could drink and play poker and shit. When we got there, it wasn't like that. Dogs were fighting, and the energy . . ." He closed his eyes. "I know it sounds bad, but the energy in there was overwhelming. It felt good. I haven't felt like that since . . . Anyway. The betting was easy. I made some decent money that night, so I kept going back.

"There was poker too, but it was mainly fighting. Dogs, sometimes people. I never bet on the people." He locked eyes with me. "I swear."

I had to ground myself, freezing every muscle and not allowing myself to move thanks to the anger that was simmering through me. *Only* betting on the animals did not make this better.

"I kept going back, and this one fight, it was so obvious who was going to win. It wasn't just me. There were a lot of people that bet big that night. Easy money. But it was a bait and switch. This little dog that seemed like it was about to die took down a dog three times its size. When I didn't have the money, they threw me in the pit with both of them."

Brandon looked down at his hands. "You know the rest about the money."

"The people," I said. "Did they choose to fight?"

"I don't think so."

I steeled the rage that boiled in my chest. "Did you see anything else? Drugs? Guns?"

He looked at me again, and now I didn't see the angry soldier. I saw the scared kid who was barely old enough to be dealing with any of this. "There were drugs and guns. Not the kind that you're talking about, just in general. But it wouldn't surprise me if they were doing that too."

Finally, I turned away from him. I very much wanted to be in the Resting Warrior gym pounding on a bag right now. That would have to come later. As angry as I was, and as bad as this was—worse than we'd originally thought —Brandon needed help. We hadn't been able to get through to him the first time. Maybe we could now.

"You can help us find these guys?" I asked.

"Yeah."

I pinned him with a stare. "No more lies. Or hiding things. It's one thing when it's just you, but now Kate is in it. They know where you live, they definitely know about her. Understand?"

He nodded.

"I'm going to pay for the next two weeks of this payment plan," I said. "That should give us some breathing room to figure out how to take them down."

Both of their voices spilled on top of each other, telling me I didn't need to give them money.

"Yes," I put enough power into the word to quiet them, "I am. Unless you want to be in a world of hurt, there's not really another option. I have the money, and we'll use it."

Brandon aside, I wanted to help Kate. She needed it. I'd seen the desperation and misery in her eyes earlier today. It wasn't the same, but I knew what it was like to be desperate, alone, and everything spinning out of control. It was the exact feeling that haunted me at night and chased me from sleep on a regular basis. I knew my friend Jude felt the same.

I thought about what we knew. We couldn't reveal our hand to the Riders before we got inside and figured out how to shut the operation down. And that meant doing something I didn't want to do.

The last thing I wanted was for Kate to have more direct involvement. But with Brandon in the hospital, if she wasn't the one to deliver the money, then they might be suspicious and go to ground. Members of groups like these usually acted first and thought later. If there was even a chance they knew who we were and what we wanted to do, we'd never see them again.

Yet, if we had the opportunity to take them down, I was going to make sure we didn't waste it.

"The 'week' is up tomorrow, right?" I asked.

"Yeah."

"Okay," I said. "Let's get something set up then. I'll call in the guys so we can follow these assholes once they pick up the money from Kate."

"Hey," Brandon snapped. "You can't let her do that. She doesn't have anything to do with it."

I leveled him with my gaze, but my words were as kind as I could make them. "I don't want her to have to, but the fact that it's necessary is on you. There's nothing we can do about it now if we don't want them suspecting how much we know." I looked over at Kate. "Are you okay with that?"

"Yes." Not even an ounce of hesitation.

"We're going to do everything in our power to keep you safe in this," I said. "If everything goes smoothly, it could all be gone in a couple of days."

She smiled in relief. "I like the sound of that."

I nodded to Brandon. "Set it up. Somewhere open where we can have full visuals. I'm going to call Daniel and fill him in."

"Wait, Noah," Kate followed me out of the room, "are you sure about this? The money? That's not a small amount."

"I'm sure." Living simply, along with my military retirement, gave me more money than I knew what to do with. "If we get these guys, I'll get the money back. If we don't," I shrugged, "then I'll call it an investment in your brother's future. Everyone needs that at some point, no matter what they've done. People have done it for me, and I don't mind doing it for others."

"Okay." She bit her lip, worrying it between her teeth like she wanted to say more but couldn't. There was no disguising the relief in her eyes. "Thank you."

"You don't have to thank me for anything, Kate."

"I still want to though," she said. "This is more than a lot of people would have done."

I smiled, resisting the urge to touch her. Pull her into an embrace and tell her everything was going to be okay. But I couldn't. "Set up the meeting with Brandon. I'll be back shortly."

Kate looked at me for a long moment before she retreated. I blew out a breath. Every time she looked away from me, it was like being released from an electric shock. And I was starting to crave that shock.

I was in trouble.

Chapter 9

Kate

The park bench was cold even through my jeans. I tried to keep my breath even, but it was impossible to not be nervous. When you watched movies with things like this, it seemed so far away from real life. You never imagined it could be in your city, let alone *you* participating in it.

In my jacket pocket there was an envelope with four thousand dollars. Cash, at their insistence. I'd expected some kind of account number or routing information. Wasn't that the way the bad guys did it on TV? They always had their account numbers memorized and at the ready.

"Noah?" I tried to keep my lips as closed as possible so it didn't look like I was talking to anyone.

The park was open and empty. Not many people hung out in parks in late November when there was already snow on the ground. Behind me, the river moved under a sheet of ice. In the distance to my left there were occasional cheers and announcements from the baseball stadium. Some kind of concert in the off-season. And there, across the park near some apartments and a small cafe, was a van that contained Noah and at least two other Resting Warrior guys.

Others were in separate vehicles at other potential exit points.

"Kate." His voice was low and calm in my ear. The smallest earbud that I'd ever seen, but the connection was crystal clear. "You're doing great."

I swallowed. "Doesn't the fact that they want cash kind of reinforce the fact that they're into bad stuff?"

There was a pause. "Not necessarily, but likely, yes."

"I just want this to be over." Done, so that Brandon would be safe. It wasn't like managing house sitters had set me up for a lot of intrigue in my day-to-day life.

"It will be soon," he promised. "Thank you again for doing it."

He didn't have to thank me. There was very little that I wouldn't do for Brandon. No matter how much he made me angry or messed up, he was all I had. If doing this would save our family, then I was going to do it.

Across the park, a man started walking toward me. He was tall and broad. Wearing mostly black. It could be a coincidence, but there wasn't anyone else in the park besides me right now. Odds were this was the guy.

"Coming from the baseball side. Near the main road."

"We see him," Noah confirmed.

I didn't move from where I sat until he was close. And not even then, in case it wasn't him. But he slowed and looked at me. Looked a little too long even though I was bundled up in a down jacket and hat.

"Do you have it?"

I stood to cover my reaction. His voice. I knew his

JOSIE JADE & JANIE CROUCH

voice. He was the guy from my apartment, the one who'd promised to put Brandon in with the dogs if he didn't pay.

"How do I know you're with them?" I asked.

His gaze sharpened. "You want me to go visit your pissant brother in the hospital and ask him for an identity check? I'm sure he'll be happy to see me."

Okay, then. In my ear, Noah swore softly.

I took the envelope out of my jacket. "This is for the next two weeks," I said.

He went for it, and I don't know what the hell I was thinking when I pulled it out of reach. "I want you to tell me this is for two weeks and you're not going to show up next week claiming that I didn't pay you."

"If you question my word again, that's exactly what I'll do." He snatched the envelope out of my hand.

"Careful, Kate," Noah said in my ear.

While he flipped through the bills, counting them, I tried to get a really good look at him. His chest might as well be a barrel for how large it was. Medium skin and tattoos on his hands. More were creeping up from the collar of his dark shirt.

I memorized his features as best I could. If I needed to recount them, I wanted to be able to.

He closed the envelope and tapped it against his hand. "Well, it looks like your brother is off the hook . . . for now."

The smirk on his face didn't give me a lot of reassurance, but I wasn't going to ask what that meant. In this situation, it was better to take the simple win rather than worry about anything else. We'd bought some time with these couple of weeks, and hopefully it would be over by then.

He moved, putting the envelope inside the pocket of

his jacket. That single movement made the gun he was carrying crystal clear.

Don't panic. He has no reason to use that on you. But the knowledge that he was armed and the Resting Warrior guys were not close enough to prevent a shot had my heart racing.

"It's done, Kate," Noah said in my ear. "You can leave."

"You know," the man said, "when I found out Brandon had a sister, I didn't think anything about it since he's an ugly fucker." His laugh was rough, like a person who'd started smoking way too young and hadn't stopped. "But now I wish I'd known about you from the beginning. Would have kicked him out in favor of his hot sister."

He laughed again, but it wasn't funny. Nausea swam in my gut. I gave him a tight smile. "We'll text you for the next payment in two weeks."

Stepping around him, I walked.

"Good," Noah said. "Head toward the coffee shop so you can be around some people. We'll watch him and get you out after."

But the footsteps behind me told me everything I needed to know. I wasn't getting out of this that easily. Speaking as softly as I could, I forced the words out quickly. "He's following me."

"Hey," he called. "Wait up."

"No thank you."

"I said *wait*." A hand grabbed my arm, yanking me to a stop so quickly I nearly fell. "Why are you in such a rush?"

I said nothing, pulling my arm out of his grip. Just because he wasn't touching me didn't mean this wasn't a bad situation. We were still far enough away from Noah that it would be hard for him to intervene.

"I have places to be," I said, managing to keep my voice far calmer than I felt.

"You didn't even listen to my other offer," he said with a grin. "Your brother's debt—it could be paid off in other ways. Ways that I'm sure would be fantastic for both of us."

The fact that I didn't throw up right there and then was a miracle. He reached for me again and I took a step back. "No way in hell," I said. "You have your money, as agreed. You're going to let me walk away now, and you're not going to follow me."

I didn't recognize the voice that came out of me. Whoever was speaking wasn't afraid of this very large, armed man.

He smirked again, and I could practically read the thoughts on his face. There was no need to follow me when he already knew where I lived. "I'm sure I can convince you otherwise. I'm throwing a party tonight, and rumor has it, payment plans can be very . . . *flexible* for anyone who accepts an invitation."

The emphasis made it clear what he meant.

"You already said it. No way in hell, Kate." Noah's voice. "Tell him no."

This man was a part of the Riders. We wanted to take them down. How many times had Noah said we didn't have enough information to do it? Even with Brandon providing details, there wasn't enough. This was a perfect way to get more information.

We needed it to end this.

So I smiled. I softened my body and looked him up and down the way he wanted me to. "I could probably do a party. Is there a dress code?"

Noah was talking in my ear so fast I could barely hear him.

"No official dress code, but the place is warm and we like our women to look nice. I'll come pick you up."

Nice, in his mind, clearly meant provocative or worse.

"Kate. Please don't do this," Noah begged. "Get out."

"Oh, no," I said. "You don't need to do that. If I'm going to a party, I want to make an entrance. What fun would it be if you spoiled the surprise?"

That excuse was flimsy as hell, but I was not about to get into a car with this man. I might not be doing what Noah said, but I wasn't going that far.

He looked at me for so long my lungs froze. Would he go for it? Had I just screwed myself entirely?

Finally he looked me up and down one more time, not disguising the kind of interest he had in me, and thankfully not calling out my complete changing in attitude. "Fine. But there are conditions."

"Oh?"

"Give me your number," he said, pulling out his phone. I didn't want to give it to him, but I was in this now. Slowly, I let him put my number in. "Okay, Kate."

"You know my name," I said. "But I don't know yours."

"Max."

"Max," I repeated, and he grinned.

"I like it when you say it. Maybe I'll hear it at a much louder volume later."

I didn't respond.

"The conditions. I'm going to text you an hour before you have to be at the party. That's enough time to get there from Missoula."

"That's . . . specific."

He stepped into my space, and I froze. I didn't want to show fear, but he was probably three times my size and if he chose to grab me again, there wasn't much I could do.

"If you walk into the party even a minute after that hour is up, *Kate*, there will be consequences. You've already seen what we do to people who break their promises to us, right?"

"It's just a party," I said. "What's the big deal?"

"For you, it's not a party. It's a business transaction to see if we can change the terms of your brother's debt. One hour, or you won't like what happens both to you and to him."

He did grab my arm again, and this time, there was no way for me to pull away. "If you even think about bringing the cops with you, I know where you live. And I know exactly where your brother is."

"You don't have to threaten me," I said. "I'll be there."

He released me, and I stumbled back. "You'd better." Turning, he started to walk away before stopping. "I suppose if you did bring the cops, there would be one upside."

I kept silent, waiting.

"You wouldn't have to worry about the money anymore." He twisted his body so his jacket fell open to reveal his gun. More boldly than the first time. A threat I wouldn't forget.

"I'll be waiting for your message," I said.

He kept walking. The van that held Noah and the others pulled out, ready to follow him.

"He's gone," I said.

"Go into the coffee shop. Wait for ten minutes and then Jude will pick you up outside. He has your car."

"Noah—"

"We'll talk about it at the hotel, Kate."

I pressed my lips together. He was pissed and I couldn't exactly blame him. This was not what we'd agreed to do, but it was the right thing to do. He wanted information, and I could get it. It was that simple.

Hopefully, once we could talk about it, he would agree. Slipping my hands into the pockets of my jacket, I walked toward the coffee shop in the gathering darkness to wait for Jude.

Chapter 10

Noah

"Shit," Liam said from the driver's seat. "He's gone. I'm sorry, Noah."

I scrubbed a hand over my face, thrusting down my frustration. "It's not your fault."

Max—I was already growing to hate the name—was more clever than I wanted to admit. There was no way he could have known he was being followed, and yet he still took a circuitous route that had us second-guessing every turn.

The center of Missoula was a residential mess with random diagonal roads and drivable alleys running between or behind most houses. Unless you had every single one of them memorized, keeping up with someone who knew them was impossible.

We didn't. So he lost our tail without even trying to.

"Let's not waste more time," I said. "We don't know

when that asshole is going to message her, and I need to talk to her before that happens."

"Go easy on her," Liam said. "She's trying to help."

"By throwing herself straight into the lion's den? That's not helping. That's setting up for disaster."

Liam glanced over at me. There was just enough light left for me to see there wasn't any humor in his face. For Liam, that was a rarity. It also meant I should probably listen to whatever was coming next.

"Are you angry because she volunteered herself? Or because that asshole put his hands on her?"

"I—"

The instant dismissal on my lips died.

Wasn't it possible to be both? Of course it was. But was her volunteering the reason I had rage like lava swimming through my veins?

I sighed. No. It wasn't. If I'd been in Kate's position and been offered the opportunity to get the information I needed with relative ease, I would have said yes too. But those three words when I'd heard her fear . . .

He's following me.

The terror in that whisper wasn't something I wanted to think about. In that whisper lived every woman's worst nightmare. And I hadn't been close enough to do *shit*. He'd touched her without her consent. Not just once, but twice.

There was nearly a red film over my gaze when I played the sight over in my head.

"Are you going to judge me harshly if I tell you it's the second?"

A humorless laugh. "No. And if you'd decided to break cover to fix that situation, I would have gone with you. No matter the consequences."

We drove in silence, the streetlights lighting us up like images captured in a strobe.

"But, Noah," Liam said, "don't take your anger at him out on her. Is it a bad idea? Yeah, probably. And you should talk about that. But be careful."

"Yeah."

As much as her actions made sense, I still wanted to shake her. And there was the other part of me—that I was desperately ignoring—that wanted to wrap her up in my arms just so she knew she was safe.

So *I* knew she was safe.

We pulled into the hotel parking lot, and Kate's car was already there. Jude was standing outside, watching. "She's in her room?"

"Yes."

We'd stayed at this hotel last night once the meet had been set. The guys had driven down, bringing what we needed and Kate's car.

I knocked on her room's door.

"Just a second."

Taking a breath, I steeled myself to follow Liam's advice. But as soon as she opened the door, I was talking. "This is a bad idea, Kate."

She gestured to the room, and I went inside. There were bags on the bed. Makeup and what looked like new clothes. "Jude took me a couple of places on the way here so I could grab some stuff to get ready. He thinks it's an okay idea."

"It's a *terrible* idea. He threatened you. Even if he hadn't, going in there blind? Where these people operate? It's like stepping straight into the line of fire."

There was that familiar fire in Kate's eyes. "What did you want me to do?"

"Walk away."

"Where would that have gotten us, Noah? We bought two weeks' time, but if we don't know anything about them, there's nothing you can do to stop them. Can you honestly tell me you don't want to know what's going on? That you wouldn't do the same thing? At least now we'll have something concrete to work with."

I turned away for a second. There was no way to explain the fear I had for her doing this. She wasn't wrong, but at the same time, I couldn't even breathe. "An hour isn't enough time. If he's giving you an hour, then this place isn't close. That's on purpose. We won't have time to set up any kind of perimeter. The chance that we catch them is close to nothing."

Sitting down in front of the mirror again, she started putting on makeup. The open containers told me it's what she'd been doing when I knocked. "Right now that's fine with me," she said. "Because if you think that I'm risking Brandon's life by involving the cops yet? You're wrong."

"So you'll just risk your own life?"

She didn't say anything to that, but the hesitation in her body was obvious.

"Have you thought about whether they might be setting you up? That he *wants* you to fail? Because if this place is just far enough you can't make it, he'll have you. In the middle of nowhere."

That gave her pause. And it should. It was a very real possibility.

Finally, Kate met my eyes in the mirror. There was determination there. Burning resolve. "I'm going to do this. He has my number. I'm going to get the message, and I'm going to get us what we need. If you don't help, I'm going to do it anyway."

That's what I was afraid of. Her. Alone. With no way to call for help. "I know."

For a second fear flashed over her features. As if I would ever let her do this alone.

"We still have the earpieces. I'll ride with you in the trunk so I can be close by if anything happens."

Kate put down the makeup she was holding. She was fucking stunning, and I couldn't ignore it even though it was the last thing I should be thinking about right now.

"I can't let you go alone. Please, Kate."

She nodded once. "Okay."

~

This really was the middle of nowhere. The good news was we still had some time. We were a little way down the road, parked just out of sight. It wouldn't take more than five minutes for her to walk to what looked like an abandoned barn.

I suspected it was anything but.

It was more than halfway back to Resting Warrior. Way too close for my comfort. The only consolation was that the location was closer to our resources. Still not a warm and fuzzy feeling when a place like this was up and running so close to home.

Unfortunately, right now wasn't the time or place for me to deal with that anger. The stinging-cold wind coming across the field had me on edge, beside the fact I was about to send Kate into a place that I was afraid for her to go.

"Here," I said, helping her put the earpiece in again. "It's small enough that they won't be able to see it, and as long as you don't go into something with walls as thick as a bank vault, you'll be able to hear me."

It was almost the exact same speech I'd given her earlier when we'd been getting ready for the exchange. But Kate didn't say anything about the fact that I was telling her again. She hadn't said much of anything since her phone had chimed with Max's message.

The rest of the guys were on their way, along with Charlie and a whole phalanx of police. That was the second battle, getting her to let them come. She'd finally said yes after I'd promised they wouldn't make a move until we had absolute, concrete proof the Riders were up to some illegal shit.

Either way, it would take time for them to get here and all their equipment into place, especially without being spotted. For now, we were on our own.

Another gust of wind crashed into us, and I fought the flash of memory. I knew what it was like to be completely alone and not have backup—and know that the backup you needed was never going to come. Kate wasn't going to feel that. I would have her back for every second of this.

"I'm going to try to find a way inside," I said. "Walk around, see if there's a back entrance or something."

Her eyes flashed up to mine before flicking toward the barn. "Doesn't really seem like a place with a lot of options."

I forced a smile. "There are always options, promise. Besides, I'll be listening the whole time. Maybe we can pick up something that will give me an opening or an excuse and then I can just saunter in through the front door."

"Yeah, maybe." Kate laughed, but not like she actually found it funny. That was fine—I didn't either.

"I just want you to remember one thing."

"What's that?"

I fiddled with her earpiece for a moment before fixing my own. "I'll be listening to you the whole time. If you need me in there, you can tell me. I don't give a shit about anything else. If you tell me to come, I'll come and get you."

Kate looked up at me. It was dark, and the only light

was from the moon rising above the mountains, painting her face in silver. "Why?"

"Why what?"

She shook her head. "I don't understand why you would do that for me. I don't understand why you would do any of this for me."

I stayed silent for a moment before reaching for her earpiece one last time. It was an excuse to touch her at this point, because Kate . . . I didn't know what it was, but something about her called to me. I wanted to help her. But even as I thought those words, I knew it was deeper.

"I'm helping you because you're a person."

"What?" She blinked. "What does that mean?"

"It means you're a human being, Kate. Every person in the world deserves to have someone in their corner. Everyone deserves to have help when they need it. Believe me. I know what it's like to not have it."

She shuddered. "Even if that's true, you've still done more. You could have found my phone number, called me to tell me what you found, and let that be it. But you didn't, and I'm nobody."

"Not to me."

"Noah—"

I reached out and touched her arm. "You're not nobody, and you don't owe me anything. For any of it. But what I'm about to do? It has nothing to do with me helping you."

The question was in her eyes, and I knew after this, we couldn't go back. I leaned down and kissed her anyway.

Chapter 11

Kate

I saw the intent in Noah's eyes one second before he moved, and the next his lips were on mine. Gentle. Seeking. Insistent.

We were standing, freezing in the wind, and now there was no part of me that was cold.

Noah pressed me against the car, allowing both our bodies to line up. The body I'd seen that first day, I could feel all of it now, and it had my head spinning.

Love wasn't on my radar. Not in the slightest. I'd given up and resigned myself to the fact that I would be alone. Every date I went on seemed unimpressive.

There was nothing unimpressive about Noah.

After Brandon had come back, I'd been too busy trying to keep us both afloat to worry about things like dating and sex. Great job that I'd done on that front.

But it had led me here. Standing in the snow, being

kissed by one of the most gorgeous men I'd ever met in real life.

Of course I was attracted to him. I had been the second I'd seen his picture on the website. Even when I was *furious* at him, I was attracted to him. This whole time, I'd thought I'd been imagining the chemistry, and he was just helping me.

Now I didn't want to go inside that barn and face whatever was inside. I wanted to stay here and kiss Noah.

I shoved every last thought out of my head and leaned into him. Wrapped my arms around his neck so I could be closer. Tingling warmth and feelings I thought I'd buried spread from his lips all the way through me.

This was the best kiss I'd ever had.

There wasn't even a question.

Neither one of us wanted to pull away. I felt it in the way his hands tightened and he pressed me harder against the car. I wished I didn't need to breathe. When we broke apart, it felt like I'd run a marathon with the way I was trying to catch my breath.

Noah didn't move away, simply tilted his forehead against mine and breathed with me.

"I thought—" Even talking was a struggle after that. "I thought you didn't like me. Not like that."

"Kate." The roughness in his voice did things to my insides. "I've liked you since the first time we met."

"Oh."

"But to be clear, I was never helping you so that *this* would happen. It's important to me that you know that. I would have helped you either way."

Of course he would have. Because that's who Noah was. He helped people who needed it, even if they didn't deserve it. Like Brandon. "I know."

"Is this all right?" he asked.

I didn't speak. Instead, I lifted my mouth to his again. Noah took the hint. The first kiss had been soft and nearly soothing. An experiment.

This kiss?

This kiss was hot, hard, and hungry.

Noah's hand slipped behind my neck and pulled me closer. Lips slipped over lips. The way his tongue danced with mine had my mind imagining things I couldn't keep in my brain when I walked through those doors. Even though it was the last place I wanted to go now.

I couldn't get enough.

"Now," he growled, "you know when I say that I don't want to let you go in there alone, it's not only me being concerned about wanting to take these guys down. If you're in there and something happens—"

"I'll be okay." Despite wanting to stay here and kiss him until the sun rose, the anxiety I'd felt earlier had disappeared with the touch of his lips. I didn't care that it didn't make sense. I could do this. "You'll be in my ear the whole time."

"I wish it were more than that."

"It's just a party," I said with a shrug, taking on the confidence I was going to need inside. "Just some people. I'll be fine. And as soon as I get what we need, you call in the cavalry and this will all be over."

Noah took out his phone and glanced at it. "You have to go, or you'll be late."

But he didn't step away. He kissed me one more time. Just as hot, but this was slow. Deliberate. And over way too soon. "An incentive," he whispered.

"For what?"

He grinned. "For you to come back quickly."

That was the kind of incentive I could get behind.

Now he stepped away, and I straightened my coat. "Lipstick okay?"

"You're perfect."

I was glad it was dark enough that he couldn't see me blush. Taking a deep breath, I started the walk.

"Kate?"

It was hard turning back, knowing I couldn't stay. "Yeah?"

"Remember, if you need me, I'll come get you. Fuck everything else."

There was a darkness in that promise that made me shiver. He would do it. I didn't doubt it. Every man at that ranch was a warrior through and through. Noah was no exception. "I remember."

I felt his eyes on me as I headed down the road.

To the outside world, this place looked abandoned as I approached. Where were all the cars if this was a real party? Maybe they'd all parked and walked the way I had to keep things low-key?

Or maybe Max had sent me on some kind of wild goose chase so he'd have an advantage.

"You okay?" Noah asked.

"Yeah," I said quietly. "But it really doesn't seem like there's anyone here. Literally no signs of life."

Like I'd conjured it, a door opened in the wall of the barn. I jumped back as a guy even bigger than Max stepped out, looking me up and down. "You lost?"

I swallowed, summoning the confidence that I'd had back at the car. "My name is Kate Tilbeck. Max is expecting me."

He smirked. "Just in time."

My stomach dropped. He'd known who I was and was

testing me. Because of course he was. I put on a smile. "I told him I'd make it."

The man stepped back and gestured behind him into utter blackness. My heart picked up speed, pounding in my ears. I was the heroine in a horror film going into a dark basement alone.

Behind me, the door thumped shut, and he brushed past me to shove open another. This one opened on light and sound, blinding after the brief and total darkness.

I stepped into the party and looked around.

It . . . was normal?

I'd been expecting to step into some kind of den of horror. Chains hanging from the ceiling and a bunch of people screaming over an animal fight. This seemed more like a house party than anything else.

The bouncer stepped out from behind me. "Max will be with you in a minute. Don't wander off."

"Okay." I grinned at him, relieved I would be left alone for a couple of minutes.

There was a dance floor to my left, a bunch of people dancing to electric music that pumped through the floor, vibrating. They must have some amazing sound insulation, because no noise or vibration made it outside.

A few tables dotted the rest of the space with people playing poker. There was an extensive bar, well stocked and with a gorgeous blond serving the drinks. But nothing here looked remotely illegal.

"Noah," I whispered. "This isn't what we thought."

"Are you okay?"

"I'm fine. There's nothing here."

I heard the shock in his silence. "What do you mean?"

"I mean there's nothing weird in here. People dancing. Drinking. Playing poker. But this party could be in anyone's basement. The only thing that's weird here is that this barn is in the middle of nowhere."

Noah swore softly. "Well, that alone is enough to make me think they're hiding something."

"Right," I said quietly, aware that if I talked to myself too much, someone was going to notice. "But nothing I can see right now. But I'll keep looking."

"Kate—"

"I'm in now. Can't back out when I told Max I'd be here. Too much on the line either way, especially when he went out of his way to get me here."

"He threatened you," Noah said flatly.

"Glad you could make it," a loud voice said behind me.

I turned. Max was walking toward me. Same clothes, same gun, completely different attitude. "I said I would."

He reached out and yanked me toward him, embracing me and patting me down at the same time. The scent of alcohol was obvious. "I thought you might chicken out."

"Of course not."

"Well," he smiled, "I'm certainly glad that you're here."

The glint in his smile told me he was glad for a very different reason than I *wanted* him to be glad. "Here. Give Aaron your coat, and I'll get you a drink."

So the bouncer's name was Aaron. I made a note as I handed him the coat, wishing that I could keep it on. The shirt I'd bought when Jude had taken me to the store was pretty, and not revealing, but Max was drunk enough that I didn't think it would matter either way.

I was right.

A low whistle landed in my ears as he came back with a red plastic cup. "You clean up good, Katie."

I fought the nausea in my stomach and smiled. "Thank you, but my name isn't Katie."

"It is here," he said with a laugh. "Come on, I've got money on this game, and I'm not about to lose. You'll be my lucky charm."

He watched as I pretended to take a sip of the drink he'd handed me. There was no way in hell I was actually going to drink it. Even if I could use the alcohol to steady my nerves, I wasn't about to take that chance.

We walked around the dance floor to a poker table all the way in the back and nearly hidden. If there was a VIP section in this place, this was it. The men sitting around the table were like Max. More guns and dark looks, but they mostly ignored me.

A couple of other girls were standing behind chairs, watching the men play. I had to fight not to roll my eyes at the obvious sexism. But Max hadn't lied. A huge pot of money was in the center. Enough that the four grand I'd given him earlier seemed like pocket change.

"Wow," I said. "That does look like a lot."

"And when I win it, I'll use it to take you out on the town."

I smiled and pretended to take another sip.

"Remind me to make sure he gets arrested," Noah muttered in my ear.

Max downed the rest of a glass that looked like whiskey. He was clearly already drunk, and that wasn't going to help matters much. "This," he said with a gesture back at me, "is Brandon's sister. Told her we would have kicked him out a lot earlier if we'd known how hot she was."

The guys around the table laughed as they looked me up and down. I tried to react like it was a compliment. "How could I resist an invitation like that?"

Max burst out laughing, as if he hadn't threatened me with violence to get me here. Had he forgotten that? He forgot something. As soon as the cards started to move again, I was invisible.

It was a relief, but also a trap. I couldn't leave without him knowing, and I couldn't go poking around for stuff they might be hiding without getting myself into trouble. But then again, it really didn't look like there was anything to find.

"*Yes*." Max roared the word so loudly every person at the party looked over. He'd surged out of his chair, knocking it backward and nearly into me. "Read them and weep, you fuckers." He tossed his cards down on the table. With the cards already on the table, he'd managed a full house. Not bad.

The other men rolled their eyes, but they started to toss their cards and get up to leave.

"You don't want to play?" Max asked.

"I've lost enough money for one night," a man in a leather coat said as he slung an arm around one of the girls' shoulders. "Now it's time for something I could never lose to you. Ass."

Max laughed and turned to me. "I don't need your ass, Greg. I have my own."

"The fuck he does." Noah's voice was dark in my ear. I wanted to say something, but I couldn't.

"Come on," Max said. "I need another drink. So do you."

"That's okay." I put on my best flirtatious smile. "I'm still working on this one." But I followed him to the bar and watched as he slammed back another shot of whiskey.

His eyes were fully on me now. "You seem like a girl who likes darts."

"I've never really tried." That was the truth.

"Let's go." The next shot was ready for him, and he grabbed my hand, pulling me to the opposite side of the barn where a dart board that looked like it had been made in the last century hung off the wall.

It was everything I could do not to rip my hand out of his. "Are you sure?"

"Of course. Darts are fun. Especially when I get to teach you how."

I was already imagining the way he planned to "teach" me darts. His hand on mine, probably pressed up against the back of my body so there was nowhere that I could go. Forcing a happy moment into my brain, I laughed. "Actually, I need to use the bathroom first. Where's that?"

"Other side." He pointed before tossing back the shot still in his hand. "Come back soon."

"Okay."

The bathroom was small and dark, but thankfully it was just one room, so I knew I was alone. "Noah, we need to call it off."

"Why?"

"Because there's nothing here. A few guns maybe, but you and I both know a couple of unregistered guns aren't what we need. So having this place raided only puts Brandon in more danger."

And me too, probably. But I didn't say that part out loud.

"Yeah." I heard the frustration in his tone, but it wasn't directed at me. "You're right. I'll let them know it's a bust."

"All right. I'll get out soon."

"Be careful," he said. "Max sounds like he's ready to take you into a back room."

Noah wasn't wrong. "He's drunk. Hopefully I can use it."

"I'll be waiting."

I pushed out of the bathroom and went back to Max, watching him throw darts and missing the board completely. "It's getting kind of late," I said. "And I have a long drive back to the city, so I think I'm going to go home."

The look he gave me sent a flash of fear rolling through me. He looked sober. Then he smiled. "That's fine. I'll be in touch."

The way he said it made me anxious, but right now? I was going to take the win and leave. Aaron gave me my coat and let me out through the strange dark door back into the incredible silence of the Montana countryside.

Max hadn't said anything about knocking money off of Brandon's debt. But I hadn't really expected him to. It was just an excuse to get me here.

Don't run, I said to myself. *Don't run.*

There wasn't a reason to. Nothing in the barn had been awful. Well, not awful enough to call in the cops. It was still dangerous, and I knew that. I'd used up all the confidence I'd mustered, and now I wanted the hell out of here.

Noah paced near the car, clearly feeling the same nervous energy I was. As soon as he heard the crunch of my boots, his head snapped up. He didn't wait for me to reach him.

He was there, and he was pulling me to him. Not a gentle hug. This was a fierce embrace. Noah's arms crushed me against his body, and it was exactly what I needed. I was out. Nothing had happened. That was good.

"I'm sorry," I said into his coat. "We didn't get what we needed."

"I don't care."

I laughed once. "We both know that's not true."

"It is," he said. "I don't care about that right now. I'm

just glad that you're out of there and that, for now, it's over."

I closed my eyes and let my heart slow to normal, enjoying the rare feeling of being held and cared for. Yet I couldn't help but notice the undercurrent of failure to my thoughts—as good as this felt, it didn't solve anything.

Chapter 12

Kate

The couch in the Resting Warrior lodge was arguably the most comfortable that I'd ever slept on. But it was still a couch, and I couldn't sleep on it forever. At some point, I needed to go home, and it seemed like today was as good as any.

I'd shown up just like Max had wanted me to. They knew where to find me. There was no reason to think they were following me now. Why do that when they could just call me?

The coffee I made was still steaming in my mug as I stared into the morning fire. I didn't want to go home. There was a peace at the ranch I didn't get in Missoula. But my apartment wasn't going to clean itself, and the longer I put it off, the longer I would dread it.

The door opened and Noah came in. My stomach fluttered with brand-new butterflies. Last night when we'd come back here, he'd kissed me good night before going home.

I didn't regret those kisses. Not at all. But seeing someone for the first time after kissing them in the dark always felt strange. Those moments last night had felt intimate and different because of where we'd been and what we'd been doing. Was that all it had been?

"Good morning," he said with a smile.

"Morning. There's more coffee, if you want it."

"I'd love some."

I forced myself not to look back and drink in every part of him in the daylight.

He groaned when he took the first sip. "You make good coffee."

"As well as anyone who can put grounds in a maker," I said with a laugh.

"You're right." He sat in the chair near me. "There's no logical reason why it should be better, but trust me. I drink that coffee every day, and this is the best coffee I've had in months."

My cheeks suddenly felt hot with the compliment. "Thank you."

Noah looked at the fire before he looked back at me. "How are you?"

"Good. As much as I don't want to, I thought I'd go back to Missoula today. Start cleaning up the apartment so it's actually livable when Brandon gets out of the hospital. Plus, work."

His eyes sharpened. That was the only way to describe it. Like he was suddenly looking at all of me—inside and out. "I don't like it, but I also can't think of a reason you shouldn't." He let one side of his mouth tip up into a smile.

"Can't stay on the couch forever."

"I'd be willing to test that theory."

I laughed. "It is a very comfortable couch."

"Do you have to leave now?" He took a sip of coffee. "Or can you stay a bit?"

"What did you have in mind?"

There his real smile. "Well, I thought you might help me with the animals, if it's something that interests you at all. You said you'd never really been around them. This would be a good chance."

Did he really want me to help with the animals? Or was this simply a way to spend more time with me? Did that matter?

No. No, it didn't matter. "I'd like that."

He smiled wider.

"But I don't want to deal with poop."

Noah laughed, the sound echoing off the rafters and coming back. "Don't worry. That's day two."

"Perfect."

"Whenever you're ready," he said. "Come meet me at the stables. Take your time."

I did take some time. There wasn't any rush for me to get back to the city. All that waited for me there were cleaning products and broken glass. Quickly, I checked in on work to make sure the sky wasn't falling before I packed up and put my laptop and suitcase in my car so I wouldn't have to worry about it later.

Noah was at the stables, just like he'd promised. "Ready to get dirty?"

"Are we?"

He grinned. "No. We're not. Just feeding everyone and making sure they have water and that it's not frozen. I took care of the messy part already."

"Oh, okay." That was a relief. I wasn't sure how to act now. It had been a long time since I'd done this kind of thing with anyone, and I felt like we were dancing around it.

I followed Noah across the barn, expecting to see where the food was. What I didn't expect was for him to turn, catch me around the waist, and press me back into a pillar between the stalls. My breath caught. "Hi."

Noah raised one eyebrow. "Hello."

"What are we doing?"

"Right now? We're talking. After that, we'll see."

This was so much like last night that I shivered. The way he had me pinned up against something hard. I liked it. "What are we talking about?"

"Well, I was going to ask you why you feel as skittish as one of our new arrivals this morning. Are you all right?"

"I'm fine." Better now I was in his arms, but I didn't say that.

"Fine usually means not fine."

Blowing out a breath, I looked up at him. I liked being this close during the daytime. I got a chance to really *see* him. Those dark blue eyes I could drown in. "I just don't know how to do this. I'm out of practice."

"This?"

I lifted my hand from where it rested on his arm and gestured between the two of us. "After last night."

For a moment his face darkened. "Any regrets?"

"No." The answer was immediate. "None at all. It's just been a long time since I even thought about . . . that."

He leaned in an inch. "May I kiss you again?"

"Yes."

I'd barely whispered the words before his lips were on mine. Now that it was familiar, neither of us held back. Noah deepened the kiss, stroking his tongue along mine in a way that made me shiver. Every anxiety dropped away.

After the tension of last night, I'd been worried

daylight would somehow make this less real. But the same chemistry sang between us now. Solid. Physical. Just like then, I didn't want to break away from him.

"Okay," I said when he pulled back, my eyes still closed. "It's real."

"Did you think it wasn't?"

"Yes. No. I wanted it to be, but I wasn't sure." My cheeks flamed with a blush.

Noah was smiling. "If you want me to stop, let me know."

"Definitely not."

He laughed, actually guiding me to the food this time. That slight awkwardness was gone, and now helping him with the animals was fun. Noah didn't touch me again, but I felt his eyes on me the whole time, watching.

It felt like he *was* touching me.

The animals were amazing. The horses were gentle, the alpacas had me laughing, and the dogs were so joyful they nearly knocked me over. It didn't feel like we spent hours together, but it was afternoon when we finished. Even if I didn't want to, I had to leave.

Noah walked me to my car.

"Keep me in the loop," he said. "Please. If anything happens with Brandon, you, or the Riders, I'd like to know."

"Or you'll show up in Missoula again?" I teased.

The look on his face didn't look remotely like teasing. "Please promise me, Kate. I know there wasn't anything there last night, but we know these guys aren't messing around. No matter what, they're dangerous."

"I promise."

"Thank you."

We stood there for a moment, something stretching between us. Whatever this was, it was still breakable.

Leaving like this, I was glad he didn't step forward and kiss me again. Because if he did, I wouldn't be able to make myself go.

He watched me as I drove away, staying in my rear-view mirror until I couldn't see him anymore.

The drive wasn't bad, but it was getting dark by the time I'd checked in with Brandon at the hospital, stopped for some cleaning supplies, and pulled into the parking lot. This wasn't going to be fun.

I forced the door open. It wasn't sitting right on its hinges anymore. That was one of the first things that I needed to fix. But looking at the damage, I wasn't sure I shouldn't just buy a new door. The handle wasn't working properly, the hinges were bent, and even the doorframe was worse for wear.

I definitely wasn't getting my security deposit back.

Was that a thing? Could you tell a property management company your apartment had been destroyed by gang members looking for your brother so you couldn't be held responsible for the damage?

Yeah, I didn't think so.

My suitcase was still in the car. I wasn't entirely convinced I would be able to stay here yet. It was going to take way more than one night to fix all this.

Standing in the middle of the living room, I looked around. There was almost nothing that wasn't damaged or broken. It was just *stuff*, but emotion rose up in me anyway. This was the one place I was supposed to feel safe . . .

I let the tears build and spill over. Pushing them down wasn't going to do me any good. I needed to get them out. Only a few minutes. That's what I allowed, wallowing in the pain, the fear, and the sadness.

Then I got the broom and started with the glass first.

It wasn't the things, exactly. It was what they'd meant. I

JOSIE JADE & JANIE CROUCH

was proud of the fact I'd built a business on my own. That I could support myself and pay my bills. Help Brandon when I needed to. This? Helpless and standing in the wreckage of what I'd built?

It made me feel like none of it mattered.

The sound of my phone ringing made me jump like a startled cat. I had to stop and put a hand on my chest. Was I really that on edge? I needed to calm down if I was reacting like that to the phone ringing.

I found it where I'd left it in the kitchen, and my stomach dropped. Maybe I wasn't overreacting after all. Max's name was on the screen. I very much didn't want to talk to him. Should I let it go to voicemail?

An instinct deep down told me that would be a bad idea. I needed to take this call even if his name made me want to take the phone to the river and hurl it in.

I swiped answer on the screen. "Hello?"

"Hello, Kate." That voice was a far cry from the slurred happiness of the night before.

"Max," I said carefully. "Good to hear from you."

He laughed. "I hope so. You passed the test."

My stomach plummeted into the core of the earth. "The test? There was a test?"

"There was. The first party is always a test to make sure you're not a liar and end up bringing the cops."

"Oh."

I could almost hear him shrugging. "But you were a good girl. You passed. Now, you have to come to the real party, and we'll actually discuss your debt. But the same rules apply. Since I'm surprising you, and I'm a nice guy, I'll give you an hour and fifteen minutes this time."

"Now?" My mouth went dry. This wasn't part of the plan. We had nothing in place. Noah wasn't ready. Nobody was ready.

"Right fucking now," he said. "Your time starts as soon as you get the text with the address."

The line went dead, and I stared at the screen for a second. It lit up with a new address. Clicking on it showed me a new location, but still in the middle of nowhere. This wasn't good.

What did I need? A different shirt. I sprinted to my closet and tore through it, looking for something that said I was ready for a party but that hadn't been destroyed by Max's rampage through the apartment.

I found one. Blue and silky that showed just enough skin that it would look like I'd dressed up without doing too much. I threw on mascara and lipstick and grabbed my phone before sprinting to the door. Noah's number was already dialing.

"Kate?"

"Max called me," I said, trying to catch my breath as I slammed the car door behind me. "Last night was a test."

"*What?*"

"To make sure I didn't bring the cops. There's a new address." I recited it to him. "Gave me an hour fifteen. I think I used up seven getting ready."

On the other end of the line I heard the sounds of him moving too, and he cursed.

"I don't want to do this," I told him. "But I can't afford not to."

"I know." His voice was rough. "Believe me, I don't want you to do it either."

I sighed. "We both know that we don't have an option."

"You still have the earpiece?"

It was in my pocket. "Yeah. I do. I'll make sure to turn it on, but if I run out of time, I can't wait for you."

In the background, Noah's truck roared to life. He was

already coming. Pure relief flowed through me. "I know," he said. "But I'm on my way. You won't be able to hear me until I'm in range, but I'll let you know the second that I am."

"Okay."

"Kate," he said.

"Yeah?"

"Please, please be careful."

I took a shaky breath. "I will."

We hung up. I slammed the address into the GPS at a stoplight on the way out of town, eager to reach the highway so I could pick up speed. So I could go in the last direction that I wanted to go.

~

Noah

The steering wheel creaked under my hands.

Fuck.

Last night I'd been frustrated as hell it had all been for nothing. Now I truly wished that's all it had been. That we'd been wrong and all of it had been a misunderstanding or some kind of dream. Because this was far, far worse.

If last night had been a test, then everything we'd feared would be at the party last night would be there *now*. And Kate had no backup.

I shouldn't have let her go home alone. Something had told me that I shouldn't, but I'd ignored it. I'd thought it was wanting to keep her close and kiss her into oblivion that was clouding my instincts.

When was I going to learn to just listen to them?

Shaking my head, I let out a brand new string of curses. On the surface, there hadn't been any reason to prevent her from leaving the ranch. But I had *known* I shouldn't have let her. Or at least I should have gone with her.

Now this was happening. She was walking into danger alone.

After last night, there was no chance I'd be able to get Charlie to muster the troops. They weren't going to do that again without hard evidence. They were certainly going to have that by the time we were done.

All the guys were away. Lucas was taking the shift at the ranch. Harlan and Grace had gone camping out of cell range. Grant, Liam, and Daniel were on an overnight drop-off of some animals down in Colorado. I didn't know where Jude was, but for this? I needed more than one-man backup.

I dialed Lucas.

"What's up?"

"We're fucked," I said. "That's what's up."

His voice changed, and I knew his entire focus was on me now. "What's going on?"

I quickly relayed everything, along with the address.

Lucas let out a breath. "That's really out there."

"Yeah." I was familiar with the general area, and signal was notoriously spotty. Which was exactly what they'd want for something like this. A space where it was hard to track signals? Perfect for something this far underground. "The transmitter should be fine though," I said. That was a different kind of signal.

"I'll let everyone know," Lucas said. "They're going to be pissed."

"They can get in line."

"You want me to call Charlie?"

I shook my head even though he couldn't see me. "They won't be able to do anything. Not in time."

"And you think you will?" Lucas asked. It wasn't sarcastic, it was a genuine question.

"I don't know. But there's no way in hell I'm just letting her go in there alone. We'll get what we need, and then we'll make sure the next time Charlie rallies the troops, it's not a test."

"Right. Keep us in the loop. Should I send Jude your way?"

"Keep him on standby."

I hung up and tossed the phone on the seat next to me. All I could do now was hope I made it in time before anything got worse.

Chapter 13

Kate

There were similarities to last night. The barn I approached seemed just as abandoned. And without Noah in my ear yet, I was very much aware of how alone I was. There was nothing but the wind sweeping across the fields and the clouds moving over the moon.

And a couple other people walking toward the barn. Men. Chills ran down my spine. I knew there were people inside and that I wasn't actually alone. But that didn't mean I was safe. Every cell in my body knew that I was anything but.

Parking a short distance away gave me a little time to procrastinate. I couldn't wait any more though—I was out of time. Where was Noah? Was he close?

Another invisible door opened, and there was Aaron. He asked the men in front of me for a password, but I wasn't close enough to hear the answer.

I didn't have the password. Did I need one?

Last night Aaron had looked at me warily. Like an enemy. This time, he was smiling. "Welcome back."

"Thanks."

He waved me through without a password.

It was much harder to muster the persona I'd created last night. Every step was shaky, and I didn't know what I was going to do once I got in there. All I knew was that I had to do it.

The inner door opened, and everything was different. This. *This* was the nightmare my brother had painted.

No one was dancing at this party. Music still pounded through the air, and there was still a bar with a beautiful woman behind it. But the entirety of this place was centered around a pit. Railings ringed it, and there were bodies pressed up against those railings. They were cheering and screaming. Through the gaps in the bodies I could see movement, and I heard the squeal of a dog.

Dogfighting.

I was going to be sick.

This wasn't something I wanted to see.

Clearly, people were betting. I'd only been looking for thirty seconds and I'd already seen money change hands twice. This was what we needed. Hard proof that these assholes were doing something illegal. Only this time, no one was coming to arrest them. We were totally in the dark.

Aaron took my coat and walked away.

"Kate?" Noah's voice crackled to life in my ear.

I inhaled so fast I almost choked. The music and cheering were loud enough that I risked it. "I'm here."

"Good." He sounded as relieved as I felt. "Is it bad?"

"Yes."

That's all I could say, because Max was making a

beeline straight for me. "Kate." His smile was sharp. "Glad you made it."

"Of course." I grinned at him. "Wouldn't miss it."

He wasn't drunk tonight. In fact, everything about him seemed honed. Sharper than a knife blade. That made him about ten times more dangerous. I wouldn't be able to rely on the fact that he wouldn't remember things in the morning.

I was here. What did I do now?

"This is quite the party," I said, trying to look the part. It wasn't hard to act overwhelmed. I was. "And I'm amazed anyone can find this place. It's even worse than the one last night."

"You found it, didn't you?"

Grinning up at him, I ran my fingers through the end of my hair. "I did. But I'm special."

Max's eyes roved down my body, just like I knew they would. I could have been wearing a bikini the way he looked at me, but I did my best to ignore it. "You are that." Reaching out, he grabbed my arm. It wasn't gentle. "Let me give you the tour."

"Okay."

"First, let's get you a drink." We went over to the bar, and he signaled the bartender.

She dropped what she was doing the second she saw him signal. "What can I get for you, Max?"

"Nothing for me. Kate here can have whatever she wants."

"A beer," I said quickly. "I'll take the bottle." It was the only thing I could think of that was sealed. Far less likely they'd spiked all the beer bottles on the off-chance a woman drank one. Still, I didn't plan on letting my senses down.

"Kate," Noah said. "We don't have backup this time. I

don't want to leave you in there alone. If you can, find out enough to get me in."

The bartender passed me the beer with a smile. I'd watched her open it. I turned to Max and locked eyes with him while I took a long sip. Leaning against the bar, I tried to pretend that he wasn't a man who was threatening me. He was someone I was interested in. What would I do if it were Noah standing there?

I shoved the thought out of my head. There were plenty of things I would do—that I wanted to do—with Noah that would not be a part of this. I brought out my flirtatious smile anyway. "You never answered my question."

He leaned against the bar too, mirroring me. "Which question was that?"

"How the hell do people find this place? I don't think everybody at this party has you on speed dial like I do."

That got me a laugh. "No. Not everyone is so lucky. I suppose since you passed your test, I'll tell you."

It wasn't lost on me that he'd said *my* test. So there were others, and some people got a different one.

"It honestly depends. Sometimes we have people who've heard about this place from a friend of a friend and they reach out. Sometimes they come to parties like last night's, and if we like them, then we give them the password. Sometimes they have to earn it."

I frowned like I was confused. "If they heard about it from friends, then why don't the friends give them the password?"

Max's eyes took on a nearly feral glint. "Because the password changes. And they know if they give out the password without permission, there are consequences. Your brother would know all about that."

Swallowing, I took another sip of my beer. The sour taste grounded me. "Is that what he did?"

"No," Max said. "But the results are similar."

"What's tonight's password?" He looked at me, like he was wondering what I could want with the info. Anxiety zipped along my nerves, and I shoved it down. I rolled my eyes. "You said the password changes and I'm already here. Who am I going to tell?"

Max grinned. "Fine. You're lucky that I like you."

I giggled, putting on a show. "I am."

"Tonight the password is 'tangerine.' "

Noah was immediately in my ear. "That was amazing, Kate. I'm on my way. Just keep him going, all right? I'll be there soon."

Making sure nothing showed on my face, I laughed. "Tangerine? Why tangerine?"

"Why not?"

I shrugged. "I don't know. It doesn't exactly match the vibe."

"Exactly. The more random the password, the less likely someone will guess it."

"You have to admit," I took another sip, "that if someone came and just randomly guessed the password, out of all the words in the English language, that would be really impressive."

Max chuckled. "I guess."

"I'm ready for the rest of the tour."

"There's not much to it." He pointed. "Over there we do have a couple of poker tables, but we don't really use them on fight nights. Over there is the in-house betting. People can make bets with each other all they like. But we pay a lot better."

He didn't have to say they took a lot more too. We both

already knew that. My brother was still sitting in the hospital with those consequences written on his skin.

"And of course, there's the pit."

I glanced toward the crowd of people surrounding the dip in the ground. That was the place I was the least interested in. So of course it was where Max was going to take me.

He took my arm again and pulled me away from the bar, guiding me with a hand on the small of my back all the way around the pit to a back corner. There was a small elevated platform with a table and what looked like a comfortable restaurant booth.

This was VIP, I guessed.

A sound of pain came from the pit, and there was a visceral reaction in the crowd. I didn't look. Didn't want to look. If an animal had just died—

I focused on the ground in front of me and climbing the stairs to that platform. Settling on the couch. Taking a small sip of beer. Anything to keep from looking into that pit and seeing something I wouldn't be able to unsee.

"Don't be shy," Max said, pulling me up off the couch and over to the railing that overlooked the fighting pit. I couldn't look afraid. Couldn't be afraid. I still didn't look directly into the dip in the ground, instead looking at the surrounding crowd and trying to focus on what Brandon had said. That he'd felt alive.

His hand was still on me, around my arm, but now he stretched it out around my shoulder. It was a casual movement, but possessive. I wouldn't easily be able to shrug him off without giving offense or letting him know all of this —*all of it*—was an act.

"Any interest in making a bet?" he asked.

I laughed. "Already have one debt to take care of. I'll think about that after."

"If you're sure. We have some good candidates for the next fight." He pointed with the hand that wasn't pulling me into his body.

Following his gesture, I saw two dogs in cages. Neither of them looked healthy. But one was obviously angrier than the other, snarling at anyone who came close. The other dog looked small and weak. It was pressed to the back of the cage, trying to sleep.

Tears pressed at the backs of my eyes. I had to get it together. I couldn't cry right now. I blinked them back. "Are you going to bet on one of them?"

Max thought about it. "The house odds are on the dog on the right."

The angry one.

"But what are your odds on?"

One side of his mouth went up, and his hold loosened as he turned toward me and leaned on the railing. "I usually bet on the quiet ones. They tend to surprise you."

"Good to know."

He was looking at me too closely. "We never got to discuss your debt last night. My original offer is still on the table."

Hell no. "You mentioned there were opportunities to reduce it for people who came here. Are there?"

"There are. But that involves betting against your debt."

Of course. In my ear, Noah swore. So the options he was giving me were to sleep with him, or to bet on a fight that had no guarantees and possibly dig myself deeper into trouble. Neither of those were good options. "I'll be here for a bit." I sipped my beer. That was probably the last time that I could. No part of me wanted my senses impaired in this place. "If I see a bet I like, I'll think about it."

"And the other thing," he insisted. "Think about the other one. I promise you your debt will evaporate. Give me three nights."

I raised an eyebrow, but I looked at him. Really looked at him like I was considering it. I wasn't, but he didn't have to know about it. "It's early. I'll think about it."

Max grinned like I'd just given him a cookie and pulled me back against his side. It took everything in me not to push him off. As long as his hands stayed neutral, I could handle it.

Across the room, there was a shuffle of bodies and a voice. Someone asking to see who was in charge.

There he was. But he looked different. Dangerous. There was a predator on the loose now, and it was coming straight toward me.

Noah.

Chapter 14

Noah

I'd been to places like this before. Not for a long time. Never so close to home. I hadn't had the pleasure in years, and I wished that my streak had been longer.

The fact that this place was even closer to Resting Warrior than last night was shocking. It made me question what else we might be missing, if an operation that ran so diametrically opposed to our mission could get away with it. But that was a question for another day, when I wasn't in the middle of this.

Right now, my focus was like a laser pointed straight at Kate and Max. The asshole was already treating her like a piece of property. The fact that his hands were on her made me want to grab him and throw him into the pit.

Hopefully at some point in taking them down, I could.

The flash of darkness in those thoughts gave me pause, but I pushed it aside. I'd gotten my wish. I was in. Now I had to make the most of it and live with the consequences later.

A cheer went up from around the pit. Another fight starting. My jaw creaked I was clenching it so hard. I didn't let it show. Instead, I funneled every bit of anger I had into an arrogant stride. Confidence that made people get out of my way as I strode toward Max.

Kate saw me and froze. I would look different. I'd slicked back my hair and had on darker clothing. A leather jacket and dark jeans. If I'd had the time, I would have put on some tattoos to blend in more with the crowd. As it was, I'd been lucky that I had some clothes in the emergency kit in my truck that worked. This party was no place for a rancher.

Still far enough away that I could disguise my words, I spoke. "I'm no one to you, Kate. Don't let it show."

Her eyes flicked away from me toward the fight, and again away from that. I didn't blame her. It wasn't anything I wanted her to see.

I stopped in front of their little balcony and looked up at Max. "They say you're the guy in charge."

"Who's asking?"

"Someone who heard you do more than just animal fighting in this pit, and if that's true, then I want in."

Max looked at me, sizing me up. What would he bet on me? We were about to find out.

His gaze turned suspicious. "How did you get in here?"

Thanks to Kate, I could make this work. "I had the password. Been around for a bit, some of your other parties. Finally got hooked up."

"And your name is?"

I raised one eyebrow. "The kind of places we're talking about don't usually use names. Didn't expect to need one here. Just interested in making some money. If that's not an option, I can find somewhere else."

He stopped me before I could fully turn around. "So you want to fight?"

"I do. I'll even put a big fucking wager on myself so you have nothing to lose."

He pulled Kate tighter to his side, and I fought the urge to curl my hands into fists. All I wanted to do was sweep her away from this place and these people, but I could barely afford to look at her in case this asshole thought I was being too interested.

"I'll see what we have for tonight," Max said before glancing at Kate. "Stay here."

He came down the stairs and disappeared behind the platform. I just barely caught a glimpse of him going through a door, and there were more people back there. That was interesting.

What was he actually doing? If he had to confer with other people, then maybe Max wasn't who we thought he was. That could make sense. Have him be the front man and the face of things while someone else pulled the strings. If I were inclined to have a business like this, it's what I would do.

Kate looked at me before turning her head away. "You can't do this." Her voice was breathless in my ear. "Don't put yourself in that position."

"Stop." I said the word as gently as I could, and it was still too harsh. The character I was playing was hard to let go of in one breath. "Don't give him any reason to doubt. I can handle this."

She looked at me then, and there was terror on her face.

"Kate," I tried not to move my lips, instead leaning on the base of their little VIP platform and pretending like I was bored. "You haven't seen this side of me, but this isn't anything I haven't done before."

"Okay." Her voice was small, and I hated that. It drove all my protective instincts to the surface, and it hurt like hell to have to beat them down.

Max strode around the corner and saw me. "You're in. Could use a bit of a mix-up in tonight's entertainment. And besides," he looked me up and down, "it's always fun to see a newbie get their ass beat."

I smiled, letting it take on a dangerous glint. "We'll see about that."

"I like confidence," Max said, slapping me on the arm. "But we like money better. You said you would wager on yourself. That's what's holding your spot, so you better make good."

"Lead the way."

I followed Max back through the crowd to their bookie. The second I'd walked in, I'd marked where he was, but the longer Max spent with me, the less time he spent pawing Kate like an animal.

The bookie looked at me as Max shoved me forward unnecessarily. "Which side are you betting on?"

"My side."

"He's the next fight," Max told him. "Wants to make a bet on himself, and I'm going to let him."

The man couldn't look more bored. "How much?"

"Twenty grand."

He looked up at me. "Come again?"

"I want to bet twenty grand on myself."

In my ear, Kate gasped. She knew what that meant. It meant that if I lost, I'd be getting the same kind of visit her brother had. But I had the money, and I wouldn't need it. I could take whatever they threw at me, and I would win.

Max laughed. "That's not what I thought you meant."

"Is it going to be a problem?"

"Not at all. Just want to make sure you know what you're getting into. Throwing away twenty k ain't nothing."

"I'm not throwing it away."

He laughed again and clapped me on the shoulder. "Whatever you say. But if you lose, and it turns out you don't have this money? You're going to answer to me. Understand?"

Only for him, I put on a show of fear. Nervous energy. I swallowed. "I understand."

"Good. Mark him down."

I watched as the bookie did exactly that, along with my nameless phone number, and then stalked away toward the side of the pit opposite Kate to prepare myself. My confidence wasn't false, but I also couldn't afford to take this lightly.

In the arena, there were sounds I needed to block out, otherwise I was going to descend into pure rage. Actually, that wasn't a terrible idea.

I'd spent a long time confronting the horrors that lurked in my memory. Months of torture were written on my body and in my mind. And I'd spent a lot of that time overcoming the violent impulses that those memories brought to me.

But other times they became too much to bear. In those moments, I usually ended up in the Resting Warrior gym. Sometimes Jude joined me in fighting that battle. Sometimes the others. Because as much as I'd mastered those memories, they were always, *always* fighting to get out of the box I kept them in.

Time to let them out.

Raucous cheers exploded behind me. The fight was over, and they were pulling the dogs back from each other.

The smaller, calmer dog had won. That was why you never underestimated any opponent. It didn't matter if they looked like they couldn't beat you. There was every chance they could.

Exactly the way the man climbing into the ring was about to underestimate me.

"Got something special," Max called out in my direction. "Newbie over there came in and wanted a fight. We're going to oblige him."

Cheers.

"Place your bets."

The man that had already dropped into the pit was a giant. I wasn't short, but he had probably four inches and easily fifty pounds on me. That didn't bother me. I'd fought bigger men than him and won.

I stripped off my jacket, and then the shirt underneath it, letting my mind sink down into that place of darkness I worked so hard to keep it out of.

Gasps rippled through the crowd as they saw my scars. Let them look and wonder what the fuck I'd done to get them.

I couldn't stop myself from glancing at Kate. This wasn't the way I'd wanted to show her these. But nothing about this was what I'd wanted. I hoped that she would let me explain. And that once I did, she would still look at me the way she had this morning. Like I was someone worthy.

She looked nervous, staring at my opponent. If she looked at me, I would try to convey that it was going to be okay, but I couldn't do anything else. With a movement that looked like I was scratching my ear, I took out my earpiece and slipped it into the pocket of my jacket on the floor.

This was a fight. Anything could happen. I couldn't afford for it to be knocked out or discovered.

Enough stalling. I stretched my arms and made my way over to the ladder that led down into the pit but didn't bother to use it. I dropped straight in, landing on the balls of my feet.

"Last call for bets," the bookie shouted. People moved. Now that they saw the comparison between me and the guy across from me, they were more than willing to bet. On him, I imagined.

My back was to Kate. Which meant that she would see some of the worst of my scars.

Not now.

I thrust my mind into darkness and breathed in the terror, anger, and desperation that were always so close by. I would take it and use it. Wield it. Excise it.

"That's it," the bookie's voice reached me. "Bets are closed."

"Then let's do this," Max said.

The guy across from me moved. I didn't. Let him make the first move. I wanted to watch him. It wouldn't take long to pick up what kind of style he was used to.

He ducked and charged. Okay then.

I lunged to the side, avoiding his attempt at a hold, and used my elbow in his back to drive him into the wall. The crowd stilled. This was already more interesting than they'd anticipated.

Smiling, I gestured to him. *Come at me.* He did, and again, he missed. That was the thing about big opponents. They didn't always know how to use their mass to their advantage and ended up flailing.

"Fucking pussy," the man spat at me. "You just going to jump around and avoid me?"

He threw a punch, and I pushed it to the side, using my other hand to land my own, straight up into his jaw. That was the answer to that.

New anger flooded my system. My opponent took on more darkness than he had. He was one of the specters that haunted my nightmares, and I saw exactly where I could hurt him. I saw where I could kill him.

It would be easy.

He was still recovering, and I had just enough humanity left to know that I needed to end this quickly, before I went too far.

I only let him turn. Running to the wall, I pushed off it and up, giving me enough height to land another punch directly in the giant's face. He crumpled like dirty laundry. I followed him to the ground, punches still flying.

Blood spilled from his nose, and I punched him again. And again. His eyes would be black.

It would be so easy to keep going until there was nothing left. Let this darkness and hate burn me alive until I pressed it all into this man's body.

But when he went limp, I managed to pull my hand back.

There was nothing but silence around me.

I could hear a pin drop. It wasn't the outcome they'd been expecting, and not many—if any at all—had bet on me.

Smiling, I looked up at Max. "How's that for a newbie getting his ass kicked?"

I didn't wait for his response, climbing out of the pit and grabbing my clothes. I put the shirt on, and the jacket. I didn't bother with the earpiece. We were close enough now that I didn't need it.

"Guess I was wrong about you," Max said.

He was behind me, Kate at his side. Her eyes were wide, and I couldn't figure out what was behind them. Did I scare her? That was a possibility.

"Yeah, you were."

Max pulled Kate under his arm possessively. She stiffened, and my hands itched to throw him into the pit along with the guy who was currently being dragged out of it.

But aside from blowing our cover, all the eyes in the room were on us.

"Mark was undefeated," he said, too casually. "Never seen him get taken down like that. Ever."

"Not my fault your guy screwed up." *Or that you underestimated me*, I added silently.

"Congratulations. I mean it. But," Max seemed nervous now, "as far as your payment, we don't have that kind of money on site."

I could give a shit about the money, but this gave me an opportunity. Max in my debt put us in a position of strength. "So you let me bet that much, expecting me to pay it, but you can't do the same?" The disgust dripped through my voice. "Some operation you've got here."

"You'll get your money," he snarled. "You just have to come back next fight night to get it. We pay our debts, and we collect them. Just ask little Katie here about that. She knows all about it."

Kate smiled weakly, even as Max tightened his arm, practically pulling her against the front of his body.

"Fine," I spat. "I'll come back and collect. But I want something now."

He looked pissed, and I didn't care. "We can give you five."

I shook my head. "No. I want something from *you*." My eyes fell on Kate. "I want her."

"What?" she gasped, eyes angry. "I'm not a thing that you can buy—"

He shook her once, and she went quiet.

"I'll even knock three grand off the total," I said. My gut wanted to go higher, but I also didn't want to tip him off that I was more interested in Kate as anything more than a business transaction.

Max glanced back in the direction of the door he'd gone through earlier. I wasn't even sure he realized he'd done it. Then he looked down at Kate, long and hard. All I could see was the anger on his face when he made the decision. "Fine."

He shoved her at me, and I caught her.

"Are you serious?" She played her part perfectly. "You can't just sell me to some guy I don't know."

Max smirked. "I think you're forgetting what you owe me, Katie. Let's be honest about this. You were already jumping into my bed to pay off one debt. No point in being upset about paying off another. We'll have our moment."

Kate lunged, and I held her back, acting like I didn't even care that I'd just bought a woman. "You have my number," I said to Max and pulled Kate toward the door.

The look he gave me was lethal.

In my arms, Kate put up a good show of resisting. But that's all it was. A show. Beneath everything, I could feel her relief, even as I held her still and put her coat on her before marching her outside.

Until we were around the corner of the barn and no longer in sight.

Chapter 15

Kate

I was shaking, and I couldn't seem to stop. Snow came down hard around Noah and me as he marched me out of the party and into the darkness.

He waited until we were out of sight before wrapping me up in his arms. "Are you okay?"

That wasn't an easy question to answer right now. Was I okay? I didn't know. What I did know was that I hadn't been prepared for this.

The awfulness of the dogfights. Max touching me —*selling me*—and Noah's fighting . . .

I had known Noah was a former SEAL, and a warrior, but knowing that and seeing that in action were two very different things. The scars he had? I had no idea what they were from. But those weren't the kinds of scars you got from climbing trees or playing sports. Someone had hurt him.

The way he'd taken that man down was brutal. The sound of Noah's fist hitting his face would stay with me for a long time. I'd never seen any kind of fight up close before, and it wasn't like I'd thought.

It wasn't like what you saw in the movies. Which was a stupid thing to think, but it was the truth. On screen, it seemed exciting and easy. Watching it up close had let me see the true nature of it. The life and death quality. The reality that at any second, one or the other could no longer be alive.

It had needed to happen. I knew that. But I still didn't know how to process any of my thoughts about it, let alone say anything.

But at the same time, Noah had gotten me out. If he hadn't, I would have been in an impossible situation with Max, who thought me giving him my body was a done deal. Noah had risked himself for me. Risked *everything*. And that wasn't something I was going to forget either.

I still hadn't said anything out loud. Right now, I wasn't sure how.

"We need to go, Kate," he said gently. "We can't leave the cars for those guys to find. We'll talk about it, I swear. I'll make it right. But we need to leave."

He walked me to my car. Of course he'd found where it was.

"You know the way to the ranch from here?"

I nodded.

"Go straight there. Don't stop. I'll be right behind you."

That, I could do. Simple, easy instructions. Noah aside, Resting Warrior was the only place I wanted to be right now. I craved the calm peace that filled the entire property.

The snow was so thick I could barely see out the front

126

of the windshield. It was the kind of snow that no one liked, even if you were a Montana native, born and raised. This was snow that caused accidents, so even on abandoned back roads, the going was slow.

In my rearview, there were lights in the distance. Noah.

Thankfully, the concentration I needed on the road was enough that I couldn't sink into the mountain of questions I had, or give in to the sickness in my gut from being confronted with the worst of humanity.

I knew it hadn't been much. Not by comparison to some things. But it was enough to terrify me. I'd thrown myself into it and thought it would be easy to do, the way it had been last night. It wasn't. It didn't matter that I hadn't had a choice.

Now I understood why Noah hadn't wanted me to go at all.

Too late for that.

Finally, I pulled into Resting Warrior, and the relief I felt . . .

It was like I was melting into the seat of my car. I could just stay here and fall asleep. That would be fine. Parking in front of the lodge, I wasn't even fully sure I could make it up to the steps to that comfortable couch. All the energy had gone out of me, like I'd run a marathon.

Noah's truck pulled alongside my car a few minutes later. It didn't shut off. But there he was, at the door to my car, opening it and pulling me out into the snow. I didn't resist when he lifted me off my feet and up into the cab of his truck.

It didn't bother me. In spite of the violence I'd seen him dole out tonight, I knew he wasn't going to hurt me. Noah was *good* all the way down to his core. I knew that. He had darkness, but so did we all.

I leaned my head against the window as we drove.

Why did it feel like this? Why couldn't I seem to find my voice where it was buried all the way down in my gut? Why did it feel like I'd just walked a hundred miles in the desert without water?

It wasn't a long drive before we pulled up to a small two-story house, just barely visible in the swirling storm. Noah didn't carry me, but he didn't let me go either, making sure that I was on my feet as he unlocked the door and brought me inside.

It was dim in the entryway, but it was warmer than outside. "Come in, please," he said.

I took off my boots and my coat, following him into a comfortable living room. Coals were banked in the fire, so it took him only minutes to get a fire roaring.

A squeak distracted me seconds before an orange blur flew into my lap. I startled before I realized it was a kitten, another small black one following close behind.

"Oh my goodness," I said. My voice had reappeared for them.

Noah smiled at them like he was looking at naughty toddlers. Affection and frustration in equal measure. "That's Garfield and Salem. Currently my fosters."

The orange one—Garfield—batted at the ends of my hair and lost his balance, falling over himself and onto the couch beside me. "I didn't realize you were a cat person." Now I remembered he'd mentioned the kittens that first night when he'd given me the tour.

Noah laughed softly. "I'm not, really. But they had nowhere to go. And they're adorable. So against my better judgment I said I'd foster them over the holidays. My curtains regret that decision."

I picked up Salem, who snuggled into my arms. The

warmth of the fire was nice, and I curled deeper into the couch. This was good.

"Kate, will you look at me?"

It took me longer than I wanted to meet his eyes. When I finally did, he took a shaky breath. "Are you okay?"

"Yeah," I said. "But . . ." My words ran out.

"Yeah." He echoed me and cleared his throat. "I know. That was more than either of us expected or planned for."

That was an understatement.

"I'll be right back—I'm going to make some tea."

With Noah out of sight, I took a deep breath, holding the kitten closer, his small, warm body cuddling into me.

Why couldn't I get my shit together? No one had hurt me. Max touching me, despite what he'd thought was going to happen, could have been worse. I was *fine*. So why did the world feel like it was shifting under my feet?

How could I have missed something this big with Brandon? Was I that stupid? Or so blind I couldn't see that he was hurting? That he was struggling so much he'd go to *that* length just to feel like he was okay? Why hadn't he talked to me?

The spiral of my thoughts were pulling me deeper, and I wasn't sure how to find my way out of it. What did it say about me that my own brother couldn't even talk to me when he wasn't okay? We were all that the other had. We were supposed to be able to rely on each other.

And now?

It was clear he didn't trust me. Or hadn't. I didn't know if I could ever trust him again either. If I could, it was going to take a long time to get there.

Noah came back into the room carrying two steaming mugs. He placed them on the coffee table and disappeared again, coming back with cream and sugar. "How do you take it?"

"I can do it."

He looked at me with the ghost of a smile. "Looks like you have your hands full there."

That was true. "A little cream, a little sugar."

He made my tea and then his—cream with no sugar—before sitting on the other end of the couch. "Are you going to tell me what you're really thinking?"

I could feel everything bottled up coming to the surface, but I didn't want to scare this kitten, or the other one that was now curled up against my leg. So I let it out as quietly as I could.

"I just don't understand how Brandon could do that. Be a part of that. Help them . . ." I shuddered. "Help with those fights. Watch them and bet on them. Was he fighting too? Was he putting the animals in there? How far did he go? I just can't imagine why he would need it. Or if he was having such a hard time, why didn't he come to me?"

Noah took a sip of his tea. "I have an answer, but I need to ask you a question first."

"Okay."

Salem stretched in my arms and nearly tumbled out of them. I resettled the little black furball on my lap and reached for the tea. Noah had made it perfectly.

"What I did back there." The vulnerability in his voice was plain. "Did I—do I scare you?"

"No," I said. "It was hard to watch because I've never seen anything like that. But no, you don't scare me. I know that you wouldn't hurt me. What happened was necessary. You did it for me, and I'll never really be able to thank you for that."

He smiled the ghost smile again, and it dawned on me that he wasn't okay either. What happened in there wasn't something he craved, it was something he avoided.

"You saw my scars." He waited, but I said nothing. Whatever he was going to tell me, he needed to get it out without interruption. "When I was still a SEAL, my unit . . . we were ambushed in Iraq. We never saw it coming. And those of us that they didn't kill, they captured.

"Jude was in my unit too. We were the ones who survived. There were others, and they didn't make it. A rescue came for us, but there was a problem. They got me and couldn't get Jude. I was there for two months. Jude was there for six. The scars—" He cut himself off. "War will do things to you that you never imagined. And the pain that comes from that? It can make you seek out things that would have revolted you before, simply because seeing that kind of pain is the only thing that makes *your* pain feel real. Because most of the time, your pain isn't the kind people can see."

"Noah—"

He held out a hand, and I let him keep talking. "I've been dealing with my past for years. I know what it does to me. I know where it can take me. And even after this long, it's a struggle every fucking day. Brandon doesn't have the benefit of that experience. Maybe he went there to feel something and then he couldn't get out. Maybe he got caught up in something he didn't realize he couldn't control until it was too late. Either way, what he's done has nothing to do with what kind of sister you are."

I looked away. It made sense, but the reality of it still stung.

"And no matter what happens with these people, I am not going to let anything happen to you, Kate. I promise you. I would fight a hundred fights like that one if it kept that asshole from touching you again."

Between us, Garfield rolled onto his back, at once stretching and nuzzling against my leg. It was an overload of adorable. The fact that these kittens were so loving and so affectionate at such a young age was just another piece of evidence that Noah was good. And kind. And so much more.

"I know," I said.

Tension spun out between us. I was in his *house*. The whole thing with Max had just been a ploy to get me out of the party, but now that I was here, it wasn't exactly crazy for me to wonder . . .

I wanted that.

Noah felt like safety. And more than that, he made me feel things I'd forgotten.

Leaning forward, I placed my tea back on the coffee table and gently moved the kittens so they were curled in the blanket slung on the back of the couch. They woke up for a second but were so sleepy that it was only seconds before their eyes closed again.

Noah's eyes were on me the whole time. And they were still on me as I slid toward him. Took his mug and put it on the table. Leaned close and kissed him first.

Arms came around me and hauled me against his body, making sure I didn't doubt he *wanted* to kiss me. And kiss me, he did.

This one felt different. It rode the line of desperation and the things we both wanted but hadn't been able to say. My lips opened under his, and my whole body shuddered when his tongue danced with mine.

Abruptly, he broke away. "Fuck." The word was so soft that I barely heard it. "If I don't stop now, I won't be able to."

My stomach fluttered with nerves. "That was kind of the idea I had."

Noah lifted one hand to my face, the other tightening around my waist so that we were still pressed together. "I want you. You have no idea how much I want you."

My heart skipped a beat. "But?"

He leaned his forehead against mine. "But we're both still reeling. I don't want the start of this to be because of those assholes."

I hated that he was right, but he was. It didn't change the disappointment I felt, but this would be better. Leaning my head on his chest, I let myself breathe with him. "As long as this isn't no forever."

"It's not," he said, shifting beneath me. All of a sudden I could feel exactly how much it wasn't. He was fighting this want and need right along with me. "I don't have a guest room. You can take the bed."

"Noah." I looked up at him. "I can't sleep in your bed. *You* need your bed. I survived on the lodge couch—I'm sure your couch is just as comfortable."

"I don't sleep much," he said. "Because of . . . all the things I told you about. If anyone is going to get good use out of a bed right now, it's you."

"Are you sure?"

His eyes shifted away from me. How much was he having to hold in right now? How much had being in that fight really cost him? "I am."

"Okay."

I didn't want to pull away from him. It was the last thing I wanted, even if he was right.

With a little squeak, Garfield woke, stretching. "Are these little guys allowed in your bedroom?"

Noah laughed. "As if I could keep them out."

"Then I'll take them with me." Neither of the little furballs protested when I gathered them up in one arm. I grabbed my tea with the other. "Up the stairs?"

"Can't miss it."

I looked at him. "Good night, Noah."

The fire, heat, and hunger in his eyes as he looked at me were almost enough to make me beg. "Good night, Kate."

Chapter 16

Noah

I watched Kate disappear up the stairs with the kittens and scrubbed my hands over my face. There was nothing about this that was ideal. I wanted to follow her up the stairs and show her exactly how terrified I'd been for her, and how much I wanted to make sure she was okay.

And *continue* to make things okay.

Being on this side of things? I couldn't give the other guys shit anymore. I finally understood what it was like to want nothing so badly as to protect one person. One woman.

I leaned my face into my hands for a few more seconds before I dug out my phone. Lucas answered right away. "You okay?"

"Yeah. We're back. Did you track down Jude?"

"I did."

I sighed. "Can you come over to the house for a few minutes?"

"We're on our way."

Plenty of people would say we were too paranoid about things like talking on the phone. But with our collective history, we all preferred to talk about things in person when we could. There was far less chance anyone was listening. And with this group—the Riders—I was taking zero chances.

It didn't take the guys long to make it here and step inside. "We have to stay a little quieter."

"What's up?" Lucas asked.

"Kate is upstairs sleeping. She was pretty shaken up by everything."

Jude nodded. "Tell us what happened."

I did, running through what I knew. There was some stuff missing that could only be told from Kate's point of view, but I'd heard and seen enough.

"This is bigger than we thought. Max having to ask permission is a clear sign. And it's obviously not just down in Missoula—it's here."

"Yeah, no kidding. Glad you were able to get Kate out without too much trouble."

I was leaning forward, elbows on my knees, still staring into the fire. Looking at the fire was easier than looking at them and knowing they were wondering about me and my past. How I was handling it. "As long as she's in this, I'm in it. I need to help her and her brother, and I promised nothing would happen to her."

Their looks were boring into me now, but I ignored them.

"We already know they have more than one location," Jude said. "There's probably more, and if they're all rural, then it's possible there's one even closer to home. I don't like the idea of that."

"Especially with the animals," said Lucas.

I nodded. "I thought I'd follow up on who's adopted the animals that have come from the ranch and make sure none of them have ended up there. If any have . . ." I let myself drift off and not finish that sentence. Because all the things that I wanted to say seemed too brutal at the moment.

"Can't say I disagree," Lucas said.

"Same," Jude added. "But at the moment, I'm more concerned about you, Noah."

"I'm fine."

Jude laughed once. "You don't look fine."

Of all the people on this ranch, Jude was the one who could look at me and tell. I was fine, and I wasn't fine. The urge to fight back and *strike* and *hurt* the people who had done this to me—to us—was something I fought all the time. Most of the time, it was easy to ignore that bit of it. Especially in a life filled with caring for animals and people who cared about me.

Fighting brought all of it to the surface. I'd experienced it before when I'd had to fight. A switch would flip and suddenly I wouldn't be in the here and now. I would be back there in those fucking wind-soaked caves, fighting for consciousness and barely able to hold on through the pain.

But that hadn't happened tonight. I'd stayed on top of the memories and hadn't lost myself. Even as I felt it pushing up from the place I kept them, I felt solid. "I'm okay," I finally said. "It was good to have that kind of outlet for those few minutes. Just kind of let it happen. But I don't need or want that regularly. Just glad that I got through it."

"Glad to hear it," Jude said. "If that changes—"

"Then Dr. Rayne will be my first call," I said with a smile. "Then probably you."

Lucas looked out one of the windows. "The snow is

slowing down. You want to go to the gym and work off some of the excess?"

I shook my head. "No, thanks. Not while Kate is here."

"Wait," Lucas said. I saw the wheels click for him. "You don't have another bedroom."

"She's in my bed."

His eyebrows rose into his hairline. "Okay then."

"Nothing happened tonight. I know better than that."

Jude chuckled. "We know. But are you going to be okay with that? When it happens?"

He wasn't asking about sex, but if my PTSD would rear its head while I was sleeping in the same bed as Kate. It was something he worried about. And was just one of the reasons he hadn't dated anyone in years. Not even the woman he'd been blatantly in love with since we'd all come here.

"I don't sleep enough that it would be a problem. If anything, she'll be the one who decides it was a good idea nothing happened. I . . . didn't hold back in that fight. I wouldn't blame her if she was scared of me now. She said she wasn't, but—"

"If she said she wasn't, then you need to believe her," Lucas said.

"A lot happened. She may not have processed it all yet."

Jude stood. "That could be true. But what you're not going to do is process it for her and decide she can't handle it. That woman is strong and smart. It's not exactly a huge leap to see what you did tonight isn't who you are, Noah."

He wasn't wrong.

"If you need us," Lucas said. "You know we'll be here."

"I know."

"We'll fill in the others about everything while the two

of you rest. Tomorrow, maybe we'll be able to come up with a plan."

When they left, I locked the door behind them, leaning against it for long moments.

Everything inside was swinging back and forth like a pendulum. One second I was fine and grounded, the next I was spiraling down into panic and darkness.

I was okay, but I wasn't *fine*.

Kate might be able to handle what I'd done and how I'd acted, but at the moment, I wasn't handling it well. This far past retirement, the fact that violence of that kind came so easily to me wasn't something that made me comfortable.

Nor was the fact that it had felt *good*. Like I'd stepped into an old skin that fit so well it made me question why I'd left it behind.

One thing was for sure, if I tried to sleep right now I wasn't going to stay that way for long. Right now, the past was too close.

Returning to the fire, I finished off the tea and stared at the flames once again. I was tired, but it was easy to fade into the haze of gray between awake and sleeping where I let my mind drift and do what it wanted. This was one of the things Dr. Rayne, and others, had taught me.

Just let it pass through. If it was a bad memory or a good one. Whatever thoughts, dark or light, let my mind be a conduit for them instead of a container. Thoughts couldn't hurt me. They weren't a physical thing. A thought didn't have to be acted on. It could just be let go.

Once the thoughts were settled, I could pull back and go to my vault. A single, imaginary place in my mind. For me, it was a rainy forest clearing. Mist drifted along the ground, and the air was so humid it was sticky.

In the center of that clearing, out of place, was a giant

safe. It looked like a bank vault. Or an overgrown gun safe. Large, dark, metal, with a slot going in, and a mechanism like a faucet coming out.

And everything that was inside there were things and feelings that were better left alone.

Dr. Rayne had helped me create the vision, and though it felt counterintuitive that a simple visualization could help so much, it did.

In my head, I approached that vault and slid all the thoughts about my past that had managed to slip out back inside the slot. They couldn't come out without my permission, and most of the time, it worked.

Up close, there was an engraving on the metal that Rayne had had me put there. *Not to be opened unless it serves my healing.*

Wasn't that the truth?

I was no closer to sleep, but there was relief in my chest and my limbs. I was still here, and still whole. My past hadn't gotten the best of me yet.

Chapter 17

Kate

A chill across my skin woke me.

I sat up in the bed, my mind taking several seconds to remember where I was. What happened?

Noah's house. This was Noah's house, and this was Noah's bed. I shuddered. The reason I was in Noah's bed was still in the forefront of my mind.

I felt better, but there was a part of me that was still shaken. Bruised and vulnerable from what we'd come up against tonight. Was it tonight? What time *was* it?

As I reached for my phone, something squeaked. Garfield was curled up halfway on the screen and barely moved when I slipped the phone out from underneath him. Utterly adorable.

I tapped the screen, the light bright in the darkness. Three in the morning. But I didn't feel sleepy. I felt clear. If I stayed here staring at the ceiling, that's what I would do. Stare.

The temptation to see where Noah was overtook me. I still wasn't all right, and he probably wasn't either. But I hoped he would at least be asleep, since he'd said he had trouble with it.

I tiptoed down the stairs. They led straight into the living room, and I wasn't about to be the reason why Noah lost some of the precious little sleep that he did get.

But the couch was empty. The fire was low in the fireplace, and Noah was nowhere to be found. Where was he? After what had happened tonight, I knew better than to think that he'd gone anywhere else. Even within the safety of Resting Warrior, I didn't think he'd leave me alone. So where was he?

I shivered as a breeze hit me.

That's why I was awake, I realized. It was *cold* in here.

At the back of the house, I found the source of the dropping temperature. The back door stood open, knocking against the house in the stiff breeze. It wasn't snowing anymore. The white covering the ground was fresh and shining under a clear moon.

And out in the yard . . . Noah.

He was far enough that it was hard to see him. But there he was. I didn't bother being quiet now, grabbing my boots and my coat from by the front door before heading out the back and shutting the door gently behind me so the house and kittens wouldn't get any colder.

Noah faced away from me, staring into the distance. He didn't seem to be aware I was approaching at all, so still that he looked like a statue.

I was almost to him when I stopped. "Noah?"

He whirled, faster than breath, taking a step toward me before he stopped. It had taken him a second to realize who I was and that I wasn't an enemy. His gaze was dark in the moonlight.

Those were shadows I recognized. I'd seen them in my brother's eyes too. After what he'd told me, I didn't doubt he was caught up in a storm of memories.

"Noah," I said again.

"Kate." My name was a ragged breath in his mouth. He exhaled, some of that darkness fading.

But not all of it.

"Are you okay?" I asked.

Turning away from me, he looked back past the fence, and I realized that Noah wasn't actually alone out here. A dark, fluffy shape was standing by the fence. One of the alpacas. I hadn't known their enclosure came so close to Noah's house.

"When I came back. From . . . captivity." The word seemed hard for him to say. "I wasn't the same. I was . . . broken. In some ways, it was worse than what they did to me."

I didn't dare say anything. I didn't want to break the spell of his vulnerability. Noah was trusting me with this. I was honored. And terrified. Not of him, but of the enormity of it, even as it felt right.

"I felt so fucking guilty I'd gotten out and Jude hadn't. And that I'd survived at all when everyone else hadn't. They—" He swallowed thickly. "They wanted information from us. What plans did the United States have? Where were we stationed? What did we know about them, and how much? Some of it we knew, and some we didn't. Of course, that doesn't matter in an interrogation."

Noah tilted his face back to look at the sky, the moon illuminating his face with cool light. I drank in the image. So raw and open. So striking. Painted like this, he was all sharp angles and planes. Right now? I didn't think I'd ever get enough of just *looking* at him.

That was terrifying too, in its own way.

"We're trained to withstand it," he said softly. "There's a reason that SEALs are talked about the way they are. They put us through hell so that we're able to withstand it. But until you're actually there? In hell? You don't have a fucking clue what it's like. What it will do to your mind. Your body."

It was my turn to swallow. I wanted to touch him. Wrap him up in my arms so he could feel as safe with me as I did with him.

I didn't move, but I did find my voice. "They tortured you."

It wasn't a question.

"Yes." Then, slowly, "It was cold in those caves. There are thousands of them, and some connect. Create wind tunnels. And people don't realize how cold it gets in the Middle East. Especially in the winter."

He wasn't wearing a coat. Just the shirt he'd had on earlier. "It's freezing. You must be cold, and—"

"I go back and forth with the cold. Every time there's a gust of wind and it throws me back there. Fuck, even when I kissed you the first time—" He broke off and glanced at me. "And then there are moments when it makes me remember what I came back from. It was working with the animals that helped me."

Reaching out, I took his hand. Noah didn't pull away. His fingers wove through mine. Wrapping us together. That small movement—that trust—felt like the most intimate moment we'd had.

"This guy," he smiled for a second, "is Al Pacacino."

A laugh burst out of me. He hadn't told me the names of them when we'd walked around the other day. "Really?"

"Really." The ghost of a smile was on his face, but his eyes were still haunted, lost in the maze of memories that *still* held him captive in those caves. "Animals are simple.

They like you or they don't. They respond honestly to whatever you offer them. Whenever I'm struggling, I come out and spend time with them, and they help me find my center. Animals don't have the complex motivations that make some people want to hurt others."

He reached out and ran his free hand along the alpaca's neck. "But I do. I have them."

"Noah—"

"I spend so much time pushing against that part of me. Those instincts. And I can't pretend it didn't feel good to let that all go. If I hadn't stopped?"

"You did stop."

"It would have been easy not to."

Pulling on his hand, I turned him to face me. "I told you I'm not afraid of you, Noah."

"Maybe you should be." The sadness in his voice broke my heart.

"No. I absolutely should not be. There's no part of me that believes you can't tell the difference between what you did and what you would have chosen if you'd had another choice. You did that to help me. To *save me*. From what might have happened. You didn't leave me alone in there." I reached up and took his face in my hands. "And what I said earlier is just as true now. *You don't scare me*."

Noah leaned down, touching his forehead to mine. In the cold air, our breaths mingled. He took a long, shuddering breath. "Thank you."

"Come inside with me," I murmured. "It's my turn to make the tea."

Half of his mouth curved into a smile. "Okay."

Our hands were still linked as we walked back to the house together, the only sound the crunch of snow beneath our boots. I reached the stairs of the back porch first and turned to face him. This was the first time I'd ever been the same height, since he towered over me when we were on level ground.

"I need to say something."

Noah's eyes were clear now, and his gaze dropped to my lips before flicking back to mine. A curl of heat rolled through me when he looked. Like he already knew what I was going to say before I said it.

"Am I completely over what I saw tonight? No. I'm not. But I'm not going to pretend that anything that happens between us is because of them." I lowered my eyes along with my voice, half afraid he would say no again. "We were already heading in this direction before tonight, and we both know it. Right now, you need me as much as I need you." Physically. Mentally. In every way.

I dared to raise my eyes again. "Please don't make me sleep alone."

A teasing smile appeared on his face. "If I'm not mistaken, you're not talking about sleeping."

"No," I breathed. "I'm not."

He took the first step up.

My breath was short. "Do you still want the tea?"

"Do you?"

I shook my head.

A new light lit his gaze, lighting me up in turn, like embers being sparked into flame.

It wasn't clear who moved first, and it didn't matter. Noah's mouth met mine, and our groans of relief matched. That same desperation I'd felt earlier was leaking through the both of us.

My arms were around his neck, his arms around my waist, and then I wasn't touching the ground anymore. I gasped into his mouth, dizzy with the sensation of being lifted and held.

God, how long had it been since I'd been kissed like this?

Who was I kidding? I'd *never* been kissed like this. This wasn't the way Noah had kissed me before. There was no restraint here. We were no longer toying with the edges of something, instead barreling toward the inevitable explosion that I wanted to be right in the center of.

My back hit the door, and I hadn't even realized that we'd moved. That Noah had carried me up the stairs and pressed me there. His hands slipped down further, letting me wrap my legs around his waist. I didn't want to let him go, but there was still a whole flight of stairs in front of us.

"I can walk," I managed to say in the fractions of moments our lips weren't connected.

The sound that he made was nearly a growl. "If you think I'm letting you go, Kate, think again."

The words sank through me. I knew he meant right now. These moments. But it felt like more than that. Like an admission neither of us had the time to think about because getting him closer was the only thing that fucking mattered.

We only broke apart to get the door open and closed behind us. He wasn't even watching the stairs as he carried me upward, lips on my neck, tongue leaving traces of fire behind.

My heart thundered in my ears. This was what I needed. *This* was what made me feel safe and grounded. It was him. Noah.

"The kittens," I gasped. "They're on the bed."

His low chuckle sent tingles skittering across my skin. Every cell in my body reacted to that sound. Knew what it wanted. What it needed. "They can sleep on the couch tonight."

Noah set me on the bed, kissing me hard again. Deep.

"If there weren't two little balls of fur that need attention, my hands wouldn't be leaving your skin."

I grinned up at him, aware that we hadn't even stopped to take off my coat. "You haven't touched my skin yet, Noah."

His eyes went dark, and it matched the depth of his voice. "I'll be right back."

He scooped up both kittens and disappeared down the stairs. I shed my coat and boots, tossing them aside. He was going to be back in seconds. Did I undress before he got back?

My stomach jumped. Not with fear, just . . . anticipation, excitement, and a healthy dose of nerves. It had been a while since I'd done this with anyone. And the last time, it hadn't been like this. I hadn't wanted it so desperately it felt like I was shaking.

Noah appeared on the stairs, striding down the hall toward me. There were no shadows clinging to him now. No traces of doubt or uncertainty. He came straight to me, slipping his hand behind my neck and tilting my face to his.

"The kittens?"

"Nestled in a blanket on the couch. They'll be fine."

"Okay."

He kissed away any other words, pulling me hard against his body. Now, without my coat in between us, I felt all of that strength. I'd seen how he could use it now and was ready to yield everything to him.

We broke apart, staring at each other in the dim light. Noah was breathing just as hard as I was. "What?"

"I'm nervous."

A kiss on my neck. "Why?"

"I don't know."

Noah murmured against my skin. "Just promise me one thing."

"What's that?"

"That you want this. Want me."

I nodded, desperate. "Yes."

"Then no nerves," he said quietly. "Let me take care of you."

He'd already done that. More than he could possibly know. But I held on to him a little tighter and whispered my answer.

"Yes."

Chapter 18

Noah

I'd thought about this moment. Hadn't dared to hope for it like this, or so soon. But having Kate in my arms was everything. With her hands on me, nothing crept into my head. No doubts about who I was or what my past made me. It was clear.

And she was looking up at me like I was the best thing she'd ever seen. I didn't know if I deserved it. But tonight, I wouldn't deal with those thoughts. Instead, I was going to show her that *she* was the best thing I'd ever seen. Make sure she knew I didn't take one second of this for granted.

I kissed her. Slowly this time, dragging us down into the heat that had hovered around us for so long. Kate's body melted against mine. That was all it took for my body to react—more than it already had. I was so hard that I ached.

Turning her, I skimmed my hands up her hips, finding

the edge of her shirt and lifting. Every inch of skin I revealed was an inch I'd fucking dreamt about.

Kate shivered when I pulled the shirt over her head and tossed it aside. Wrapping my arms around her, I rested my lips by her ear. "If you need to stop—"

"I don't."

"But if you do, I need you to know that you can."

She turned to me, fire in her eyes. "I would never have thought otherwise. You're not Max."

The words hit home. I hadn't even realized that was the reason I'd felt I had to say it, but it was. I didn't want her to have any regrets.

She unhooked her bra, dropping it to the floor between us like a dare. The smirk on her lips was at war with the vulnerability in her eyes. Kate hadn't lied. There was no fear there. But she was still nervous, and I guessed that running a business and caring for a brother with PTSD hadn't left her a lot of time for relationships.

I reached out, touching her. Sliding my fingers over her skin. Well then, two of us had nerves then. Not because of anything that had happened tonight. Not because of those assholes. Not even because of my past.

But because every time I touched this woman, I was drawn deeper. Toward her. Toward a place it wouldn't be easy to leave.

That I might never want to leave.

Stripping my shirt over my head, I tossed it aside.

Kate's eyes went wide. "Wow."

"Likewise."

She laughed, quiet and bright. "Okay."

"Yes," I put every bit of truth into my voice.

"This can't be real." She reached out and brushed her fingers over my chest. Everything in me tightened. More of that and I wasn't going to be able to stop myself from going too fast. "No real person has muscles like this."

"Comes with the territory," I smirked. "Ranching. Hauling things." The other guys regularly kicking my ass in the gym.

The way her eyes traced over my skin was too much. I hauled her against my body, taking her mouth again as I took us both to the bed. Her skin was so soft under mine, her body arching into my hands, and I was going to *lose it*.

"You're perfect." I dropped my mouth to her skin. The path down to her breasts was heaven, her nipples hardening just before I reached them. I loved those reactions. The ones she couldn't control and were just for me.

Did her nipples do that when I kissed her, when they were hidden and I couldn't see them?

The thought nearly struck me blind with arousal. Her skin pebbled under my tongue. That first true taste of her skin was a miracle. A marvel. Everything I'd fucking wanted.

"Oh *God*." One hand wove into my hair. "If we keep going at this pace, I'm going to explode."

I mimicked her words from earlier this evening. "That was kind of the idea I had."

Kate's cheeks flushed a pink that trailed down over her chest. Her honey-hot gaze dared me to go slow. Dared me to go fast. Challenged me. Set me on fire.

Dropping my mouth again, I continued to worship her skin. Moving from one breast to the other, teasing her until she was gasping. "Noah. Please."

"Please what?"

"Please *anything*."

I laughed into her skin, dropping further down her body. Already, I'd decided I wanted to hear her come before anything else. Even if it was going to be pure, delicious torture to hold myself back.

Her jeans slid off her hips under my hands, leaving nothing but a thong that was lacy and sheer and took my breath entirely. It wasn't what I'd expected.

That blush was on her cheeks again. "Is this something you wear often?"

She shook her head slowly.

"Did you wear this for me?"

The slight tensing of her body under me, the little intake of breath, told me everything I needed to know about that. She'd thought about me when putting on this scrap of lace that was going to make me die of blood loss because it was all currently racing to my cock. Thought about it even though it was such an unlikely possibility, and she'd still wanted it.

I couldn't wait any longer.

Pushing Kate's thighs apart, I licked her straight through the lace.

Her moan could bring a dead man to life. As it was, it might kill me. The taste of her, even through that thin piece of cloth. I was going to remember the fucking taste of her until the day I died.

"Noah." Nothing but a breath of a moan. *Yes*. That was what I wanted. Desperate and wanting, begging for more of me and it and us.

I stretched the lace over her clit, dragging my tongue behind it, using the fabric to tease her. Feel her. Tell her that every second she'd spent thinking about this moment was worth it.

As fun as it was, the thong had to go. It joined the rest of her clothes on the floor and was forgotten. Because there she was. All of her. Already wet and shining, and it was my groan this time as I yanked her hips toward my mouth and truly tasted her.

Her hand was still in my hair, and then there were two, pulling. Hard. It wasn't pain, it was permission. There wasn't one part of her I didn't taste or explore, listening to the way her breath caught and voice escaped when I slid my tongue inside her. When I licked one side of her clit and then the other, finding the exact place that made her hips arch off the bed. When I sealed my mouth over the little bud of nerves and sucked, not stopping for one fucking second.

I placed one hand low on her stomach, holding her in place for me. My tongue wasn't the only thing I wanted to explore with.

"Oh, God." Kate's hands dug into the comforter on my bed. That one simple movement, driven by my mouth and the single finger that was now inside her, was the hottest thing I'd ever seen.

She was pure heat. Silk and softness. One finger wasn't enough. I added another, stroking, seeking the spot that was elusive enough to make me want it.

Her hips jerked as I felt a touch of roughness. *There*.

"Noah." My name was a plea and a prayer and everything in between.

"Kate." I whispered it before my mouth was once again occupied. The way she was moving—writhing—I wanted more of it.

She tried to say my name again as I thrust my fingers deep, hard against that single spot. Licked her where she'd groaned. Pressed my hand harder on her stomach to create more friction, more pressure.

And I didn't stop.

Whatever words she'd been trying to say disappeared into nothing but moans. Her body squeezed my fingers, begging me for what her mouth couldn't ask for. But I did nothing. Not more or less. Exactly the same. Over, and over, and over, and over as she began to shake.

One breath she wasn't there, and the next she was, shuddering and gasping, coming over my fingers and tongue and letting herself go.

Her body eased, sinking back onto the bed in the aftermath of pleasure, and I pulled back. Just for a second, just so that I could strip out of the rest of my clothes and find a condom in one of my drawers. It had been a while for me too, but I liked to be prepared.

Kate was looking at me when I turned back to the bed, propped up on her elbows. That pale hair was wild and messy, and I loved that I'd been the cause.

"You're, uh . . ." She cleared her throat. "You're good at that."

"Glad you think so."

Her eyes dropped down my body. It was the first time either of us had seen the other like this, and watching her turn red while taking in my body made me impossibly harder. Kate's eyes didn't leave my hands as I stroked the condom on. "Want to find out if there are other things that I'm good at?"

"I'm starting to think there's nothing you're not good at," she breathed.

"Definitely not true," I said, pulling her to the edge of the bed. "You've never tasted my cooking."

Kate laughed. It was a pure sound. Only joy. Which was the thing we both desperately needed.

I couldn't stop touching her, moving my hands over her skin as I pulled her close. In turn, that gave her permission to touch me. Kate's hands were more hesitant than mine. But every place she touched burned. Like her touch marked me invisibly. Only I would be able to see it, but I would never fucking forget.

"Kate."

She looked up at me, and I lost my breath. It was another moment, like the one before I'd kissed her. The sense of something bigger. This was something we couldn't take back, and I didn't want to.

"I need to feel all of you."

We moved together. I guided her onto her knees, because the need to touch as much of her body as possible was overwhelming. I could—did—wrap myself around her. Her back to my chest, our legs pressed together, my mouth brushing her neck.

And we were right there. I sank into her, crossing that line that we couldn't step back over, and we both shuddered.

There was no holding back now. It was impossible. The feeling of her around me drove every rational thought out of my head. I was feral for her, and she for me. We came together with the force of thunder. Lightning.

Kate drove herself back onto me as hard as I was driving into her, both of us giving in to need we couldn't escape.

Those same instincts rose in me. The ones that had let me take down a man who should have put me on the floor tonight. Hazy, animalistic *need*. But this instinct didn't take my control from me. It gave me more. It honed everything into sharp focus.

Each breath together. The angle of my hips. The spot deep inside Kate's body I hit with every thrust. Every movement that told me how I could make it better for her.

I was an entirely different type of predator now.

Pleasure raced along my spine. There was no chance I could last as long as I wanted to this time. Everything about Kate felt too good, too much, too fast. I wanted to drown in this heat. We fit together perfectly, coming together like puzzle pieces or a key in a lock. Nothing had ever felt like this.

I needed to see her. I needed to see her face.

"Turn," I groaned into her skin, pulling out of her just long enough to help her flip before sinking into her again, grinding down with every stroke to add to her pleasure. If I could make her come again, I was going to. The only thing I wanted was to see her let go completely.

To come apart.

For me.

Kate reached for me, wrapping her arms around my neck. Legs around my hips. Pulling me deeper. Until our lips met and our breaths matched and everything about us was coming together, barreling toward the end.

She moaned softly.

"No one can hear you but me," I said against her lips, thrusting harder. "If you want to shout, do it."

She grinned, the smile instantly fading with the next thrust, pleasure overtaking her features. That expression was going to be tattooed on the inside of my eyelids for a long time. "You trying to get me to scream your name, Noah?"

"If I'm only trying, then it's not good enough."

Changing the angle of my hips, I felt her. Kate went rigid, eyes flaring wide, and I smiled. Right there.

Right. Fucking. There.

Her body clenched around mine, and I swore. Every word she tried to say melted into one delicious sound, and we were there. Kate's hips jerked, the shout I'd wanted to hear muffled by my kiss as I slammed my mouth down on hers and let it all go.

Lightning blazed down my spine, all the way through

my cock. Pleasure flashed behind my eyes, ripping its way through me like a storm. No control. I was powerless as it gripped me and held me, and finally let me go.

We were panting together, both trying to catch our breath. But I didn't care about air. All I cared about was kissing her. Kate.

Her gaze was warm. Glazed and sleepy now that everything was relaxing. No more tension in her body. Just relaxation that made her fit against me that much more perfectly.

"You were right," I said. "We both needed that."

"No." She shook her head, still smiling. "I just needed you. *That* was so much more than what I needed."

She didn't have to say it was absolutely everything. I already knew.

I kissed her again, drawing it out, tangling our tongues together in that slow dance of two people who finally know each other. Truly know.

"I'll be right back."

It was sweet torture to pull out of her body when it felt so right. But I wanted to hold her while she slept, and once she was asleep, there was no way in hell I was disturbing her.

I ditched the condom and grabbed a washcloth, soaking it with warm water before returning it.

"I—" Kate stopped and blinked like it didn't compute that I was going to help her.

"I told you I would take care of you." I let a smile break through. "Full service."

She laughed once, though she was blushing, her hands gripping my arm in embarrassment as I helped her clean up. There was nothing to be embarrassed about. But words wouldn't be the thing that made her believe that. Only actions.

I tossed the washcloth in the sink before wrapping us up together in the blankets. My hands still moved across her skin like they had a mind of their own. I wouldn't be able to get enough of her. Enough of *this*.

Kate curled toward me, tucking her face into my neck. "Thank you."

"I think I should be the one saying that." She'd brought me out of my memories. Shared her body with me. Looked at me like I was more than what I'd done and what had happened to me. That was worth far more than a couple of orgasms.

Her words were quiet and mumbled. She was falling asleep and still trying to talk. Did she even know what she was saying? "No, it's all me. For the couch and the money and getting me out and just . . . everything."

I ran a hand down her spine and felt her breathe. Drew her a little closer as that breath evened out and she eased down into sleep.

"I'm still the one that needs to say it." I said it so quietly she would never hear it.

It took some time, but I didn't stare at the ceiling. I didn't collapse back into the memories she'd pulled me out of. With Kate in my arms, I slept.

And it was easy.

Chapter 19

Kate

Waking was different this time. It wasn't fast and clear. This time, it was warm and hazy and comfortable. Because I wasn't alone.

As my brain put together where I was and who I was with, I felt the weight of Noah's arm over my hip. The gentle tickle of his breath on my neck. All the skin and muscle touching me in different places where we were tangled.

I turned my face into the pillow to hide the blush absolutely no one could see. Because I was in bed with Noah Scott. Naked.

The blankets twitched, and I smiled. There was the reason that I'd woken. The kittens had found their way back upstairs. I didn't think they were big enough to jump up onto the bed, but as kittens could figure out, blankets were climbable.

As I opened my eyes, a ball of orange fluff approached

my face. So close that he pressed his nose against my cheek before he lay down, curling against my forearm. Salem was there too, choosing to shove herself up under my chin for morning cuddles instead.

I couldn't stop the soft laugh that shook me even though I was trying to be quiet. Noah was sleeping, and he deserved every minute of it. He didn't need to wake for kitten antics.

But the low, rasping sound of his voice made my whole body respond. Viscerally.

"Something about waking up with me funny?" There was a smile in his voice too as his arm tightened around my waist.

"Not in the slightest." I arched into him on purpose, and he groaned. "The kittens who just found me, though, are very funny."

Noah's chuckle vibrated through my chest. "It doesn't matter where I put them to sleep. If the door is open, they will find me in the morning. Or this morning, you."

"They're so cute it's almost upsetting."

"I know."

Slowly, Noah moved the hand that was over my hip, slipping it up the front of my chest until it settled between my breasts and pulled me back until our bodies were flush. He kissed my neck. "Good morning."

"Morning."

It didn't seem real—what we'd done last night. Even though it had been my idea. Noah had been overwhelming and amazing. And waking up like this? I *loved* this feeling.

Safety.

That's what it was.

Certainty and safety. Now that I felt it, I was aware of how much uncertainty had been in my life lately. Especially since Brandon had come home. I was glad to have him home, but it was different. I hadn't felt this at ease in a really long time.

Never in my wildest dreams, in a million years, had I ever thought that someone from the military would be the one to make me feel safe. But Noah did, even while wrestling with his own demons.

"Your mind is going so fast I can hear it," he whispered.

I turned, moving Salem onto my chest so I could see Noah's face. "I was just . . . enjoying this."

"What?"

My heart stuttered. Why was saying things out loud so difficult sometimes? "Waking up with you."

Noah smiled. It was like the sun broke over the horizon with that smile, even though it was already up. "It does have certain benefits." He lowered his lips to my shoulder, kissing along my collarbone.

I wasn't unaware of the fact that it was the morning, and he was hard. "Too bad we have these little rascals," I said, petting Salem's tiny back.

Noah turned his head and reached behind him. "That's why I keep a stash of these." He held up a little toy in the shape of a mouse. It was fluffy and furry and Salem perked right up at the sight of it.

"Is there catnip in those?"

"Yes." He laughed and threw the little toy down the hallway toward the stairs.

Salem *launched* herself off me, kitten claws digging into my bare skin as she used me as a rocket boost to follow the toy. One more throw and Garfield was running off the bed too, the little thumps of kitten feet running away from us.

"Ow."

"I can fix that."

Now that we were free, Noah rolled over me. His

162

weight pinned me to the bed and he kissed the fiery pinpricks that Salem had left. "Am I bleeding?"

"You are not."

"Good."

He glanced up at me. "No promises for the future though. Their claws are sharper than my razor."

"Gotta have their weapons. Keep themselves safe," I murmured. Noah's face evened out, eyes searching mine. "The way you keep me safe."

The smile on his mouth didn't make it all the way to his eyes. "You're not a kitten."

"Thank goodness."

The air hung breathless between us, leading to something. Finally, I broke the silence. "Last night—"

"Wasn't nearly enough," Noah growled.

The words that were on my tongue disappeared under his. I'd already known that he could kiss. Kissing him while pinned by his naked body was another experience entirely.

I tested, seeing how far he'd let me go. Pushing on his shoulders, he moved with me, letting me flip us until I was sprawled across him. "You did all the work last night. I didn't get a chance to see you. All of your ridiculous, unreal muscles."

Those already dark blue eyes grew a shade darker. "Keep saying things like that and I may not be able to give you the chance right now."

I smirked before leaning down, mimicking what he'd done to me just now by kissing his chest. The dusting of hair there that led toward his already hard cock. Which was exactly what I'd imagined. Better. But there was no way a man like Noah could be anything less than perfect when it came to that.

There was big dick energy, and then there was the energy that Noah carried. Easy energy. So confident and secure in himself that he didn't even need to joke about having that energy.

And no, he most certainly didn't need to joke about the size of his dick.

I ran my hands over the lines of his muscles, tracing along his ribs where even there it seemed like he had some. His abs contracted under my fingers and Noah's breathing sped up as I explored him. I pretended not to notice his hands curl into fists, desperate to reach for me, fighting the just-as-desperate urge to let me do this.

"How do you like it?" I asked.

His voice was barely in control. "I like whatever you do."

I rolled my eyes. "Noah."

Wrapping my hand around him, I watched his face as I stroked. Soft and gentle. Teasing. There was pleasure there, but it wasn't what he loved.

A little harder, then. He jerked in my hand. "Getting closer."

Noah pressed his lips together to keep from smiling. He was enjoying this.

I gripped him harder, squeezing him as I drew my hand back up, and he groaned. His eyes rolled back in his head. "There it is. Two can play this game."

"I have no idea what you're talking about," he said. Far too innocently.

"Sure you don't."

Of course he didn't know. After he'd found every little place on my body that made me jump and moan and used them to make me see fucking stars.

I didn't wait longer, leaning down and pressing my lips to his skin. Dragging them up his shaft until I could slip my mouth over him and savor the sound that he made. Dark.

Raw. Like last night when we'd given in and nothing had mattered but how hard we could drive into each other.

Every muscle in Noah's body was taut with that same tension, ready to take and fuck and make sure we both drowned in pleasure again. I wanted him to.

But this came first.

I slid him further into my mouth, and he swore. "Kate."

A blaring, ringing sound made us both freeze. A phone ringing. Not mine—Noah's.

"Fuck," he whispered. "Let me make sure it's not an emergency."

The man had the willpower of steel. I saw it in every line of movement, because moving his cock out of my mouth was the last thing he wanted.

Noah dug into the jeans he'd discarded last night and froze. "It's not a number that I know."

"Then we can ignore it."

"I don't think we can," he said, staring at the phone. His face was strained, but he hit answer on the call at the same time that he came over to me. The phone was on speaker. It was early still, and Noah made himself sound sleepy.

"Hello?"

"This the asshole who beat my best fighter last night?"

Max. Everything fun and sexy drained out of me. Noah grabbed my hand and squeezed. "Yeah, that's me. Why the fuck are you calling me? And why is it at this hour of the morning?"

An ugly laugh came across the line. "You are the same asshole. There's a special event tomorrow night. Unplanned, but it gives us a chance to settle our business. Wouldn't want to let a debt hang over my head."

No, he wouldn't. Not with what people like him did to people with unpaid debts.

Noah looked wary. But we needed to catch these guys, and this might give us the chance. "What kind of event?"

"One you'll like."

"Fine." Noah made an annoyed sound. "Send me the details. I'll be there."

He went to hang up, and Max spoke again. "Wait. The girl I gave you last night."

I couldn't look at him, but I felt Noah's eyes on me. "What about her?"

"You left with her faster than I'd thought you would. I'd promised people some introductions . . . if you know what I mean."

Noah squeezed my hand again, and I squeezed back. I knew this was a part that he had to play. It didn't have anything to do with me or what had already happened between us. "Do I care about who you want to introduce your groupie sluts to? No."

Max's voice went hard. "I need to know where she is."

Leaning back on the bed, Noah brought me with him, tucking me against his side. It let him make stretching sounds like he was getting out of bed, and he laughed. "I have no idea where she is. I fucked her and made sure she gave me everything she was good for. But it wasn't good enough for me to have seconds."

"Where did you last see her?"

An angry sound came out of Noah. "I don't know, and I don't care. We fucked in my car. I let her out on a street corner. Are we done?"

Panic laced Max's voice. Concealed, but there. "I need you to bring her back. With you. Tomorrow. It's not negotiable."

Noah shrugged, though he couldn't be seen through

the phone. "The only thing that's not negotiable is that you owe me seventeen thousand dollars. That's minus the fee for the fuck. I'll bring it back up to eighteen if you don't let me get off the fucking phone."

"Look—"

"No, asshole. You gave her to me. I used her. Don't even remember her name."

"Katie."

I ground my teeth together.

"Whatever," Noah said. "I'm not helping you find some random chick. I'll be there for my money. And if you make it interesting, maybe another bet so you can make it back."

He ended the call before Max could say anything else and tossed the phone on the bed.

"That wasn't what I expected."

"No," Noah said. "I don't like that he still wants you."

I snorted. "Yeah, I'm not exactly a huge fan."

He still held me close to his side. "Something doesn't add up here. It doesn't make sense. He should already know where to find you. He has your number. Knows where Brandon is. Knows where your apartment is. So why ask me?"

It didn't matter. All that mattered was making sure every single one of the people who were there and involved with what was happening in that underground club went to jail. "It's fine," I said. "I'll go."

He rolled over me, resuming our position from earlier. "No. You don't need to. Why put you back in danger when I just told him I don't know where you are? This is already a win. We have a chance to take them down now, and we'll make sure they're all arrested."

The fervent passion on his face made me smile. I reached up and ran my fingers through his hair. "Okay.

But if you need me to, I will. I want these guys gone too. And I already know you'll do whatever you can to keep me safe."

The light in his eyes that had dimmed when Max called came back in full force. "Yes."

The single word was a promise, backed up by his hands on my body and his skin on mine. Solidified by the fact that we were here together. In his bed.

He started smiling at the same time I did. "We were in the middle of something before he called."

"We were," I breathed. "Are you going to let me finish it?"

Noah leaned closer until his lips brushed mine. Not kissing, but barely a whisper away from it. Every hair I had stood on end. "On one condition."

"What's that?"

"That after you complete your exploring, I get to have my wicked way with you." His smile promised more of that wild pleasure that we'd both fallen into last night.

I rolled us, ending up on top and already moving downward. If he was going to shower me with pleasure, then I sure as hell was going to do the same for him.

"Deal."

Chapter 20

Noah

The sun seemed brighter today. Maybe that was insane to say, but it felt that way. After waking up with Kate—even with our brief interruption—the world seemed to sparkle.

I was in so much trouble.

The other guys were going to see it on my face, and all the shit I'd ever given them about women in their lives was going to come back on me.

But I didn't mind. I chuckled, filling the food bowls for the dogs before heading over to the alpaca enclosure. Kate was worth any amount of teasing I could possibly endure.

She was in my house right now, working at my dining room table and keeping an eye on the kittens. She hadn't wanted to get up after I'd worn her out all over again. But I certainly wasn't going to apologize for that. Having her in my bed . . . there was a certain bone-deep satisfaction, a settling in my chest that I couldn't explain.

It was on a visceral level. Not a conscious thing and certainly not something I could avoid.

"Hey, guys," I said to the alpacas. They approached me at the fence line and I stroked their necks. Al Pacacino gave me a look which was entirely too human. Like he knew what happened when I'd left him outside last night. "Don't look at me like that."

I cleaned up the enclosure and fed them, stretching after I exited the gate. That was that. All the normal chores were done. Just in time too. As much as I wanted to go back to the house and see Kate, I had another appointment. One that would affect the both of us.

As I jogged up the lodge stairs, Liam and Daniel were already there. "Did I keep you waiting?"

"No," Daniel said. "We have time, and we wanted to let you get stuff done."

Liam was uncharacteristically serious as he sat at the table. "You're sure about this, right? Because Charlie is already going to give you hell."

"I'm sure." I held up my hand as evidence. The bruising there was darkening. It hurt. Not badly enough that I needed to do anything about it or that I would let it stop me from doing anything *fun* with Kate, but it was a reminder. "When I walked in, there was a dogfight happening. They were taking illegal bets. There were guns. And Max basically sold Kate to me like he owned her. There's more than enough."

He held up his hands. "I'm with you. Just want you to be prepared."

"I can have Kate come if you want," I said. "She's at the house, and I can guarantee she'd be more than happy to tell Charlie what she saw."

Liam's face returned to his normal teasing grin. "She's at your house?"

Lucas and Jude hadn't told them everything then. "She is." He laughed, and I cut him off. "Feel free to get all of it out now."

"Oh no," Liam smirked. "I'm going to take my time. Really curate some of these jokes that I've been saving."

Daniel laughed and stood. "You can let them simmer on the way."

There had been times when Charlie came to meet with us. But especially for this, it felt important that we go and meet him on his turf. We were asking him to muster a huge amount of resources that we didn't have. And he'd already done it once with nothing to show for it.

The Riders were a good target. But especially in places like rural Montana, there weren't infinite resources, and pulling a lot of cops and even wrangling a SWAT team wasn't a thing you could do over and over.

"Coffee on the way back?" I asked.

"We're probably going to need it," Daniel said.

Daniel's eyes were on the road. He hadn't seemed off back at the lodge, but there was a tightness in him now. "Something I don't know?"

"No," he said. "But Liam is right. When I told Charlie what we were coming to talk about, he wasn't thrilled. I'm guessing the way the meeting goes, we're probably going to want something to take the edge off."

"If that's the case," I said, "then coffee might not be strong enough."

"We'll see."

The Garnet Bend police station was small but secure. Thankfully, everyone knew us. We didn't have to waste time getting checked in, we were just waved back. But I did note a couple looks we got. Had I really fucked up our reputation that badly by calling in a false alarm?

I probably had. Until now, we hadn't done that. When

we told people there was something wrong, they believed us.

Daniel knocked on the door to Charlie's office. "Come in."

We entered, and he looked up from a stack of papers on his desk, glasses slipping down his nose. I doubted many people saw this side of Charlie, where he seemed more like an old-time newspaper editor than a chief of police. But Charlie wasn't a man who belonged behind a desk. He was skilled, sharp, and in shape. It was good to have him as an ally.

If he still was.

"Take a seat." He looked between each of us, one at a time. "You're coming to set up another sting?"

"This time it's credible," I said.

Charlie sighed, his face softening. "You said that last time, Noah. What's different?"

I held up my hand like I had for Liam. "Last night, we went in again. There wasn't much choice in the matter. I saw enough to put people away, and I doubt that you'd have to dig very far to find a hell of a lot more."

He looked at me for a long moment before nodding again. "Tell me."

I did, trying to outline the evening as objectively as I could, despite the fact that I felt far from objective. The emotions connected to that . . . Kate and my past and feeling good taking that guy down. They weren't going to go away with one night.

"He called this morning." Daniel and Liam looked sharply at me. "Told me that there's a special event going down tomorrow night. That's where he expects me to collect the money. I gave him the impression I might fight and bet again if he makes it interesting. He wanted me to bring Kate back too, but I pretended I didn't know where she was."

Charlie raised his eyebrows. "Where is she?"

"Safe."

Taking in my face, he nodded once. "All right. I'll bite. I didn't doubt you the first time, and you couldn't have known it would be a test. This kind of operation is still not something I can tolerate. Tomorrow night?"

"Yeah. I have an idea of where it will take place this time," I said. "But they're still skittish, so we'll have to verify once I get the information."

"Noted."

Daniel relaxed in his seat. "Thanks, Charlie."

The police chief chuckled. "You guys always manage to get yourselves into trouble. I suppose it's just my good luck that you manage to get yourselves out of it again too. And help me put away some bad guys while you're at it."

The fairly public arrest of a local wealthy man who'd nearly killed Grant and his fiancée had brought attention to Charlie and the entire Garnet Bend police force, small as they were. That attention was part of the reason he was able to set up the operation we were asking for in the first place.

"We'll keep kicking trouble's ass as long as it keeps looking for us," Liam said with a grin.

Charlie raised an eyebrow. "Hopefully that's tomorrow."

Meaning, please don't let this be another cry of wolf.

Daniel was right. I did want coffee.

I breathed in the sharp cold air as I stood near my truck, waiting for the signal that everything was ready to go.

Fiddling with my earpiece, I looked up at the sky. Unlike the last time we'd been here, it was clear. The stars were so close I could reach out and touch them.

"You realize that every time you touch that earpiece the rest of us hear it?" Liam asked.

I laughed once, softly. "Sorry."

He was in a van farther down the road with Kate, in case we really did need her to go in. It was my goal to make sure that didn't happen. I didn't want her anywhere near Max or anyone who thought they could use her as a pawn. Not while I was here and could help it.

"ETA?" I asked quietly. If someone drove by and saw me, I didn't want them to see me talking. In one hand, I had a lit cigarette. An alibi and an excuse. I wasn't actually smoking it.

"Probably five more minutes," Liam said. "Teams on the far side are getting into place."

I wasn't on the comms of the bigger teams so I wouldn't get distracted or react to something unexpected in my ear. Even with our level of training, you didn't mess with instinct and surprise. Not when it could give you away.

The only people I could hear were Liam and Kate.

"You okay?"

Liam knew I wasn't talking to him.

Kate's laugh was like fire in my blood. I could probably melt the snow with the heat she gave me. "I'm fine. By the way, you weren't wrong. Garfield and Salem *love* your curtains."

I swore under my breath.

"Had to rescue them a couple of times this afternoon."

"They think they're superheroes," I muttered.

Her smile was audible. "Completely adorably superheroes."

"If this is what the two of you sound like when you're flirting, then I'm going to vomit from the cuteness," Liam said.

"It's not," Kate said without hesitation.

It was my turn to laugh, though I tried to suppress it.

"Okay." Liam's voice was in operation mode. "They're ready. Anytime you are."

The text tonight had confirmed it was the same location. And this time with a new password. Turtle. I hoped for all of our sakes that they'd act like turtles when I gave the signal to crash the party. Slow and clumsy.

"All right. I'm on my way in." I dropped the cigarette into the dirty snow at the side of the road and crushed it with my boot. Couldn't be too careful.

There were a couple of cars here and there. But even with cars spread along the road, it didn't raise that much suspicion. Out this far into unpopulated land? A couple hundred reasons for cars on the side of the road could present themselves. Most people weren't going to ask. And the ones that did weren't looking deeply enough to question any answers that they got.

I shoved my hands in the pockets of my jacket and modified my gait, taking on the character. This time I'd been able to get more into costume, and I looked the part.

The door slid open in front of me. Not the same bouncer. "Password?"

"Turtle."

The only response was a grunt as he waved me through. The darkness grabbed me by the throat, and I forced the instinct back as light spilled out from the inner door. My shit needed to take a back seat right now.

"Thanks," I said, and passed him.

The door closed behind me, and the party in front of me . . . was nothing.

Shit. *Shit.*

This was the same space. But where the fighting pit was last night, it was covered in flooring that looked seamless. It was a dance floor tonight, some people using it. Not that many, but then again, it was relatively early.

Still, the people that were here . . .

These weren't the same kind of people. A couple hovered in the corners, and they looked like me. Darker, furtive, and constantly looking around. The rest were just people looking for a good time. Carefree people who'd gotten wind of a barn party and decided to come check it out. You could see it.

Nothing illegal was happening here. At least not in plain sight. Sure, we'd be able to find the fighting pit if we uncovered the floor, but that alone was nothing. Especially if there were no arrests to go with it.

No one from their command structure was here. Max wasn't. The bookie. Even the bouncer was someone I didn't recognize.

"Noah?" Liam asked. They could hear the sounds of the party through the earpiece. All they needed was my go-ahead and everything was ready to go.

I moved to the side, fading into a shadowy corner. Was this another test? Had I just failed it? Was there a way to save it?

Dread pooled in my stomach. There had to be a way to save this, or we'd just blown everything that we had. And I'd brought Charlie and the boys in blue all the way out here for nothing.

"Noah," Liam said, falling into military cadence. "Tell me what's happening."

My throat worked. "Nothing is happening."

I heard Kate gasp. "What?"

"Nothing is fucking happening," I growled. "Just like the first party. Fighting pit is covered with a dance floor. Nothing illegal going on except maybe some underage drinking and alcohol without a license. Max isn't here. No one that is involved is here, as far as I can tell."

"That doesn't make any sense," Kate said. "Why would he do that?"

"I don't know." I sighed. "Tell them to call it off, Liam."

He sounded firm. "Get out of there, because they're going to come in."

"Liam."

"Noah," he said. "If we can't catch them tonight, at the very least they have one less location where they can do this shit. Charlie can have some arrests."

He was right. It might be the only way to salvage the situation. "All right."

I made my way out of the barn, the bouncer looking bored when I left only minutes after entering. "I'm out. Going to do some damage control with Max. I'll see you back at the Ranch."

My phone was already in my hand. I knew what to say. I would say that I'd gone outside for a smoke and seen the cops before they had a chance to make the raid and that I'd got away. I'd rip him a new one for still not giving me my money. It could work.

All I got was a shrill tone and a voice that told me the number had been disconnected.

Fuck.

I tried one more time, just in case, but the number was dead. The damage was done. However they'd known what we were up to, they'd gone to ground. What had tipped them off?

Behind me, shouts went up as the cops raided the barn.

Somehow, I'd fucked this up.

Again.

Chapter 21

Kate

The days slid by. I didn't go back to Missoula, instead staying with Noah at Resting Warrior and keeping tabs on Brandon with phone and video calls.

Noah was protective. Going with me whenever I left the premises to go into town, making sure that I was never isolated or alone for too long. Was it a little overprotective?

Yes.

But I understood it. I knew it wouldn't last forever, and remembering the terror I'd felt when I'd encountered Max and his friend in my apartment, I was grateful for it.

Aside from that, I wasn't complaining about the fact that I got to stay in his house, where there were two adorable kittens and an abundance of amazing sex.

The first couple of days, we pretended that Noah was going to sleep on the couch. On the third day, I looked at him and asked him if he was going to come to bed. He only hesitated for a couple of seconds before following me up the stairs and showing me that he was indeed coming to bed.

But not to sleep.

It was addictive, having that at my fingertips. I was a little drunk on the feeling of going to sleep with him and waking up with him and falling beneath the sheets together and coming apart with him. Because of him.

There was not one sign of the bad guys since the night Max had pulled one over on us. Even with the two weeks we'd "bought" coming to a close, there'd been no contact to try to get us to pay more money. It seemed too good to be true.

Who was I kidding? It was definitely too good to be true. That was why both Noah and I were constantly looking over our shoulders and the reason he held me tighter at night.

Today, we were driving down to Missoula. I was out of clothes, having never finished the apartment cleanup after Max had called me that night. If there was anything left to salvage, I wanted it. That, and Brandon was well enough to leave the hospital. It was a good thing—he was practically climbing the walls with boredom.

The apartment was the first stop, and Noah went silent when we pushed in the door.

I shoved down the immediate sadness and anger at the sight of everything that was still broken. "It was worse. I managed to do some cleaning."

"That doesn't make me feel better."

Turning, I went up on my tiptoes to kiss him quickly. "I know. But we're not staying long. At some point I need to get this cleaned all the way up and hope that I can do it enough to get some of my security deposit back."

"They wouldn't give it to you if you told them that you'd been violently burglarized?"

I took a breath. "Maybe. But having someone who was targeted like that in the building isn't a great thing for them either."

Noah looked around, and I could see thoughts on his face. He didn't say them out loud though.

"Let me just grab some clothes."

Brandon's clothes were entirely destroyed, since they'd been torn apart in the search for money. Max was enough of an asshole that he probably laughed at the idea of Brandon getting out of the hospital and having nothing to wear. At least some of my stuff had survived.

I grabbed what I could. When we stopped to pick up some stuff for Brandon, I'd pick up something too. My thoughts flickered to the fact that my underwear was all utilitarian, with the exception of that one thong Noah had seen. He didn't seem like the kind of guy that would really care if I put on fancy underwear—none of my clothes remained on once we reached the bedroom.

But the mental image of his surprise was enough to make me want it.

He was standing in the wreckage of the living room, sweeping up dirt and glass.

"Okay, I'm ready."

One more look around the place showed that he was more troubled than he was letting on.

"Noah, I'm okay."

"I know. But if you'd walked into the middle of this?"

It wasn't something I wanted to dwell on. I took the broom from him. "Come on. I still have more than enough stops without wallowing."

He caught my arm and pulled me back to him. His eyes were serious as he looked down at me. "You're allowed to be upset about this."

I avoided his gaze, looking straight through him instead. "What good does it do?"

"I know a thing or two about pushing down feelings." There was a gentle smile in his tone, but it wasn't funny.

"They're just things, Noah."

"They're not. This was your *home*. The place that you were safe."

That last word lodged in my chest, and I looked up at him again. He was my safety now. We'd said as much, but to say that out loud here? It felt like a statement deeper than I was ready for. A declaration.

Instead, I leaned into him and let him hold me. "Thank you."

These moments of silence and rest sometimes happened, and every time they did, I treasured them. Just the two of us, existing where nothing else had a place.

It was beautiful.

I didn't want to, but I pulled back. "Time to go get my brother?"

Noah nodded.

We took separate entrances into the hospital. For now, we had to keep up the charade that we weren't together and hadn't known each other the night that Noah had "bought" me. If they were still watching—and we had no proof that they weren't—then it was necessary.

Brandon looked so much better in person. His bruises and bite marks were still garish, but it was a far cry from the warmed-up death he'd looked like when I'd first gotten the call.

"Thank fuck," he said. "Can we please get out of here?"

"Yeah, in a couple of minutes."

"What are we waiting for?"

Like it was his cue, Noah walked in. It wasn't a secret

from Brandon that I'd been staying at Resting Warrior. He'd recognized I wasn't at home when I called him each day, so I'd told him the truth. Not that Noah and I were together, but that I was up there in case anything happened.

Brandon's face fell. Clearly, he hadn't been expecting another visit from any of the Resting Warrior guys. "I know I owe you for the money you lent us. Coming to collect?"

I expected Noah to bristle. To get angry. But he didn't. He simply smirked. "No. We're here to jailbreak you, get you some clothes, and then head up north."

My brother looked at me. "I'm not going up there."

"Yes, you are."

"I'd rather just go back to our apartment. Please?"

It was hard to resist that please. Small, broken, and the little brother that I'd long since thought I'd lost. "I wish I could let you," I said. "But I just came from there. I haven't been able to clean it all the way up, and it's not ready for anyone to live in."

"Aside from that." Noah's voice was gentle but firm. "Just because it's quiet doesn't mean they won't come back. They know where the apartment is, and it's the first place that they'll look. It's an unnecessary risk while you're still healing."

Brandon tensed, ready to argue, but Noah spoke again before he could. "You can have one of the cabins at Resting Warrior. No strings. No therapy or anything you don't want to do, just a place where you're safe so you can move around without being in pain. Believe me, I under-stand you want to go home. We'll try to make sure that happens sooner rather than later."

Brandon wasn't happy, but he nodded.

Noah left before us so we wouldn't be seen together

leaving, and I helped Brandon through the discharge process and outside before we met Noah in an out-of-the-way corner of a dark parking garage.

He held my hand when I slid next to him, tension in every line of his body.

Noah hated this. He didn't like that we'd lost the Riders, even though there was no way he could have known they were playing him. He was frustrated—had told me as much—that they'd gone to ground. They would just go somewhere else and start over. Idaho or Colorado or Wyoming.

If they did, there was no way to stop them.

He was good at hiding it most of the time. But right now, when we were on alert, it was in the forefront of his mind. Even though there was some other catalyst, he blamed himself for losing them, and it bothered him.

I was selfish. Because the fact that it bothered him benefitted me. He'd put all that aside and focused on me throughout the last week. And being the sole focus of Noah's attention was a heady thing. He'd let me help with the animals and drilled me until I knew all of their names.

We'd gone on snowy horseback rides and come back soaking wet from the exploration, only to warm up in the shower. Together.

Our tangled fingers were low between our legs. Brandon was already nervous about Resting Warrior. Today wasn't the day to tell him that I was . . . what was I doing with Noah? I didn't know if it could be called dating. But I'd tell him another time.

We pulled into a mall parking lot, and Noah's voice was quiet. "I'll be circling. Take your time. Call if you need me."

"I will."

Brandon groaned getting out of the truck. "Going shopping really wasn't on my list of things to do."

I shut the truck door behind me and gave him a look. "Considering most of your clothes are in shreds? You need something that doesn't have blood on it."

Not counting the hospital, this was the first time that we'd been alone in weeks. And the awkwardness was practically visible in the air. We stepped into the department store, and he started to walk away. "Not long, okay?"

"Sure."

I rubbed my chest and the tension there. I hated that it felt like this, but I didn't know how to find my way back. Because I loved my brother, but I didn't trust him.

That thought alone made me feel like shit. Hopefully we could find our way forward and I *could* trust him again. But that was going to take time. And confirmation the Riders were no longer after him or me.

Brandon glanced back toward me, and I caught the tinge of regret there. He knew we were broken too.

Blowing out a breath, I shook my head. Clothes. That's what I needed.

Not much. But I grabbed some comfortable sweats and some jeans. A few shirts. I didn't need to be fancy, especially if I was staying in Noah's house most of the time.

How I found myself in the lingerie section, I pretended not to know, as I looked over things that were made of lace that I'd never worn before.

A deep blue set caught my eye. The sheer panels fluttered down from the pretty bra and had a matching set of panties. That was perfect. One more set—black and strappy—joined the pile.

"Really?" Brandon was behind me with his own pile of clothes in his hands. But now the tension was gone, and he was smirking at me in the way that only a brother could. "You need these?"

"None of your business."

He rolled his eyes. "Yeah, okay. Because the way you two were pressed together in the truck was really subtle, Kate."

My whole body turned bright red. "I was waiting to tell you. Until you'd had a few days out of the hospital."

"I'm not going to tell you how to live your life," he said. "Clearly, I'm not a person who can judge someone's life choices."

"Brandon . . ."

He cleared his throat. "Just be careful, okay?"

"What the hell happened?" I asked. "Noah isn't here, and nothing—*nothing*—that I've seen from him or any of the Resting Warrior guys has warranted your reaction to them."

Whatever had made him feel comfortable enough to joke with me disappeared. "I don't want to talk about it."

I huffed out a breath, counting to five in my head so I didn't lose my cool. No one could get under your skin like family. "That's fine. You don't have to talk to me about it. But you *should* talk about it with someone. I'm not saying it's the therapist that they work with, but Resting Warrior has saved your life. The men there, who had no reason to help either of us, have put their *lives* on the line for both of us."

Brandon looked shaken. "What happened?"

I'd avoided telling him some of the details, glossing over them because I didn't want to upset him. And in the middle of a department store wasn't the place I wanted to tell him that his buddy Max had sold me. "Not here. Later. But when I say I trust them? I have good reason to."

"Okay." The answer wasn't sullen. It was accepting.

All of today, even arguing in the hospital, he'd been better. I'd been so wrapped up in what we had to do, I hadn't noticed until this second that he seemed so much clearer.

Like the Brandon I remembered.

"Let's pay," I said.

It took long minutes for the cashier to put everything together.

"I'll pay you back," Brandon said, voice quiet. He was embarrassed.

Reaching out, I wrapped an arm around his shoulders —or as well as I could with him being so much taller. "Don't worry about it," I whispered. "Let's take care of the debt that actually matters first before we worry about stuff like clothes, all right?"

He nodded.

I called Noah. "We're done."

The truck pulled up a second later, and I turned to my brother. "If you say anything about the lingerie, *I* will throw you back in with the dogs."

Brandon laughed louder than I'd heard in years. "Don't worry, sis. I won't tattle on you buying sexy under-wear. Trust me, I don't want to think about that at all."

"Good."

We slid our bags under the covered bed of the truck before climbing back in. Noah relaxed as soon as I was beside him, and deep in the pit of my stomach, I *loved* that.

"So, Noah," Brandon said, climbing into the truck and closing the door. I gave him a glare, but he just smiled.

Noah raised an eyebrow. "Yeah?"

"When do I get to give you the 'if you hurt my sister, I'll hurt you' talk?"

For one second, all the air in the cab went taut. Then Noah was laughing, and Brandon was laughing with him.

"After you can spar with me and win? Then you feel free."

"Deal," Brandon said.

Whatever happencd between Brandon and Resting Warrior wasn't resolved. But this was a good start. Even if it was at my expense.

The rest of the drive was much less awkward.

As we rode, I leaned my head on Noah's shoulder. Despite everything that was hanging over our heads and nipping at our heels, this was the happiest I'd ever been.

Chapter 22

Kate

Noah was somewhere in a meeting with the Resting Warrior guys, and I was sick of being in the house. Instead, I found my way to the alpaca enclosure. They were fascinating to watch.

I liked the animals. The more time I spent around them, the more comfortable I became, and the more I felt they liked me.

Movement to my right startled me, and I whirled, heart racing, to see Mara coming from the direction of the stables. All the adrenaline left me. I was way too fucking jumpy.

Resting Warrior was safe. And I *felt* safe here. But it was hard not to be jumpy when things were quiet. Too quiet. Like there was something you'd missed and it was about to jump up and bite you.

She smiled and waved.

I waved back. "Hey, Mara."

I'd met her a couple of times now. She lived on the property and took care of some small tasks. When there were clients in residence, sometimes she cooked for them. She cleaned the guest cabins and did gardening when it wasn't snowy.

"It's nice to see you," Mara said.

"You too."

Not once had I heard her talk, which Noah said was normal. But she had a pretty, musical voice, and her presence was soothing. It was easy to tell she had a good soul.

"Kate!" Liam jogged down the road toward the two of us.

Mara looked down. "I'll see you later." She continued on her way to wherever she was going.

"Bye!" I called after her.

Liam caught up with me but was looking after Mara. Naked longing rested there. Sharp and true.

He caught me looking, and his face shifted through embarrassment and vulnerability to begging me not to say anything.

I smiled. "Your secret is safe with me."

"No idea what you're talking about." He grinned. "You have some visitors."

"I do?"

"Yup," he said, popping the *p*.

I followed him. "Am I going to like these visitors?"

He laughed. "Hopefully. Either way, they're going to suck you in and not let you go."

Tonight, there was what Noah called a "family dinner." All the Resting Warrior guys, their partners, and their friends gathered in the main lodge for a big meal. Apparently, it was a thing they tried to do weekly. And if that couldn't happen, then every month. This time, I was included.

There were people on the lodge porch. Not people—women. And as soon as they saw Liam and me walking over, they waved. "Do I know them?"

Liam only laughed as a petite, curvy woman with colored streaks in her hair bounced down the stairs to meet us. "You're Kate, right?"

"Yeah," I said, bewildered.

"I'm Lena Mitchell," she said. "And that's Evelyn, Grace, and Cori. We're here to rescue you from this nest of testosterone and let you have some girl time. With sugar."

My face must have looked ridiculous. Mouth open in shock, unsure what to do with these women who were all smiling at me. I knew the three women on the porch by name. They were the wives and partners of a few of the other Resting Warrior men. Evelyn was Lucas's fiancée, Grace was Harlan's wife, and Cori was engaged to Grant. Lena, however, I didn't know. "Okay."

"Great!"

I looked at Liam. "Does Noah know?"

Lena cocked a hip. "Girl, you don't need his permission."

The sheer attitude in her pose drew a laugh from me. A real one. Okay, I liked her. "I know," I said, still laughing. "But I'd rather him know where I'm going instead of causing him to panic."

Lena's face darkened. "Why?"

Liam smiled innocently. "No reason."

She only cocked an eyebrow. "Don't worry. I'll find out."

"I'll tell Noah." Liam winked at me.

The other women came down the steps and there was a flurry of hellos and I was shuffled into the back of a classic car that sounded like it needed to be put out of its misery. "This is Bessie," Lena said. "She's my baby."

Grace and Cori slid into the back with me, and Grace said, "Just cross your fingers that *Bessie* makes it all the way into town."

"I will not tolerate any Bessie slander," Lena sang. "I can and will withhold sugar from you."

There was no slander after that. And the sugar was because Lena owned the coffee shop in town, Deja Brew. I'd passed it several times and thought that it looked really sweet, but I hadn't had the chance to go in. Evelyn worked there too.

We weren't even in town yet when the attention turned to me. "So." Evelyn turned from the front seat. "We wanted to come and meet you before the family dinner tonight because that can already be overwhelming with so many people."

"I appreciate that."

"But," Lena glanced at me in the mirror, "I won't be taking it easy on Noah for hiding you for an entire week. We could have done this days ago!"

I laughed, unsure how much all of them knew about what was happening. Evelyn looked like she knew. So did Grace. "He's had some things on his mind."

"From what Lucas said, he's had *you* on his mind." Evelyn grinned over her shoulder, and I blushed.

Last night, I hadn't had the courage to pull out the new, fancy underwear that I'd bought. Maybe tonight I would do it. It wasn't doing either of us any good buried under the rest of the clothes in my suitcase.

"I'm not sure what I'm allowed to say," I admitted.

Grace reached over and touched my hand. "We all know. At least the basics. You don't have to keep any secrets here. Nothing leaves the group."

That little tension between my shoulders relaxed.

"Okay. Well, yeah. Noah's been worried that it's not over. They could still be watching me and my brother."

"You're in good hands," Cori said as we pulled outside the coffee shop. "The boys, as we like to call them, will do anything for their women."

I froze, getting out of the car. Was that what I was? Quickly, I tried to cover my shock as Grace and Cori followed me out. But they saw it and grinned. Suddenly, I understood one of the reasons they were doing this.

They were the feminine half of Resting Warrior, and they thought I was the next member of their group. Unexpected warmth filled me. I didn't know where Noah and I were heading. Regardless, that they'd made time to reach out and spend time with me meant more than they could know.

Losing my parents so early, and being the oldest, had made me grow up fast. That meant responsibility and leadership—which didn't leave a lot of time for innocent friendships. I'd had some friends in college, but they'd dropped off when I was trying to get my business off the ground. Until Noah, I hadn't even realized how empty my life had become.

"You want coffee?" Lena called to me.

Deja Brew smelled amazing. Sugar and tea and coffee were all wrapped up with a layer of *comfort* that defied words to do it justice. "I'd love some."

"Tell her your order, and she'll never forget," Cori said. "Lena is legendary like that."

The woman herself took a bow. "Lena the Legendary has a nice ring to it." She focused on me. "Any allergies? I don't want to kill you with pastries the first time we meet."

"I'm good," I laughed. "No allergies."

My coffee order was simple, but when she set the cup

down in front of me, it was delicious. "How did you do that?"

"You'll never know," Grace said. "She's magic, and no one knows how she manages to make it that much better, but it's a gift."

I laughed along with them.

"I'm very lucky," Evelyn said, "that I get her cake-making skills for the wedding."

"Seriously," Grace said. "No regrets on mine."

I glanced at Evelyn's hand. A sparkly ring sat on her finger, and just visible under the cuff of her sleeve were scars. "When's the wedding?"

"This spring." Her smile told me everything I needed to know about how she felt. She was absolutely glowing.

Lena noticed me looking. "They're absolutely sickeningly adorable. You'll see tonight."

"It was really nice of you to do this. You didn't have to."

"The girls have to stick together," Cori said.

Finally settling with her own coffee, Lena turned her gaze on me. "Tell us everything."

Everyone turned.

"What do you want to know?"

Grace rolled her eyes. "Don't let her force you into anything you're not comfortable with. Whatever you'd like to tell us, you can. If you don't want to talk at all, that's fine too. But I imagine she's talking about you and Noah."

I smiled. The sudden, high dose of female friendship was overwhelming in the best way. "Well, the first time I saw him, I basically accused him of putting my brother in the hospital. I was angry, and I found Noah's number in my brother's pocket- while he lay unconscious in a hospital bed."

While we ate cookies—that had no freaking right to be

as good as they were—and drank all the coffee, I gave them a rundown of what happened. None of the dangerous or more graphic details seemed to faze any of them. If Evelyn had scars like that, then she had seen some shit.

They all probably had.

"So now I'm . . . staying with Noah and enjoying having kittens around."

Cori snorted into her coffee. "Yeah," she coughed. "I'm sure it's just the kittens."

I'd skipped over the sex. I wasn't quite ready to talk about that in the open yet. "What?" I asked innocently. "Is there something else I should be enjoying?"

We all dissolved into laughter at that.

"What's for dinner?" I asked.

Cori sighed dramatically. "I don't know. But it will be good. Grant volunteered to cook."

The rest of them laughed at something, and Cori glanced at me. "Before we were together, I teased Grant about not being able to cook. He very thoroughly proved me wrong."

"He very thoroughly does a lot of things to you," Lena said under her breath.

Cori blushed and busied herself with the rest of her cookie.

Grace stood. "We should probably go so we're not late."

"Who's late?"

Noah walked in the door, and all the air rushed from my lungs. Thinking about him around them, I was able to step back and look at him the way I had when I'd first seen him. Jeans that were tight enough to show off what I now knew was a perfect ass. Broad shoulders that filled out the leather jacket he was wearing. Windswept dark hair and eyes that were on mine, showing me what he felt with the intensity of his gaze.

"No one's late," Grace said. "We're just heading back to the ranch for dinner. You came all the way here to make sure she was okay?"

He laughed, still looking at me. "I came all the way here to make sure she hadn't been thrown to the wolves."

"As if we had anything but the best intentions," Evelyn said, winking at me. "Want to ride with us or him?"

"Good luck with Bessie."

The flurry of activity as they gathered their things again felt separate from the two of us. I hadn't seen him since this morning, and the way he looked at me felt like we were the only two in the room.

Finally, I broke that connection as I stood. "Thank you again for this. It really means a lot."

"Don't say it like it won't be happening again." Grace pointed at me. "Because it will. As long as you're here? You're part of the family. Hell, we like you. So you get to stay no matter what."

I couldn't wipe the smile off my face.

Noah extended his hand, and I took it, very aware of the eyes on us as we left the shop.

"My truck is around the corner," Noah said.

But we didn't make it that far. As soon as we made it out of sight of the front doors and Bessie, Noah pulled me against him, against the wall of Deja Brew, and kissed the hell out of me.

Desperation leaked through his kiss. If we weren't standing in the wind, I would have had his shirt off by now so I could feel his skin on mine. It was overwhelming, this feeling. Like I was coming home every time he touched me. Breathing was secondary to pulling him closer.

"Liam told me he'd tell you where I was."

"He did."

"Then why—"

Noah slanted his lips over mine again, silencing me. I got lost in the pleasure of lips and hands and breath. "Because I wanted to see you," he breathed when we finally pulled apart. "I wanted to do that without an audience. And I wanted to make sure you were okay."

"Why wouldn't I be?"

This close, I felt the way his breath moved. Fast, like mine. I saw the vulnerability in his eyes that he often tried to hide. "Because I love my family. But they're also a lot. Them bringing you here, it makes some assumptions. And tonight at dinner, I wanted to make sure you were comfortable before going. I'd planned to ask, but you were already here."

I slipped my hand behind his neck, pulling him back down to me. "I like being part of the family. No matter what happens."

Whatever happened with us. Or the Riders. Or my brother. This was as real a family as I'd ever had with Brandon. Or my parents. The fact that they'd pulled me in and made me feel welcome only made me love them more.

"Other than that, we don't have to think about it right now. All I want is to enjoy tonight with you."

Noah smiled as he kissed me one more time.

Chapter 23

Noah

The lodge was full of warmth and laughter before Kate and I even walked in, because the others had ended up leaving before us from Deja Brew. I hadn't been able to drag myself away from Kate's lips. Not even the cold and the wind had been able to do that.

Right now, we fit together like two pieces. As soon as she got out of my truck, she was at my side, and I had my arm around her waist, as if neither of us could imagine anything else.

I'd already asked her if she was okay with this, and she'd said yes. There was a part of me that wanted to pull her back and ask again, but nothing in her face showed any hesitance.

"You know about Jude and Lena?" I asked as we climbed the stairs.

Kate looked at me. "What? No. There's something to know?"

I laughed softly. "You'll see what I mean. Just . . . don't mention it."

Jude had his reasons for not getting involved with Lena, much as we all knew that he wanted to. A lot of those reasons were similar to—worse than—my own past. He didn't want to hurt her. But there was only so long they were going to be able to avoid it.

At least that's what I thought. If they wanted each other any more, they'd spontaneously combust.

"I'll keep an eye out," she said.

"We're here," I called, opening the door and letting Kate go through before me.

"About time," Grace said with a smirk. "Thought you guys would have beaten us here."

She was sitting on the couch with Harlan, leaning her head on his shoulder. There wasn't any tension in the embrace. Just . . . pure relief after so long at odds.

"Small detour," I said.

"I'm sure it was," Harlan said with a raised eyebrow, and Kate's cheeks turned pink.

Pulling her a fraction closer, I whispered, "If their teasing upsets you, I'm happy to drag them out back and teach them a lesson."

"I heard that," Grant said from the kitchen. "As if you'd be able to take on all of us."

"Try me." But I was smiling. This was what I loved. A real family. No matter where we'd been born or how we'd made our way here, we all belonged here together.

Brandon stood in the far corner, looking out of place.

"I'll be right back," Kate whispered, excusing herself to go talk to her brother.

I went over to the table, where Lucas sat with Evelyn on his lap. They didn't fit into the dining chair in any way, but that didn't stop them. If they were in the same room, it was a marvel if the two of them weren't touching.

A couple of weeks ago I'd thought it was a bit much, although sweet. Now I felt Kate's absence where she'd been pressed against my side like a physical ache, and all I wanted was to go over and make sure that she was real again.

Lucas, perceptive bastard that he was, caught the line of my thoughts. The corners of his eyes crinkled in amusement, and I cleared my throat before any of them could make another joke about Kate or me. "Has he been okay?" I asked softly.

"He's more skittish than some of our new intakes," Lucas answered at the same volume. "But fine. Quiet."

I nodded. For all that had happened with the Riders, Brandon wasn't someone who actually wanted trouble. I recognized the deep hurt he was trying to reconcile, and it wasn't an easy thing.

Kate reappeared at my side, taking in the way Evelyn and Lucas were entwined. Then, her gaze bounced to Grant, who was working at the counter, and Cori, who was teasing him while stealing bites of food. I caught a flash of longing there before she glanced at me and smiled, any trace of that disappearing.

Lena was sitting at the table too, while Jude was over by the bar—watching her, as he always did when we were in a group.

Kate leaned up and kissed my cheek. An excuse to whisper. "I see what you mean about them."

I laughed quietly enough that only the two of us heard.

"Grant," I called. "What's for dinner?"

"Steak, potatoes, and greens if *someone* doesn't stop stealing them."

Cori didn't look guilty in the slightest. "I can't help it that you're an amazing cook."

"I am," he said. "Don't forget it."

Liam stepped inside, shivering and grinning before he took off his coat. "So Kate survived the lion's den."

"If that's the new nickname for Deja Brew," Lena called, "then I'll take it."

"I don't know," Kate said, leaning into me. "Lion's den seems a bit harsh. I would have expected you to at least try to fight me. Maybe take my bones for a soup or something if that were the case."

Lena sighed. "Yeah, I haven't cornered the soup market yet. Unless you're willing to volunteer some bones for the broth?"

They both broke into laughter like they'd known each other for years, and I couldn't keep the smile off my face. Hope I hadn't known I needed bloomed in my stomach, the idea that not only would Kate fit in here, but that she'd *want* to be here. Everything between us so far had been rushed and circumstantial. But as the days passed with no more contact from the Riders, my mind had started to relax.

Started to think about the future, and what it meant that Kate had folded into my life so easily it seemed like she'd always been there.

"Do you want a drink?" I asked.

"Sure."

It was an effort not to get lost in those eyes. "What would you like?"

"Umm." She glanced toward the bar. "I'm a bit of a lightweight, so if you have wine or something, that's perfect."

"Coming right up."

I made a mental note to find out what kind of wine she really liked and get some for here and the house. Everyone else had their favorites here, and if she was going to stay with me for any length of time, she needed hers.

Jude inclined his head as I approached.

"Where's Daniel?" I asked.

"Phone call with a prospective client. Guess it was the only time it could happen. He'll be down shortly."

That happened sometimes. We also knew that wasn't all of it. While we all harbored our own pasts, Daniel carried guilt. And that guilt made it hard to participate in "family" activities. He'd join us, but if he didn't, none of us would give him a hard time about it.

"Wine?" Jude asked.

"Yeah. I'll get her some of whatever she likes for next time."

Jude smiled as I grabbed the bottle and poured a glass. "I'm glad that you found someone."

"We don't know where it's going yet." The immediate defensiveness I felt wasn't because I didn't *want* that with her. I did. But I didn't want to declare something and have it go up in flames. Something deep told me that it would hurt more that way.

"It's okay if you don't," Jude said quietly.

"I know." A long pause. I put the glass of wine down on the bar and looked at him. "The same goes for you."

The thin smile didn't affect anything but his mouth.

Across the kitchen, there was laughter as Grant finally started to cook the steak. I could hear the sizzle of the meat from here.

The room was so much lighter than it should be. It was always dark in the caves. And not laughter. *Screaming.* Always the screaming.

That sizzling when they hit a nerve of the man in the next room and had to cauterize it before they killed him.

Sizzle.

Sizzle.

Sizzle.

That sound and the way it faded always seemed to echo more than any sound had a right to. The screaming stopped for a little while after that. Good and bad. If they stopped screaming, that meant they were coming for me, and I couldn't take it anymore. I didn't want to break, but it was coming.

I couldn't do this.

I couldn't do this.

The door to the cell opened and that freezing wind flooded in. It was never going to end, and I needed to *fight*. I jumped at the man and got nowhere. He was holding me down and it was going to start all over again. I couldn't breathe and I was going to *kill him*—

"*Noah.*" My name was a sharp lance in my brain, clearing everything from my head.

I was still in the lodge, which had gone dead silent. Jude had me up against the wall by the bar. Because I'd tried to attack him just now.

Shame crawled up through my body like a snake, anger following on its heels. The whole room was silent, everyone looking at me. And there was no judgment there. Only concern. Which somehow made it so much worse.

Brandon was looking at me too. If nothing else, this should prove to him we understood what he felt.

Everything had been going well. I was dealing with everything. Why now? Why tonight when Kate was getting to know everyone?

She was the one that I couldn't look at. I needed to get

out of here. Because if I looked at her and saw pity . . . or *fear* . . . I would never recover.

"I'm sorry," I said to Jude, pushing his hands off me. I was halfway to the door before I could really register that I was moving.

"Noah," a voice said, and I didn't listen. "Noah!" The second one was muffled by the door closing behind me. I didn't stop. Didn't look back. I needed to get away from here.

The cold winter wind sliced through my clothes, carrying me back to that moment and threatening to drown me all over again.

Rage and pain, that's all there was in the center of my chest. I didn't want to feel this way anymore. I'd thought I was past having that kind of attack—that I was stronger than the memories. Even with everything that had happened up closer to the surface, I hadn't had a full-on blackout in years. It terrified me. I could have hurt Jude, or, if it hadn't been at dinner, Kate.

Now I understood why he didn't want to risk Lena. If I hurt her? I wouldn't be able to live with that.

Restless fire seethed under my skin. I didn't want to go back to my house where there was nothing but the gentleness of the kittens and my memories of Kate. The scent of her on my sheets. I wasn't even sure I wanted to be near the animals right now. They were so sensitive to moods, I would disturb them.

Maybe I could go to the gym and work it off.

"Noah," Kate called from behind me.

I was already a ways down the road in the direction of my house, so she was far behind me. Guilt clawed at my throat. I'd left her there with everyone, on top of what she'd just seen.

Shoving my hands in my pockets, I hunched my shoulders lower against the wind, and kept walking.

"Noah, wait." She was out of breath.

I slowed out of instinct, because even if it was just her being winded, no part of me wanted her to hurt. "You can go enjoy dinner," I said, doing my best to keep my voice gentle. "I don't want you to see me like this."

The crunch of her boots on the snow got closer. She'd brought my coat. "Like what?"

The question made me stop dodging her gaze, and none of the emotions that I'd feared were in her eyes. "Kate."

"Why would I care about seeing you like this, Noah? I don't mean that in a flippant sense. I mean that I know enough about what you've been through to understand. And I've seen my brother like this and *worse*."

I hadn't even thought about the fact that she might have seen an episode like this before.

"This isn't anything new to me, and it doesn't scare me. If you want me to leave because you need to be alone, then tell me. But if you're walking away from me right now because you're ashamed of what happened, then stop. It's not needed."

No words came. I just looked out over the ranch, trying to fit together the fractured pieces of what I felt.

"I just need to know that you're okay," she said quietly. Taking another step forward, she pushed my coat into my hands. I took it and put it on.

"I'm not."

Kate nodded. "I know. But you will be." She didn't wait, stepping close and wrapping her arms around me, pressing her face into my chest. "I don't know what it's like to have that kind of memory. But I try to understand. At the very least, I get it better than some people, having seen it firsthand. Please don't hide from me."

That cracked the hold on my mind. I wrapped myself around her, burying my face in her neck where I could feel her warmth, catch that light, fruity scent that always clung to her. "What if it had been you?"

"What do you mean?"

"If you'd been standing next to me instead of Jude? Would I have attacked you?"

Kate's fingers tightened on the small of my back. "You didn't attack him," she said. "He did that to make sure you didn't collapse or anything else."

"I could have attacked him."

Pulling back far enough to see my face, there was fire in her eyes. "You have enough to deal with. Don't take on guilt for something you didn't do just because it was one of many possibilities."

She wasn't wrong. It also wasn't that simple.

"Let me help you," she said, twisting upward in my arms until her lips met mine. "Just like the other night, let me help you forget for a little while."

"Kate."

"Noah." She placed a hand on either side of my face, just like she had when she brought me out of the cold the first time. "Look at me and *hear me* when I say this. I'm not afraid of you or your past. I wasn't afraid of you when you got into that fighting pit, and I'm not now. I see you, and I know who you are."

My whole body shuddered, the words striking deep. Home. "Okay," I said, though my voice was more of a rasp than anything else.

"Good. We're going home, and straight to bed." She took my hand and pulled me in the direction that we'd already been walking.

Home.

She'd said home.

First, she'd said she wanted to be a part of the family, and now we were going *home* together.

She'd never know what that meant to me.

Chapter 24

Kate

Noah still seemed distant as we entered the house, but he did follow me to the bedroom. I wanted him to know I was here for him. And if I couldn't get through to his mind, then I would get through to his body.

The kittens were deep asleep on the couch, curled up together. They didn't even stir as I tugged Noah up the stairs. At least we wouldn't be interrupted, adorable as they were.

I pushed him to sit on the edge of the bed, and I got my first glimmer of life from his eyes. The corner of his mouth tipped up into a smile.

"Shoes off," I ordered, and he obeyed. That was the last order I gave. I was the one that peeled off his shirt and touched him. Noah leaned into my touch, stealing a kiss against my cheek when he could, but otherwise stayed still.

He moved with me when I stripped off his pants and

tossed them aside. Once he was naked, a sudden thought stopped me. "Don't move. I'll be right back."

I pulled one of my mall purchases out of my suitcase and scampered into the bathroom. Noah's laugh followed me, which was a good sign. "I think we're past you having to go into a different room."

The blue lingerie was soft against my skin, and in the harsh light of the bathroom the color was almost too bright. But I liked it, and I thought he would too. "But if I didn't go into a different room," I said, "then I wouldn't be able to make an entrance."

Noah's face slackened when I stepped back into the bedroom, eyes darkening and fire kindling in his gaze. There was the Noah I knew. He was coming back to me.

The look he was giving me right now made this lingerie worth every penny.

When I was within reach, he caught me by the arm and pulled me into his lap, then turned and spilled me onto the bed so he was over me. "If that's the kind of entrance you make, you can do it any time you like," he breathed against my skin.

"I had a plan. Sit you on the bed, get down on my knees, and make you feel good until all you could remember was me." The hardness against my hip told me that at least part of my plan was working.

"I'd rather get to look at you like this," he said, "in *that*, than have it hidden with you on your knees."

Heat touched my cheeks. "So I'll just stay naked for that next time."

Noah laughed, low and dark. "Kate, you are full of surprises."

"Good ones?"

"Always fucking good ones," he murmured against my lips. "And this blue thing is going to drive me crazy."

"That was the point. I bought a couple of things when we were at the mall."

Curiosity lit his face even in the dim room. "There's more?"

"Maybe. If I'd known you'd like it this much, I would have bought some earlier."

"I like whatever you wear," Noah said. "And I especially like whatever you *don't* wear. I don't want you thinking you need a million pieces of lingerie. Wear this every night and I'd still be ready to tear it off you."

Hunger rolled through me. I'd brought him back here for him, but it was me who was crazy with need. I drew his face to mine, searching his eyes. "Are you okay?"

Noah grinned. "I am now."

I said nothing to that, and the grin faded into a sadder smile.

"I'm not actively being dragged into the past anymore," he said slowly. "And I feel better. That's because of you. I know sex isn't something I can rely on to chase it away every time. But it's not just the sex." His voice was whisper soft. "It's you."

My stomach flipped and dropped and did all kinds of acrobatics. It was as close to a declaration as either of us had come. And after meeting the girls, feeling what it was like to be around his family, it was on my mind.

"You don't have to be alone with it," I said. "They all wanted you to stay. They would have been happy to help you too."

"Not like this," he smirked.

I smacked his arm. "No. Not like this. But they love you."

Noah rested his forehead against mine. "I know. And I'm sorry for walking away. It's . . . not easy. What those memories do to me."

"It doesn't have to be easy. As long as you come back."

"I'm back." The words were firm. Commanding. "And I'm not thinking about that for the rest of the night."

With those words hanging in the air, Noah dropped his lips to my skin, kissing along the daring neckline of the lingerie. Across the skin of my breasts and lower, to the middle, where nothing but a ribbon rested, holding up the sheer fabric over my stomach.

It shouldn't feel different, dressed like this, but somehow it did. There was more to it. An intention in the way he brushed his lips over me. Reverent and irreverent at the same time.

He parted the sheer fabric, continuing his journey downward.

"You can still take me up on my offer, you know. I can give you—" My words cut off in a gasp. Noah's fingers brushed over the silk of the matching panties.

"I like that sound," he said, moving his fingers again, drawing a breathy moan from me.

"I was trying to say something."

He smirked, abandoning his downward path for a moment and murmuring words directly in my ear. "I know. Now I will. There is nothing I want more right now than to have my tongue buried inside you so I can taste you when you come for me. And then I'm going to trade my tongue for my cock, and you'll come again. Maybe more than once."

My whole body was on fire from his words. I swallowed. "Are you sure?"

The low vibration of his soft laughter did funny things to my insides. "I am very sure. You brought me out of my spiral. You don't need to do all the work."

I looked at him, still blushing, still heated. "If you're saying no to a blowjob because you feel guilty—"

"I'm not. Because being in your mouth is a whole different kind of heaven. I just can't get enough of the way you taste." He emphasized that last word with his tongue on my neck, and I swore. Just one touch made me blind with need.

"No more protesting," he said, licking my skin again.

I groaned. "Not from me."

By the time he made it back down my body to his destination, I was wet. And he took his sweet time stripping the fabric down my hips and off, kissing my legs as he did it.

"Now who's driving who crazy?" I said.

"Sorry, not sorry."

I couldn't help but smile. This was *my* Noah. Cocky. Confident. And about to rock my world.

Rock was right. There was no timidity in Noah as he pushed my thighs apart, consuming me with lips and teeth and tongue. It didn't matter whether he was taking control to forget or because he wanted to hear the sounds I was making. Either way I was slipping down into pleasure and the feeling of his mouth on my skin, lifting heat through me and up to the surface.

"Noah." His name was a groan on my lips. I shoved my hands into his hair and pulled him closer, lifting my hips.

He pushed them back down, and I felt his smile. That touch—that bit of dominance made me feel safe and treasured and turned me on more than I ever wanted to admit.

Circles with his tongue, fingers on my hips, I couldn't do anything but try to bring him closer with my fingers and ride the inevitable wave of pleasure.

Noah knew me now. He knew my body and what made it tick. Knew that when he curled his tongue under my clit just like that and stayed there he'd have me writhing in under a minute. Right now was no exception.

He had me reduced to nothing but moans and breath, unintelligible words. But it wasn't enough. I was still focused on him and the fact that he was doing this for me when I had planned on making *him* this mindless.

"Kate," he murmured into my skin. "Let go, beautiful."

One finger slid into me, curling upward to brush me where he could make flames erupt. Then a second one.

Beautiful.

Something about the way he'd said it. With tenderness, with the words that we hadn't said to each other, but I was starting to feel. It was more than just clinging to each other through trouble and fear. It unlocked the last bit of tension, and I let go.

The orgasm took me, racing up and through, lacing my nerves with light and pleasure, with deep, swirling happiness that couldn't be replaced by anything.

I collapsed back into my body, breathing hard, barely able to see in the aftermath. Noah crawled back up my body, brushing kisses across my stomach. My arms. My neck. Finally, my lips.

The words were on the tip of my tongue, but I held them back. I wanted to say them. Desperately. But now wasn't the time. Not after what happened at dinner. I didn't want any part of that to be connected to his past and to fear. Not to any of his doubts.

Instead, I traced the lines of his face. Made sure that his eyes were clear. Tried to shout what I was feeling in the way I looked at him. Imagined that I saw it in his eyes too.

This cloud we were floating on felt too delicate for words. Even the sound of the condom wrapper was loud and harsh before Noah came back to me, fitting our bodies together.

The way it felt like coming home . . .

I wasn't the most experienced with sex. But it had never felt like this with anyone else. We *fit*. More than just the way he filled me up physically.

"Wait," I breathed, grabbing his shoulders. "Wait."

Noah paused. "Are you okay?"

"Yes." I was more than okay. But I didn't know how to tell him that. How did you tell someone that you were careening out of control because you wanted them so much that it stole your breath? "I just want to feel you. Like this."

Noah's forehead fell against mine. "You feel incredible."

"Back at you." I couldn't keep the grin off my face. "I just—" I sucked in a breath. "Sometimes it feels overwhelming. In a good way. None of this was what I expected when I came here looking to yell at you."

He smiled in the darkness. "No, I imagine not. You were beautiful even while you were angry."

"I don't know about that."

"You were," he insisted. "Never doubt it. You are beautiful every second, but few things are as beautiful as someone fighting for the people they love."

My mind flashed to him dropping into that pit for me. He'd been beautiful then. Exquisite. I knew that wasn't what he meant, but it was still true. And it made me wonder if there was something more to it than wanting to help me and get me out alive.

One slow movement of his hips had me gasping into his mouth. Not hard or fast. Fluid and gentle. A motion that could build as we moved together.

That's what we did.

Noah captured my lips with his—there wasn't any more need for words. We rolled our hips together, gathering momentum until the flower of pleasure bloomed under my skin all over again.

This felt different. Whether it was the fact that we were both emotional or that we'd just learned each other enough, everything was *better*. This was building to something bigger than before.

Noah moved his hips, changing his angle by fractions until light burst behind my eyes. Oh, *fuck*.

"There it is." Pure, male satisfaction dripped through his voice. And he had every right. Every thrust of his cock sent a burst of sunlight through my body. Pleasure and fire and perfect, delicious sensation. I was drowning, and was happy to.

The slow and rolling rhythm that we'd started with disappeared. I couldn't get enough of him, scraping my nails down his back and curling my legs around his waist just so I could have him *closer*.

We were trying to crawl inside each other. Nothing felt like enough, and at the same time, it was too much. Everything came together at once. Pleasure raced toward me too quickly to even think about holding it back, and Noah the same. Our breaths were uneven as we clung to each other with each movement and took what we needed before the world went white.

The orgasm blew through me like a storm. We broke together, Noah's cock jerking inside me as I came. Pleasure gathered and peaked, so sharp that it stole my breath before spiraling down and dragging me back to earth and back into Noah's arms.

"Holy shit." His voice was quiet.

Neither of us moved. Like we were afraid to break the spell of what had just happened.

Our heartbeats faded back to normal. I still didn't want to move. But we had to. Noah was only gone for moments to clean himself up before he was back and touching me. Holding me. I wouldn't have it any other way. It didn't feel right to not be touching.

Noah covered us with blankets before pulling me back against his chest. "Thank you. For not letting me run away. For coming after me."

I grabbed the hand slung across my chest and pulled it tighter around my body. There was no need to tell him that he'd come after me first. More than once.

"I can't say that I'm glad about what happened to Brandon," I said. "Of course I'm not. But if it hadn't happened, then I wouldn't have met you."

His smile pressed against my neck. "I don't know. Maybe he would have found his way back here, and maybe we would have run into each other then."

"Maybe."

Noah hummed. "I'm not happy that your brother went through that. But I'm not sorry for meeting you, Kate. I never will be."

I tucked my head down further into the pillows, and the slow rhythm of Noah's heart at my back lulled me into sleep.

Chapter 25

Kate

I knew I was alone as soon as I moved.

Well, alone was relative. Noah wasn't in the bed with me, but there was the distinct sensation of something soft, furry, and warm on my chest.

Moving slowly enough that I didn't disturb him, I reached up and pet the little fuzzy body curled up asleep on me. I cracked my eyes and found orange fur. Garfield was there, and as soon as I started petting him, his purr vibrated through my chest.

A second purr sounded at my side as Salem echoed her brother. I didn't mind waking up with these adorable babies, especially with the purring. "Good morning. Did Noah put you in here with me?"

Garfield lifted his head and looked at me, sleepy green eyes blinking. He moved a little, snuggling up to my neck and curling up further. "Aren't you snuggly?"

What time was it? Where was my phone? I reached

JOSIE JADE & JANIE CROUCH

with one hand, trying not to disturb Salem, and encountered something crinkly. Huh?

I pulled the piece of paper closer, Noah's neat handwriting marching across it.

Kate,

I didn't want to wake you. I slept because of you. I'm still not used to that. I'll be back later. Need to do things around the property, and I have a meeting with our therapist, Rayne, about what happened last night. I'll be back later.

-N

I smiled. That was fine. I had work of my own to do.

The shower was nice, the kittens running back and forth between the shower curtains. I fed them and got myself breakfast before starting to do some work.

Thankfully, as close to the holidays as we were, I had fewer requests. People were home for the holidays, and some of those with summer homes were using them as holiday getaways.

I answered a few emails and set up a few of my watchers with new appointments. That was the beauty of this kind of business. There was plenty to do, but enough of it was decentralized that I could be hands-off when I needed to be. The women I contracted with were competent and trained, and I didn't have anyone who was new to the job right now. They could do their job without me holding their hands every step of the way.

I stretched on the couch, and Salem, seeing me, stretched with me. I couldn't stop my grin. They were growing fast, even in the time that I'd been staying here, lengthening and turning from tiny balls of fur into teenagers.

It was still early. Since Noah was busy, now would probably be a good time to talk to Brandon. Since we'd gotten back, he'd been keeping to himself. I was convinced that the actual program here at the ranch could help him, and after Noah's episode last night, maybe he'd see that what he was going through wasn't shameful or uncommon.

With a groan, I put on regular clothes. It was cold out, and staying under the blanket was definitely my preference. "Okay." I petted both kittens where they were sleeping on Noah's armchair. "I'll see you munchkins in a bit."

My brother was staying in the Ravalli cabin, the third one in the line of little houses that Resting Warrior had for people to rest and recover in while they worked with the animals. If that night with the dogfighting had gone differently, maybe I would have been staying in one of the little cabins too. But thinking back to last night, I was grateful for whatever instinct had made Noah take me back to his house. It wouldn't have been the same.

Approaching the house, I knocked on the door. "Brandon?"

Nothing. No answer.

"Hey, if you're sleeping, that's okay. I can come back later."

I knocked again, and there was still nothing—the kind of emptiness in response that usually meant there was no one at home. Okay, where was he then? Maybe he was over with the animals.

While I walked over, I called his phone and let it ring before it went to voicemail. He wasn't in the stables, nor was he in the kennel or with the alpacas. Maybe he was at the lodge?

His phone went to voicemail again.

Mara was walking toward the stables and I waved to her. "Hey!"

She nodded in response. No talking today, then.

"Have you seen my brother? I've been looking for him."

There was concern on her face, but she shook her head no.

"Okay, thanks. If you see him, point him in my direction."

She smiled as I passed by her on the way to the lodge. There was food and coffee—Brandon wasn't likely to use the kitchen in his cabin unless he absolutely needed to. I called him one more time but there was no answer.

I ran up the stairs and burst into the lodge, startling Daniel and Lucas at the dining table.

"Kate?"

"Have you seen my brother? He's not anywhere."

They shook their heads in unison. "No. Sorry."

I swore under my breath, mind already spinning out all the possibilities. Had he called Max to try to fix the debt problem or get back in with them? The number we had for Max was dead, but that didn't mean that Brandon didn't know another way to reach him.

Or maybe he'd just started walking without any thought about what that would make people think. "I—"

My phone vibrated in my hand, Brandon's name on the screen. "Where the hell are you?" I answered.

"That's a way to say hello."

"Yeah, well, I've just been all over the ranch looking for you and I was starting to panic. So please tell me where the hell you are so I don't *continue* to panic."

He sighed. "I'm in Missoula."

Closing my eyes, I pinched the bridge of my nose. "How are you in Missoula? And why?"

"I wanted some things from the apartment," he said. "Wanted to see if there was anything that I could salvage. And I borrowed one of the trucks from the ranch to get down here."

I turned my body away from Lucas and Daniel, lowering my voice. "Did you *ask* to borrow the truck?"

"Of course I did. Liam said I could take it. But I guess it was older or whatever. I'm here and the truck has a flat tire. Could you come pick me up?"

About a hundred different retorts were on my tongue. Why hadn't he told me he was leaving? Why hadn't he just asked me to take him? Why had he *actually* needed to go to the apartment when I'd told him that all of his clothes had been destroyed and that there was nothing left?

But those things weren't going to be helpful over the phone. We would have a long drive back for me to talk to him about all of this, and about staying at Resting Warrior to get the help that he needed.

"Yeah," I said. "I can come get you. You're at home?"

"Yes."

I stifled my sigh. "Okay. I'll let you know when I'm close."

"Sounds like that went well," Lucas said.

"I guess Liam let him borrow a truck. Which now has a flat tire. At my apartment in Missoula." Thankfully, both men had the grace not to look annoyed. "I'm really sorry."

Daniel waved a hand. "I know a guy down there who can pick it up and fix it. Can you write down your address?"

I did. "I can cover the cost."

"Don't even think about it," Lucas said. "Noah would have our heads."

"He can come for my head if he wants, but you guys don't need to spend money because my brother is continually getting himself in over his head."

There was a suppressed smirk on Daniel's face. "Let me get it taken care of, and we'll talk about it later."

I suspected that meant that they wouldn't let me pay, but we *would* have that conversation. "Speaking of Noah, I'm going to call him and leave a message. But if you see him before he gets it, can you let him know where I went? Don't want him to worry."

"Of course." Lucas inclined his head. "He's in a longer session, so it might be a bit."

"Looks like I'll have some time." They both laughed. "Thanks. See y'all later." I paused on my way out the door. "You guys think it's safe enough for me to go pick him up? With everything?"

They shared a look. "Yeah," Lucas said. "I think so. You're just going to pick him up and nothing else?"

"Right."

Daniel cleared his throat. "We've been looking, but it seems like the Riders have gone to ground. If they're still in the area, there haven't been any signs. But if you want one of us to come with you, we absolutely can."

"No, that's okay." I immediately felt paranoid. "We won't be staying down there long, and we'll come straight back."

They shared another look before smiling. "Then good luck," Daniel said. "We'll keep an eye out for Noah."

My car was at Noah's house. I grabbed everything I needed and made sure that the kittens were set for a while before heading out and pulling onto the highway.

Calling Noah, I let it go to voicemail. "Hey. I know

you're in with Rayne, but I wanted you to know what's happening. Brandon borrowed a truck from the ranch—I guess Liam gave him the okay—and went down to our apartment to get some things. Nearly gave me a heart attack when I couldn't find him."

"Now the truck has a flat tire, so I'm going to pick him up. Talked to Daniel and Lucas. They're going to take care of the truck, and they said they thought it was safe enough for me to go."

"I hope . . . I hope things are going well with Rayne. And I guess I'll see you later." Extra words were on my tongue and I held them back before I ended the call.

This drive wasn't a bad one. A little longer than I wanted to be making, but this section of countryside between Garnet Bend and Missoula was incredibly beautiful, alternating between wide open, snow-covered fields and midsized mountains.

Part of it required driving past the Bison Range, and though my drive was along the back side, I sometimes glimpsed some of the big animals. With all the snow on the ground, it was easy to spot them, the brown sticking out against the white.

Maybe I'd suggest that Brandon and I go when it was spring again. It was something we'd done when we were younger. Not too far from home, and inexpensive. The perfect entertainment for a pair of orphans. We hadn't been in years.

It was weird how driving into the city now felt . . . other. Like my mind had decided this wasn't home anymore. That the ranch was home, and that was that.

Don't get ahead of yourself, I scolded. It was a bit fast. To assume that just because Noah and I had been living together temporarily didn't mean that it wouldn't come to an end.

Did I want it to come to an end?

Alone, away from the passion and sex of last night, I could think more clearly. And no, I didn't want it to end. Whatever was between Noah and me, it was bigger than the Riders, and I wanted to see how far it went.

The fact that I'd been on the verge of telling him I loved him—was falling in love with him—was enough of a sign for me.

I made my way through town to our apartment and spotted the truck outside. It did have a flat tire. I hadn't thought that Brandon was lying, but I couldn't fathom my brother's bad luck. Of course he would take the one truck that would end up disabled, because it was exactly what he needed right now.

"Brandon?" I knocked on the door and reached for the knob. "Sorry, I said that I would call. I just got caught up in my own thoughts and forgot. But let's get going so it's not too late—"

I opened the door and froze.

Brandon was sitting on what remained of our ruined couch, staring at me, horrified. And pointing a silenced gun at him was Max.

The big man looked like he'd been hit at least once, and so did Brandon, fresh blood on his head over some of the older bruising. At the very least he'd fought back. That was good.

Cold fear poured over me like I'd been dunked in ice water.

"About time you showed up," Max said. "I've been looking for you."

"You found me," I said blankly.

Brandon swallowed. "I'm so sorry, Kate. I didn't know."

For the briefest of seconds, I closed my eyes. It hadn't

been Brandon's bad luck—it had been Max, or someone who worked for him. They'd been watching and had known I'd be the one Brandon would call. Why hadn't I taken Daniel's offer to have someone come with me? It seemed like lunacy now.

But there'd been nothing. *Nothing.* No sign of them still being here. Was there any way to have known? I didn't think so. And right now, it didn't matter.

"I didn't know," Brandon repeated.

Max rolled his eyes. "I'm glad we don't need you anymore."

The nearly silent sound of the shot cracked my world open. I screamed, and Brandon's body jerked. Red spilled out from the center of his chest. He wasn't moving. "*Brandon!*" I didn't recognize the sound of my own voice.

I needed to run. And I needed to help him. I was steps away from the door and steps from him, exactly in the middle.

I dove for my brother. The bleeding. I needed to stop the bleeding.

My indecision cost me. I took too long. Max caught me before I could make it to Brandon, an arm around my stomach, pulling me away. "No," I begged. "Let me help him. *Please.*"

"I didn't shoot him to let you save his fucking worthless life."

Max was too strong. He had a hundred pounds on me, and a gun. I fought, kicking out and trying to pull his arm off me. I scratched him, held on to the doorframe. Anything to *keep me here* because as soon as I left here, no one would know where I was.

The cold chill of metal slammed into my temple. "Fucking stop it."

I froze again, breath heaving. I could maybe survive

whatever he had planned for me. I couldn't survive a bullet to the head.

"Give me your phone." Dread pooled in my stomach, and Max pushed the barrel harder into my skin. "Now."

He snatched it from my hand as soon as I had it out of my pocket, tossing it to the floor of the apartment. Brandon was still. Covered in blood.

Tears blurred everything together, and Max marched me out of the apartment. Down the stairs to a dingy blue van. Please, God, let Noah figure things out. Let him feel that something was wrong and find me.

"Get in." Max pushed me, and I lost my balance. I hadn't recovered it when the butt of the gun crashed down, and everything went black.

Chapter 26

Noah

The cold air was bracing as I stepped out of the office. My soul felt ragged, but better. That session had been long overdue, and Rayne and I had both agreed that, for the time being, more frequent appointments would be good. So I could deal with this.

I pulled my phone from my pocket and had the feeling of suddenly reconnecting with the world again after a long absence. A couple of texts and a voicemail from Kate. It made me smile before I even heard her voice.

Brandon . . . I sighed.

That wasn't ideal, but I agreed with Lucas and Daniel. There'd been no sign of the Riders on anything we'd been monitoring. And if they weren't coming for the money that Brandon owed them, they likely weren't coming.

I was almost to my truck when my phone vibrated. Kate's name was on the screen. "Hey," I said with a smile. "I just got your voicemail. Are you on your way—"

"Noah." The sound stopped me in my tracks. That wasn't Kate. It was Brandon, and it *barely* sounded like him.

"Brandon."

"They have her." His voice was strangled. "She was here and—" An audible swallow and a groan. "She's gone. Max."

I swore. "You're injured?"

"He shot me."

"Hold on, Brandon, I'm sending help."

Every one of my senses sharpened to a honed point. Kate was in danger. They had her. They *had her*. The desperation in Max's voice as he'd demanded Kate's presence was clear in my mind as I called Missoula's emergency department. They were sending an ambulance to Brandon, and it was all I could do right now. He would be dead by the time I tried to help him. But I was still going to try. And I needed to find her.

I hopped in the truck, already dialing Daniel. "Hey, Noah. Kate told us to tell you where she was—"

"She's gone."

"I know, she went with her brother—"

I cut him off again. "*No.* Brandon just called me, bleeding out from a gunshot wound. They took her. I'm already driving. Grab gear. Grab whatever you can and follow me. I need to get to the apartment and see if there's any kind of sign. And hope that Brandon survives to see the ambulance. Maybe he can help us."

"Noah . . ." Daniel sounded devastated. "I told her she could go alone. That there wasn't anything to worry about."

Grim determination settled in my chest. "I thought the same thing when I listened to her voicemail. Worry about it later. Please, just help me save her."

Save her. Those words ripped out of me, but they felt right.

"We're on our way."

The drive to Missoula felt like nothing. Time collapsed like it was in an hourglass without anything to slow the sand. I was lucky I didn't get pulled over, pushing the limits as I was.

Nothing in Kate's parking lot looked out of the ordinary. No strange vehicles that told me the place was still being watched or signs of where she'd been taken.

But the door to the apartment was open, and there was a new mess inside. Blood and things from the paramedics who'd come for Brandon. Kate's phone was still on the floor. No other outgoing calls except for me. So they hadn't called and blackmailed her.

There was nothing here. I didn't need forensics to tell me that I wouldn't find Kate by looking around here. I needed to talk to Brandon.

The woman at the emergency room intake looked shocked when she saw me. "Brandon Tilbeck," I said. "I need to see him."

"Are you family?"

"If I don't see him right now, the only family he has left could die. No, I'm not his family, but I need to see him."

She went pale, her face strained with the struggle between what she was supposed to do and what she could see in front of her—that I was telling the truth. "Hold on."

She picked up the phone on her desk and made a call, turning away from me.

My phone buzzed. Daniel. "I'm at the hospital trying to talk to Brandon."

"We're almost there," he said. "Emergency room?"

"Yeah."

The nurse turned back to me and nodded.

"Gotta go."

She stood. "He's about to go into surgery, but his doctor wants to talk to you."

I followed through the halls to a man in a gown and mask, hands already scrubbed in. "You want to see my patient?"

"He's my girlfriend's brother. She was taken. That's how he got shot. He might know something that will help me get to her."

The doctor's eyes narrowed in the same appraising look the nurse had had only minutes before. "Okay. He's woozy, so I can't promise anything. But you can have a couple minutes."

"*Thank you*. Will he be all right?"

"Whoever shot him wasn't a great marksman. At that range, he got lucky. Can't know the extent of the damage until I actually look inside, but I'm optimistic."

Lucky. That was for damn sure. Lucky that Max hadn't made sure Brandon was dead before he left with Kate.

They handed me a gown and mask. The lights of the operating room made me squint, and I fought the vicious familiarity of things I'd just come up against in session. Brandon was wearing an oxygen mask, which a nurse pulled away.

"Brandon. It's Noah."

His eyes found mine. Woozy, just like the surgeon had said, but clear enough to recognize me. "He promised. Max. Said he'd kill us both if I didn't get her there, but we'd be fine if we did. He lied."

There was only panic on his face, and in the background, his heart monitor sped up. I needed to calm him down. "It's all right," I said. "I'm going to find her. But I need your help."

"It started coming back," he said. "Fuzzy, but where

they beat me the first time? It's near Moiese. Close to the river. Abandoned like the others. All I could think of."

It had to be enough. "I'll get her back," I promised. "You stay alive. Because if you die, you know Kate is going to resurrect you just to kill you again."

A flicker of a smile flashed across his face, but he was fading. They replaced the mask, and I stepped away. Back outside. The nurse was waiting. "Can you call me when he's out of surgery and let me know the outcome?"

"Of course." She was still pale. That tended to happen when people realized situations were, in fact, life or death.

I scribbled my name and number down for her, heading to the parking lot as Daniel pulled up. "Back out," I said. I told him the location, and Liam jumped in my truck to drive. Moiese was closer to Missoula than Garnet Bend, but it was still some distance. I needed to focus on other things. Like getting my bulletproof vest on and not freaking the fuck out.

"I'm sorry," Daniel said, after we'd ridden awhile in silence. Jude was in the backseat. Lucas and Grant were in my truck with Liam.

I looked over at him. "It's not your fault."

"I know. But one of us could have gone with her. It would have been so simple. Maybe we could have prevented this."

Taking a breath, I closed my hands into fists and then relaxed them. Again. I took a second to ground myself with my senses, like Rayne had been teaching me to do.

It would be so easy to put the blame for this on Daniel and Lucas. Of course, my mind was looking for someone to blame so I could direct my anger at anything except the sky. But it wasn't their fault. I'd thought exactly the same thing when I'd listened to her voicemail, that she would be fine to pick up her brother alone.

"And maybe Max would have put a bullet through your head the second you walked through that door," I said. "No point in gaming out what could have happened."

Daniel nodded once, noting my tone perhaps and saying nothing more. I had no room to think about anything but what was happening now and how to get her back. If we needed to have a conversation about what happened before, it was going to have to be later.

Jude tracked the location while we drove, accessing property records and satellite maps to identify the biggest abandoned property in the area Brandon had mentioned.

She wasn't here. I knew it as soon as we pulled up. Those instincts that were attuned to Kate—had been since the moment that we met—told me that she wasn't here. And I was right.

No one was here.

"There," Liam pointed. "Blood."

A dark stain smudged across the floor. Several places. There were doors open and patches of dirt with footprints. *Someone* had been here. The signs of movement were everywhere, but they were long gone now. There was no proof that Kate had ever been here or how old the blood was. It could have been before Kate was taken.

The world narrowed to a single point. My chest was going to explode. Kate's phone was in my pocket. Without it on her person, we had no way of finding her. This was the only clue that we had, and it was a dead end.

Nothing indicated they were still here. Jude had been all over anything he could find connected to Max. That phone number. That party. There was nothing. They knew how to hide their tracks. And if they did that now—

I shoved down the visceral, overwhelming fear. This was so much worse than my own pain. It was like hearing Jude being tortured all over again. Your own pain, you could control. Could regulate. When someone you cared about was in danger and there was nothing you could do to stop it?

The world took on a red tinge.

"Noah," Jude said. "We're going to find her."

"How?" My voice exploded in the abandoned quiet. "How the fuck are we going to do that?"

His face was grim. "We're going to do it," he said again. "We're going to get her back."

"You should know by now," Lucas said. "We protect the women we love."

Those words sent me reeling. Did I love Kate? The urge to say it had been popping up, but I'd held back because it was so fast. And a couple of years ago when Resting Warrior started, I would have said there was no way love happened that fast. But then I'd seen Lucas fall in love with Evelyn faster than I'd thought possible.

And the others who'd found what they needed.

True, shining resonance settled in my chest. There was no way it was anything less than that. I loved Kate.

I loved her.

Something small broke the silence, like a cry. They heard it too.

"What was that?" Grant asked.

The floor was the same kind as in the other barns. Close inspection revealed the outlines of boards to be removed. "Here," I said. "There's a pit underneath."

All of us heaved the pieces of wood off the pit, and I retched. This wasn't like the pit that I'd fought in. That one had been clean. Just a fighting pit. This one was more than that. The entire surface was stained with old blood. Maybe from hundreds of Brandons. He'd said this was where they'd beaten him.

So this wasn't *only* a fighting pit. It was a place of punishment. Possibly execution.

The sound came again. From the shadows where the boards came apart, where there was just enough space to crawl under the floor. A dog.

"Oh, fuck." I wasn't sure which of us said it.

And my heart dropped when I got close enough. It was the dog that we'd gotten a tip about. Animal control had said the dog was fine. He wasn't.

Alive, but that was about it. "We need to get him to Cori."

We'd called him Velcro when he was on the ranch because he'd shadowed whatever person was taking care of the dogs like he was stuck to their leg.

He'd been in a fight. That much was obvious. His fur was matted from his wounds, but it didn't look like he was bleeding anymore. Small favors.

Grant stepped forward. "I'll take him." Cori, his fiancée and the Garnet Bend vet, would have the best chance of saving him. The dog was a sweetheart. The fact that someone had made him fight for his life only added to the rage that was building inside me like a furnace.

I glanced at Lucas. "We checked on him. Right? Velcro was the one someone reported?"

"Yeah," he confirmed. "Animal control did a wellness check . . ."

It clicked in all of our heads at the same time. Animals came to Resting Warrior in all kinds of ways. From bad home environments where the owner had died or been arrested. From shelters that were full and saw potential in an animal to become a therapeutic companion. And even from animal control.

But someone who worked for animal control could easily funnel animals to a place like this with the right paperwork. They could falsify documents saying the dogs had been euthanized for being dangerous. On top of that, if they had people posing as adopters at local shelters and there were reports like the one that we'd gotten, it would be easy to give the all clear that the animal was fine even if it wasn't. Fuck.

"If someone in animal control—"

Lucas cut me off. "This wasn't just them. We'll figure that out. But we gave Velcro to the shelter. He was adopted. There was an application."

Of course there was. Troubled animals like Velcro needed patient owners to deal with potential triggers. And assholes like Max wanted them because they could be riled into violence more quickly than other dogs.

"If they had a fake ID, we can find out," Jude said. "But we don't have time for the shelter to pull the records, and I can't do that kind of digging here. I'll call Jenna."

Daniel nodded. Jenna Franklin was the best in the business. Jude came back with his laptop and Jenna on speaker. "Okay, I've got the shelter's records. They should really up their security."

Jude chuckled. "I don't think that animal shelters are particularly worried about data breaches, Jenna."

"Everyone should be concerned about data breaches so that the bad guys don't do exactly what we're doing in reverse." That was a point that we couldn't argue with. "So we're looking for anyone who doesn't belong?"

"That'll be helpful in case we don't find who we're looking for," Jude said. "But specifically a dog named Velcro." He glanced at me. "That's the name we gave the shelter?"

"Yeah."

"Found that," Jenna said. "Yeah, the adopter's info doesn't check out."

I shook my head. It wasn't the shelter's fault. They did what they could to make sure people were who they said they were, but if people went out of their way to get fake everything? Not much they could do.

"Here's a picture."

On the screen, a photo popped up. A mug shot. He looked familiar. I cursed. "It's the fucking bookie."

The guy who'd taken my bet and written down my phone number for Max in the first place.

"At least we know we have the right guy," Daniel muttered.

"This doesn't help us," I said. "Knowing they fraudulently adopted a dog doesn't get us any closer to finding Kate."

"No," Jenna said over the phone. "But this might. Pulled the animal control incident report you were talking about. The address on it matches some other reports over the last few months. Property is to the north. Isolated enough to match this MO."

I swallowed. "It's a long shot."

"It is," Jude acknowledged.

Everyone started moving at once. It was a long shot, but it was the only shot we had. So we were going to take it.

Chapter 27

Kate

I didn't know where I was.

My head throbbed where Max had hit me, and I was groggy enough to wonder if I'd been drugged. If I had, there was no way to know how long I'd been unconscious. I could be anywhere. There was a chance that I wasn't even in Montana anymore.

Oh God.

Terror ripped through my gut, and I tried to push it down. But it didn't work. I was just a vessel for fear right now, all of it spilling over like chills over my limbs.

For a moment I had déjà vu. Back to that moment in the park where I'd given Max the money, like I'd been in some kind of James Bond movie.

This part of the movie was far less fun.

I closed my eyes and tried to focus through the throbbing in my head.

Noah . . .

He would have gotten out of his session with Rayne and thought everything was fine with my voicemail. How long until he figured out I was gone? The sooner he knew, the sooner he would try to find me. My chest ached, imagining him finding out.

And Brandon—

I cut that thought off at the knees before the grief crushed me. When he'd deployed, I'd been prepared for the fact that I might lose him. And when he came back, I'd adjusted to the fact that I'd lost him in a different way. I didn't think I'd lose him like *this*.

Choking back emotion, I shoved it behind an iron wall. I needed to hold on and stay alive. Because Noah was coming. I knew him well enough now to know he would try. He would do everything in his power to get to me.

He'd walked into a place full of danger for a woman he barely knew. Now? Now I had no doubt he was doing whatever he could. It wasn't a guarantee, but I had to help him. Give him enough time to put anything together in order to find me.

If it wasn't enough . . . at least I'd know that I'd tried.

I wished I had talked to him. Told him the little words that had been on the tip of my tongue for days now. *I love you*. I did.

I'd been resisting saying it because it was too soon and too permanent. Just the situation dragging us closer and not the real thing. But now my heart was cracking in my chest. The thought of not seeing him again and *not* having said that? It might be the thing that broke me.

Focus, Kate. Is there anything that you can use?

I scrunched my eyes tight, bracing against the pain pounding in my skull. At first glance, it looked the same as the other abandoned buildings I'd been in for their parties.

But it wasn't the same. There were more signs of permanence here.

This was more storage than a space for fighting or pretend parties. There were cages on the far wall with dogs, like at the last place. But *way* more of them. A few larger cages housed what looked like exotic animals in the dimness. Was that a tiger?

I froze when my eyes reached the end of the line. On the bottom, in a cage, was a girl. The shape was undeniably human. If there were people in cages and not just fighting, then this was deeper and worse than I'd let myself believe.

Past the cages, a door was ajar. Beyond, people were packaging drugs. The fact that I was seeing all this—not blindfolded and no attempt on their part to hide what they were doing—didn't bode well for me.

I pushed back against the brand new wave of fear. My body understood more than my mind—there was a good chance I was going to die.

To my right, a door opened, and a man entered. Tall. Tall enough that I had to crane my neck in the chair that I was tied to. And it didn't matter that he was dressed casually in jeans and flannel. This was the real boss of the Riders. He exuded power and command in the same way the Resting Warrior guys did.

There was a gun on his hip, metal so dark it seemed to absorb what little light there was.

Max trailed behind him, and the comparison was laughable. Of course Max could be terrifying, but it was nothing compared to the cold stillness of the newcomer. This wasn't a person who panicked or begged. This was a man who made decisions with quick efficiency, and a man who regarded human life with disdain, if the woman in the cage was any indication.

A couple other guys with guns strapped to their chests stood near the walls. This was the real place then. The headquarters we thought we'd been hitting before.

The boss grabbed a chair and set it across from me a few feet away. When he sat in it, he was totally at ease. This was his turf. His gaze was locked on mine, and my heart sank. We hadn't known who was behind the Riders. It wasn't a face you could see and leave.

Noah, I thought out at the universe. *If you're able to find me, please do it.*

"Do you know why you're here?" the man asked. His voice was low and rough. Like he'd had a lifetime of smoking.

I shook my head and immediately stopped because of the pain in my head. "No. Not really." Pausing, I debated how much I should reveal about what I knew. "If it's about the money," I looked at Max, "then you had my phone number. You didn't have to *shoot my brother*."

"It's not about the money," the man said. "I told Max to find you again after he so stupidly gave you away. It was his job to take care of you. Loose ends aren't a thing that I allow in my organization. Especially when those loose ends are seen with ex-SEALs who have a reputation around these parts for fucking over people like me."

I sucked in a breath. They knew who Noah was. That changed everything. They knew he would try to get to me at all costs. Which meant there was every chance that they were setting a trap for him—for all the Resting Warrior men.

"I was going to take care of her," Max insisted. "Just thought I'd have some fun first. You don't think people would bet on her? Or to have her? She'd bring in ten times more money than her brother owed. But it won't happen again. Promise, boss. You heard her. I already took care of the brother."

"The other thing that I can't allow in my organization? Unreliable people." In a blink, he pulled the gun from his holster and shot Max in the head. I screamed out of reflex, every animal in the room suddenly loud with the unexpected sound.

His other guys barely flinched.

Max's body fell to the ground, and all I could do was stare at it.

"How rude of me," the man said, holstering the gun with one smooth motion. "We haven't even been introduced. You're Kate Tilbeck, and you can call me Simon."

I wasn't going to fucking call him anything. He'd just killed someone in front of me. I was going to be sick.

Max was awful. He'd killed my brother. Had *sold* me to Noah. Had destroyed my home and beaten my brother within an inch of his life. And still, seeing *another* person shot to death in front of me was more than I was ready for.

"Ignore him," Simon said. "He wasn't worth the air he breathed."

But I couldn't just ignore the way blood was seeping out onto the packed dirt floor.

"Look at me." The words were deadly soft. No room for argument. It was the voice of a killer. I lifted my gaze to the man across from me. "Do you know what you've done?"

"I haven't done anything," I said. "All I've done is try to protect my younger brother after your thugs put him in the hospital."

Simon frowned. "Your brother needs to learn what it means to be a man of his word. He said that he had the money, and he didn't. Therefore, he deserved the discipline he was given."

I bristled at the tone. Like Brandon had been some sort of naughty toddler instead of a young man struggling with things he never should have had to deal with in the first place.

"No, what you've done, Kate, is threaten the entire operation that I've built. My whole network has to hide because of you. Because your brother didn't have the good sense to just die, he brought you and the Boy Scouts into it.

"I don't like messes. Now I have to risk myself and everyone else to clean up the one that *you* created. I have to burn everything to the ground and make sure there's nothing to trace before we set up again. You have no *fucking* idea how much money it's going to cost me. Far more than the stupid twenty grand your brother sold his life for."

I felt hollow. I wasn't worth that to them. He'd already shown how little he considered the price of a life. I wasn't going to walk out of here alive.

"Unfortunately for you, the loose ends also include your boyfriend. And his friends. And you're going to help me get him if you want any chance of surviving."

Staring at Simon, I had the sudden urge to laugh. Did he really think it would be that easy? "Explain to me how I'm supposed to do that. You had me retrieved and knocked out. I don't even know where I am, let alone where Noah is. Besides, you seem like you're pretty good at finding people."

"What I didn't say," Simon replied, "was that I wanted you to tell me where he is. I know exactly where the Resting Warrior Ranch is. I know that Noah Scott is a deeply troubled man. So alike, him and your brother. The things they have in their past make them violent. It won't shock anyone when he falls into a flashback and kills you, and then himself."

Nausea hit me in a wave. He'd make it look that way.

"You can't make all of Resting Warrior disappear and make it look like an accident. That's not possible."

"That's my problem. Yours is going to be helping me get them here."

There was absolutely no way in fucking hell I was going to do that. If anything, I would tell Noah to run away and get out. Protect everyone at the ranch. Simon didn't think I was worth more than his organization, but I knew that my life wasn't worth *everyone* at the ranch.

"I can help you in a different way," I said quickly. "You won't have to rebuild your business. I can make that happen."

The only sign he'd heard me was a single arched eyebrow.

"It wasn't my plan to fuck up your business," I lied. "I was just trying to help my brother. But this can help you. I promise. I own a business that house-sits for people."

Simon scoffed. "House-sits?"

"Yes. People who go on vacation or people who have summer or winter homes here. There are tons of empty houses all across the state. They wouldn't be good for the fighting, but for that—" I nodded toward the open door where they were packaging what looked like cocaine. "It would be good for that. We'd clean up and make it look like no one was ever there. You'd be ghosts."

He glanced at one of the men near the door. "Look it up."

In the darkness of the room, the screen of his phone shone bright on his face. He flicked through a couple of pages and turned the screen to me. "This it?"

The home page of my website was on the screen. "Yes."

He handed the phone to Simon, and I watched him click through the website. There wasn't any positive or negative reaction from him, just assessment. Finally, he looked up and handed the phone back to his man. "Interesting."

I swallowed, not sure what interesting meant in this context.

"You seem to think you're in some kind of position to negotiate with me. I'm not sure why. Maybe because Max bargained with you when he didn't have the right. Let me set the record straight." Simon cleared his throat. "You and Noah Scott have put me in an impossible situation. The kind that can't be solved by offering me short-term stays in empty houses, as useful as that may be for someone with a business like mine.

"I'm willing to let you live if you help me take care of the problem. But you *are* going to help me fix it, whether or not that help is voluntary."

He nodded at the two guys, and they came for me. It took a minute to untie me from the chair, but there was no chance to run or gain any advantage—not that I would have made it more than a few steps.

Together they marched me across the space, and as soon as I realized where I was going, I fought. They were going to put me in a cage. With the other girl who was already there. Being tied to a chair was one thing. The cage made it so much more real. Too fucking real. I wouldn't go in there willingly.

Pain exploded through my side as the man holding me shoved me against the bars of another cage, close to a dog that was cowering against the back wall. "Stop it," he said.

"No!"

The other man had gotten the cage unlocked, and I unleashed everything I had as they pushed me down and shoved. I collided with flesh and metal. It was going to hurt later, and it didn't matter. What did bruises matter if they were going to kill me anyway?

It was too much. They were too strong, shoving me hard enough that I went flying into the back bars, dazed. It was enough time to get the cage locked, curse at me, and spit for good measure. My head ached and my vision spun.

Simon crouched down in front of the cage. "I'll give you some time to think about what kind of cooperation you want to give me. But one way or another, you are wiping this slate clean. I don't care if you're bloody and screaming to do it. Understand?"

I nodded. I did understand. I understood that he was a psychopath. But I had the sense not to say that out loud.

"Good."

He stood and walked toward the room with the drugs. "Tell them to go take care of the ranch. Whoever's there. No loose ends."

Slumping against the bars of the cage, I met the eyes of the girl in the prison next to mine. There was no more hope in her eyes. Like she'd been here long enough that she'd died inside.

I didn't think I'd live long enough for that to be me.

Chapter 28

Noah

Everyone was on their way. Even Harlan, who we'd pulled from the ranch for this. He was riding with Grant on the way back from dropping off the dog. We wanted all hands on deck. There was no way to know what the hell we were walking into.

I was driving again because I needed the focus. The feeling that I was *doing* something, because sitting and thinking about what was happening to Kate or if she was already—

No. Wasn't going there.

Daniel's phone rang. "Yeah?" I'd never seen Daniel gray in the way he was right now. Ashen. Now I understood the meaning of the expression. "When?" Pause. "Call the fire department. Right now. Do what you can and keep yourself safe. We're on our way."

He ended the call. "Pull over."

"What happened?" I guided the truck to the side of the road, Lucas following in the truck behind.

"The gate was rammed at the ranch. The lodge is on fire. The stables too. Evelyn and Grace are there, but no one else."

"Fuck," I said. "*Fuck*."

We didn't like to split up. Not when we were handling situations like this. Split, and you were weaker. But this was our home. We couldn't let it burn.

Liam was at the window, fury growing on his face with the information.

Daniel turned to me. "I'm not going to ask you not to go, but you can't go alone."

"I'll go with him," Liam said. "We need information anyway. Eyes on what we're dealing with. Call Harlan and Grant and get back to the ranch and deal with things. Just get to us when you can."

There was a pause as Daniel considered. Every second right now was precious. For Kate. And for the ranch. Liam wasn't normally the one to charge in and give orders, but he was right. Finally, Daniel pushed open the door. "Stay in contact," he said as Liam switched places with him. "And please be careful."

"Will do," I said, and gunned it. I would make up the time we'd just lost.

Liam cursed. "What the hell is happening right now?"

I pressed my lips together. I didn't know, but I also knew things that looked like coincidences rarely were. All I knew was Kate was in front of me, and my home was burning behind me, and I was stuck in the middle.

"We sure this is the right place?"

We parked. The large house on the property was just visible over the crest of a hill. From a distance, it looked abandoned. We knew better than to assume that. "Jenna is rarely wrong."

"Time to be sneaky," Liam said with a grin that didn't reach his eyes.

We were armed. Bulletproof vests in place. Binoculars, so we didn't have to get too close to know what was happening.

The sun was starting to set, but it wasn't full dark yet. There were fences and trees between us and them. It was enough cover for us to move without risking being seen. That was good, at least.

The closer we got, the less abandoned it looked. A low hill adjoined the back of the place, and Liam and I crept to the top of it, looking down. Several sheds and outbuildings were scattered behind the big house. Some looked newly constructed. It was also clear the house had been hollowed out, much like the barns they'd used before. A single tall door stood open with nothing but blackness beyond.

Three large white vans were parked behind a shed, people moving things in and out of it. We were outnumbered. By a lot. I didn't need the binoculars to tell me that.

"I'd like to get a closer look if we can," I said. "Knowing what's on the outside doesn't help much."

"Agreed," Liam said. "Meet back here, thirty minutes."

We split and went in opposite directions. This part was easy. This part, we were good at. The cameras had blind spots, and it wasn't too hard to get pressed up against one of the smaller sheds near the vans and listen.

"Seriously. Can't we just do this later?"

A laugh. "Don't let Simon hear you say that."

"He's busy. He's not going to hear me."

The man who laughed sounded serious now. "The man has ears in the walls, I swear to fuck. Stop complaining and get the next crate shut or we'll be here all night."

I peeked around the corner. The vans held familiar stacks of wooden crates. Just before the top came down on the one they were closing, I saw the guns.

One van was already half full, and the shed behind it was packed with more crates. So they were running guns. I'd thought that might be the case, but I'd hoped not. It made everything more dangerous for us, knowing that they likely had more than just pistols. They could run inside and grab whatever was available, whether that was a grenade launcher or an AK-47.

I moved back into cover and closer to the main house. The camera set on the corner of the house moved back and forth. I waited until it was pointed in the opposite direction before I ducked underneath it. From here, I could see both into the third truck and into the big door open to the main house.

The third truck was animals. Cages that were being brought out one at a time and stacked. Dogs, mostly. No surprise there. I forced myself to stay blank and focused. There wasn't room for anger right now.

Through the door into the house, there was more light, and tables with people packaging cocaine. They were stacking it into bins that were going into the second van. Everything we'd feared and every proof that we'd needed was here, and we were totally alone.

One breath in, one breath out. It was the full-on night-mare that we'd envisioned whenever we talked about these guys. As long as I got Kate out of here, I would be fine. They could keep the rest of it.

Stealth took time. I'd already used up half of my thirty minutes. I returned the way I'd come, avoiding the cameras and even crawling until I was back at the top of the hill with Liam.

"What did you see?"

"Not much," he said. "The front part of the house seems to be empty. Boarded windows. Moving cameras, but no other visible security measures."

I snorted. "Which means there definitely are some."

"Right. A few trucks on the other side. Other than that? Nothing."

I told him what I'd seen. "It's a piece of work. And it's a little strange they have so much in one place."

Liam agreed. "Probably brought it all here for streamlined transport to wherever they're moving it?"

"That's what I'm thinking."

I grabbed the binoculars and took another look at all the guys down the hill. I'd seen two with the guns. At least three with the animals. I hadn't gotten a count of the ones packaging drugs, but it looked busy. And there was this Simon person. Plus whoever was in the house that we couldn't see.

Those weren't great odds.

There was a good chance going down there right now would get me killed, but the thought didn't bother me. I would rather die than let Kate sit in that hellhole.

"What's the plan?"

Liam looked at me. "What?"

I reached down into the side pocket of my pants and found the silencer I'd placed there. "I'm going to get her."

"Noah, not yet."

"If you don't want to come—"

His hand landed on my shoulder. "Don't fucking start with me, and don't go there. You know I have your back. No matter what. If you go in, I'm coming with you. I'm just asking you to step back for a second. We can't win this.

And going in now will only get us killed. That doesn't help Kate."

Frustration itched under my skin with the need to move. I needed to get in there and get to her.

"Hear me out," Liam said quietly. "And if you don't like the plan, then we'll go in, okay?"

I didn't say anything. That was about as much as I could promise at the moment. It felt like I was the gun and my body was waiting for my mind to pull the trigger.

"It's almost dark. The others and the fire department will take care of things, and then they'll be back. We'll have more people, and better odds. Plus, darkness will help with the element of surprise. There's a reason we work as a team."

He was right, and I knew it. That didn't make it any easier.

Liam pulled his phone out of his pocket. It was Daniel. "Yeah?"

A long silence as he listened. Then his body sagged in relief. "Thank fuck. Yeah, we're here. We have a position and we'll hold it as long as we can. Just get here, okay?" He ended the call.

"It's okay?"

"Lena came, and the girls got all the animals safe. Helped the fire department get everything under control. There's damage, but it's repairable. None of the guys even got to the ranch before they were called off."

It wasn't funny, but I blew out a relieved laugh. The Resting Warrior women were warriors the same as the rest of us, proven time and time again. "Well, that's good. It won't take them as long to get here."

This time it was my phone that lit up, buzzing in my pocket. It wasn't a number that I recognized. Turning the volume down, I put it on speaker. "Hello?"

Interminable silence was on the other end of the line before I heard it. Her voice. "Noah."

My body shook, the relief of hearing her alive. After they'd shot Brandon, I'd been afraid of the worst and hadn't wanted to admit it. "Kate." By some miracle, my voice was steady. "Are you all right?"

Nothing.

"Where are you?"

She didn't answer the question. Which either meant that she wasn't all right or there was something else more important than the question.

"That doesn't matter. Tell me where you are. I'm going to come get you."

Liam looked at me, giving me a slow thumbs-up. *Don't give away where we are or that we're close.*

Finally, she spoke again. "I'm not sure."

I took a breath and closed my eyes. "Kate, let me talk to him."

Another too-full silence.

"Noah Scott." A smooth, cold voice.

"You got me."

"Not yet I don't. But I will. Kate here is very loyal. She doesn't want you to come get her, knowing that I'll kill you when you do. However, I think that we both know that you're going to come get her no matter what."

I said nothing. I wanted to keep him talking as long as possible. At this point, stringing out the time was important. Every second we could get until backup arrived was valuable.

"So I'll do you a favor and even give you a little incentive."

"I'm listening."

"I'll tell you exactly where we are." He rattled off the address we were currently looking at. "I offered Kate her life to help me bring you to me, but she said no. If you hurry, I'll let you say goodbye. Loose ends and all that."

"If you touch her—"

"It's a little late for threats, Mr. Scott. The two of you have done too much damage to have any leverage. I assume you're already familiar with our protocols. You have an hour. If you're not here, the next phone call you get won't be pleasant."

"Kate. Let me talk to her."

"No."

The line went dead.

"Fucking hell." My heart pounded in my chest, adrenaline swimming. "He's going to kill her."

"We have an hour. They'll be here by then."

He was right, but that would be cutting it very, very close. I wasn't going to risk him hurting Kate. "All right," I said. "I'll wait. But if they're not close enough in forty-five minutes, or there's any sign that she's in any more danger, I'm going in."

Liam looked at me in the dying light, studying my face. "All right. We'll go in then."

That was that. We flattened ourselves to the hill to wait as long as we could, and to pray the others drove fast.

Chapter 29

Noah

Fifty minutes passed. The others were still on their way. It was full dark, and we couldn't afford to wait anymore.

The vans behind the house had left, and new ones had taken their place. They were filling the second set now. More guns, more drugs, more animals.

A gunshot rang out, and the world seemed to freeze. My heart stopped. It hadn't been an hour yet. That wasn't Kate. It wasn't. It couldn't be.

Dread pooled in my stomach. The odds were against us, but we had to do this. "I'm sorry," I said to Liam.

"I'm fucking not. We're in this together, no matter what."

I nodded once. "Together?"

"Together."

The darkness made our second approach easy. We went down the side of the hill I'd scouted, down toward the weapons. My mind narrowed in pure focus. Air moved in and out of my lungs, and every breath drew me closer to my target.

Another gunshot, and another. What the fuck were they doing? It was a double-edged sword. Every gunshot brought a wave of fear I had to fight back, and yet every gunshot made it easier for us to approach without being heard. Covered by the noise, I took out the camera with a quiet shot before we struck.

We waited until they were carrying a crate and jumped. They didn't have time to drop the crate and draw their weapons. I clubbed one over the back of the head, and Liam matched me, taking down the other one.

The crate crashed to the ground. Nothing we could do about that sound, but we ducked inside the shed housing the guns, taking down two more surprised guys. I wasn't using deadly force if I didn't have to—I knew how to put a man down hard enough that he'd be out for a few hours.

I also knew that if the man on the phone—Simon— threatened Kate's life in front of me, I wouldn't hesitate.

Outside there was a shout. Someone discovering the crate and the guys. Bad luck that they'd noticed so soon. "Doors."

Liam and I each took a side, waiting for them to come in. They did exactly what they shouldn't have, rushing through the door without clearing the side, and two more went down, groaning.

We needed to move. We couldn't get pinned in this place. I flicked the lock as we slipped out, ensuring that it would take them a few minutes to escape if they woke. But they wouldn't.

"Noah," Liam called, and I dropped. A shot bounced off the shed where my body had been. Liam fired toward the house and covered me as we got up, moving to the main wall and circling. They knew that someone was here now. We couldn't take the back way in.

More gunshots that weren't aimed at us. The panic welling inside me was almost impossible to ignore, but I shoved it down. We were around the side of the big house now. "Front door?" I asked. "With the boarded windows, that might be the easiest place."

"Sounds good to me," Liam said, eyes darting back the way we'd come.

The sound of rattling metal in front of us gave them away. Three came around the corner, and I reacted. A shot in the knee took one down, and the next got an elbow to the face while Liam dealt with the third.

That same dangerous focus from the night I'd fought in the pit came back. But this had even more purpose. That night had been a calculated move to ensure Kate was safe. This was to save her life, and I wouldn't hold back.

Three more gunshots from the back of the house in quick succession, and then silence. There were different kinds of silence in battle. There was the silence when it was over—an empty sound that brought relief and release. And there was the silence in the center of chaos. An active sound like a withheld breath just before the storm broke.

This was that silence.

The front was clear, and everything was quiet. Too quiet. We cleared the other side of the house before approaching the front door, listening. There was nothing. Not a single sound to indicate anything out of place.

Liam motioned to me. Three fingers. Breach on three.

Three.

Two.

One.

I kicked the door open with all the force that I had and plunged inside.

Lights blinded me, and I fired low, aiming for the legs of the person in front of me. Shouts erupted, conflicting orders to shoot and the others to get us down.

I blinked my eyes clear just in time to duck a fist coming at my face, and in that time I realized that it was over. There were too many of them. Way more than we'd counted on. The hollowed-out house was overrun with them. Even at our best—as Liam and I were—we couldn't take on twenty.

But we tried.

They seemed happy to let us.

My gun was knocked from my hand, and I threw myself at the body of a giant man in front of me, taking him down to the ground. Three punches to the face, and he was unconscious. The next one fell away from me with a punch straight to his nose.

Liam's back was against mine, and we were surrounded. But they weren't shooting. If they'd wanted us dead on sight, they would have done it already. The slight relaxation in Liam's body meant he knew it too. The best chance we had now was letting them take us to the man on the phone and making sure Kate was alive.

We'd go from there.

I'd survived worse things than this, and could do it again.

They all moved at once.

A fist drove into my stomach with enough force to make me gag. Two of them had my arms, pushing me, marching me through the house, and I let them.

Everything in this building had been stripped back to the studs. It was just a shell—a staging area for whatever bullshit they had planned. Or maybe it had never made it past this stage when it'd been built.

They pulled me into a room darker than the rest, and

memory overwhelmed me. The scent of blood was thick in the air.

No. I couldn't go back there right now. I needed to be in this moment. Letting the horror wash over my mind, I accepted it and grounded myself. The dirt under my feet and the hands on my arms. The shapes in the dimness of the room.

An entirely different kind of horror hit me. There were cages on the walls, and the things in them weren't moving. Those had been the gunshots. They either didn't have room to transport the ones in here, or they'd decided that these animals weren't worth the trip to wherever they were going.

At the end of the row, something moved. Kate. Her pale hair shone even in the darkness, and she was staring straight at me, identical horror on her face.

She was in a cage.

A fucking *cage*.

Rage rose from the center of my being, down in the place where I kept it locked. The sight of the woman I loved in a cage blew the lock off the hinges.

I moved.

They never saw it coming.

Twisting, I broke the grip of the man on my left and turned, slamming my knee into the right man's balls before I drove it upward again, cracking my knee into his skull. The left man was so startled that he dropped like a stone.

Everything slowed. The next two that came at me didn't stand a chance. A knife flicked out, and I knocked it from his hand, returning the punch I'd been given straight to his gut.

Liam was fighting too, and went down. Not dead, but head bloodied from a blow. I turned back to the man coming at me. The only way to help Liam and Kate was to get through this army. And I wasn't sure if I could.

This kind of rage made me cold. Ruthless. Blood sprayed from nose and mouth as another went down.

It took three of them diving, bringing me to the ground, putting every limb I had in a lock to make me stop. And still I fought until they had me. Until they forced me to my knees, and amused laughter sucked the air out of the room.

"Right on time. I appreciate that you military men are punctual. Even if it does make you predictable." The man on the phone. "I was right. I knew you'd come for her."

I said nothing. What was there to say? He wanted me here and I'd come. And he'd put Kate in a cage. At the moment, I was fantasizing about the sound his neck would make when it snapped.

"I do like it when loose ends present themselves. It makes my job easier."

"I imagine so," I said. "And I did as you asked. So let me talk to her."

He rolled his eyes but jerked his head. The three of them didn't let me go until they threw me down in front of the cage, the barrel of a gun to the back of my neck a silent threat that if I tried to fight them again, it would be the end.

They didn't let me close enough to reach through the bars to touch her, and my whole body ached because of it. But this way, at least, I could buy us a fraction more time. The others had to be close. They *had* to be.

In the cage next to Kate, there was another girl. It was clear that she'd been here a hell of a lot longer.

"Noah." Kate looked terrified. Pale, and tears in her eyes. "I'm sorry."

"Don't," I said gently. "Don't be sorry. Never be sorry

for trying to protect your family." There was so much more that I wanted to say to her. How much I fucking loved her, and how, now that I'd realized it, a life with her was all I could think about. But these men would mock those words, and if I didn't make it out of here, she would suffer for them.

I wouldn't do that to her.

When we both made it out, I would tell her.

Simon cleared his throat, and they dragged me back, away from Kate. I couldn't see the fear in her eyes anymore, but I felt it as surely as I could feel my own heartbeat.

"I expected something more dramatic," Simon said. "After you fought to get to her."

"If anyone's dramatic, it's you." I tested their hold on me. It was solid. "All this cloak and dagger shit. You haven't even introduced yourself, Simon. I imagine that's not a name you ever want to get out. Because then you'd be in the mess, and despite the blood on the walls, I get the feeling that you don't like messes."

There he was. The man's face hardened. He was older, and the ease with which he carried himself told me he'd been doing this a long time. There were dead animals here, a dead body on the floor, a gun in his hand, and he was as relaxed as if he was having a fucking spa day.

"You're right," he said. "I don't. Which is why I don't leave loose ends."

"As long as my friends are alive, you'll never be rid of loose ends," I said. "They will find you."

"I took care of them."

"Did you?"

The flicker of uncertainty in his face was erased as he raised the gun in his hand, pressing it to my forehead. His men released me, backing off so they didn't get caught by the bullet meant to kill me. "If I didn't, I will. I'll kill them too."

I took a breath and closed my eyes. I'd been here before, but not like this. "Kate," I whispered. "Close your eyes." I wouldn't have her relive this over and over again.

Wetness sprayed over my face, the sound of a silenced shot whizzing through the room. Simon cursed, the barrel falling away from my skin. That was the chance I needed, and chaos erupted.

I knocked the gun out of his hand and lunged for it where it fell. More shots fired, and the men surrounding us dropped. Simon held his shoulder, backing toward the exit.

One of the men grabbed me from behind, and I dropped into action, twisting and firing. There was no more time for restraint. Daniel was there, and Jude. The sound echoing through the house was loud. Shots and screams and calls for surrender.

Now there were too many bodies to tell who was who, and I raised my hands, placing the gun on the floor. It wasn't just Resting Warrior—it was SWAT. And Charlie, looking grim as he strode in the back door to survey the damage.

Slowly, things stilled. Everyone in Simon's ring was dead or down. Subdued.

The new stillness only lasted for a second.

"Are you all right?" Daniel called.

"I'm fine." I was already moving.

He looked toward the cages and startled. "Get these women out of the cages first," he shouted.

No one would get Kate out of that fucking cage but me. I would tear it open if I had to. Jude intercepted me on the way, handing me bolt cutters, and I sheared off that fucking lock, practically ripping the door off the hinges before I could drag her out.

She was here. She was alive. She was in my arms. Her feet didn't even touch the floor as I carried her away from the blood and the cages. To the opposite wall, where I could press her against it and assure myself that this was real.

Kate sobbed once into my neck, fingers digging into my shirt almost as tightly as I was holding her against me. "I love you." The words were muffled, but audible. "I love you. For days I've been wanting to say it and I didn't, and then I was afraid I wouldn't get the chance."

I cut off the words with a kiss. As long as I lived, I would never get enough of her lips and the way she tasted. Sweet and fruity and absolutely fucking perfect. "I lost my mind," I said to her. "When I found out. And I knew. I love you. So fucking much."

This time the kiss was softer. Warmer. Like we weren't surrounded by death and the aftermath of all of this. I wanted us to be home. In *our* bed. It wasn't just mine anymore, and I was going to do everything I could to make sure it stayed that way.

"Brandon," I said. "He's alive."

She gasped, tears flooding her eyes. "Really?"

"He's the one who called me. On your phone. Told me what happened. He's in surgery, but the doctor felt good about it."

Kate sagged against me, leaning her head on my chest. This whole time, she'd thought he was dead, I realized. "Thank you."

I pulled her closer. As far as I was concerned, I was never letting her go again.

"Noah." Daniel's voice came from behind me, and I turned with Kate still pressed to my body. "You all right?"

"I'll have some bruises, but I'll live."

His eyes shifted to Kate. "And you?"

"I'm alive."

Daniel took a breath. "I want to apologize. If I'd gone with you, maybe this wouldn't have happened."

"You didn't know," she said quietly.

"The ranch is okay?" I asked.

He nodded.

"What happened to the ranch?" Kate asked.

I answered. "Simon sent people to burn it to the ground. I'm not sure what his plan was after that, but he clearly wanted to draw us there."

Daniel laughed. "We weren't even there when we got the call that Evelyn, Grace, Lena, and the fire department had it under control." He looked at me, amusement dancing in his eyes. "You know who made that call?"

"No."

"Mara." He laughed, joy and disbelief on his face. "It's the most that I've ever heard her speak."

Liam stood behind Daniel, and the look on his face— both stunned and proud—that was different.

"Liam has the license plates of the trucks that already left," I said. "We'll need to find those."

"I already put them on it," Liam said. "This is going to be a whole mess. Simon got away."

Of course he did. A man like that would have the survival instincts of a shark after years of being in this business. But I hadn't lied—he would be found.

We would take in as many of the animals that survived that we were able to, and get them the care that they needed. I was sure that Cori would want to look at them and treat their injuries.

Lucas entered from another room. "They hadn't moved the money yet. We'll get you yours back, Noah."

It was honestly the last thing that I was concerned about. Charlie was across the room, giving orders about how to clean this up. Between the drugs and the weapons, they would be here awhile. All I wanted to do was go home with Kate.

"Where's the girl?" Kate asked.

Daniel turned and scanned the room, eyes sharp. "We let her out. One of the SWAT members was going to wait with her until the ambulance gets here."

"You should get checked out too," I said.

"I'm fine. The only thing I have is a bump on the head. And some bruises."

"Still."

I walked with her out into the night, where red and blue lights were flashing everywhere. Kate did let them check her over, because I begged. But the other woman—who'd been in worse shape—was nowhere to be found.

"She'll be okay," the paramedic said about Kate. "Anything seems strange or you have any persistent headaches, head to the hospital."

"We will."

Kate made a face, and I smiled because we were alive, and she was able to make faces at me. Leaning close, I whispered in her ear. "Want to go home?"

"More than you know. But Brandon?"

I checked my phone. There wasn't a message from the hospital yet. "Let's call. He may not be ready for visitors until tomorrow."

"Okay," Kate said, shoulders drooping. She was exhausted. So was I. "If we can't see him, let's go home."

Chapter 30

Kate

I stared into the warmth of the fire, sprawled over Noah's chest on the couch. This was as far as we'd made it when we'd come inside, neither of us saying anything, and neither of us willing to stop touching each other for more than a few seconds.

The fact that I was here and breathing was a little unbelievable. I hadn't thought I was going to make it out of there alive. I hadn't thought Noah was going to make it out either, and the sight of him with a gun to his head was going to haunt me for a long time.

Everything seemed like a marvel now. A miracle. The scratch of his shirt on my cheek and the warmth of the fire. The tiny, wheezing snores from the kittens asleep on the armchair.

Noah's hand kept moving through my hair. Stroking. Like he couldn't believe we were alive either.

I looked up at him and startled. He had blood on his face. Everything had been so hectic that I hadn't noticed or processed it. "Blood."

His eyes flew to mine. "What?"

"You have blood on your face."

That spurred him into action. Sitting us up together, he swung me into his arms and carried me to the stairs.

"Noah, you got the shit beat out of you. Let me down."

His arms tightened around me. "Please don't ask me to do that." The words were soft and fervent. "I can't."

He took us straight into the bedroom, and then the bathroom. The time it took for us to strip and let the water warm up was the only time we came apart. And then we were skin to skin, drinking in the heat of the shower.

The cold tiles against my back made me shiver as he kissed me. Softly at first and then harder, mouth slanting over mine to make it deeper. I wanted to crawl inside the feeling of this kiss. It woke me up and made me *want* and now that we were both alive to want things, I was suddenly desperate.

"I love you," he said, moving his lips to my neck. "God, Kate. I'm never going to forget the sight of you in a cage."

I choked on a laugh. "Pretty sure that gun to your head is going to star in some nightmares."

"The second I got that call from your phone, and it was Brandon," he said, "I was so afraid of losing you. I've never felt anything like that. Torture was easy in comparison. Losing you is absolutely unthinkable to me."

The blood was still spattered his face, and I reached up to wash it off. Bruises were darkening on his skin, and now that all the adrenaline was gone, there were places on me that ached too. The bump on my head, and where I'd been grabbed and thrown. My wrists where they'd been tied.

"He wanted you, and I wasn't going to give you to

him. I knew that if you found me gone, you'd look for me. And find me." Unexpected emotion choked my words. For a moment, it overwhelmed me, and I was glad for the water running down my face so it would mask any tears.

"I'll always find you," Noah said. "Always." Then he smiled. "But let's try not to do that again."

"Yeah." I shuddered. "Yeah. Simon knows about my business now. I used it as a bargaining chip. Offering him all the empty houses since he'd lost his network. It was all I could think of."

Noah let his forehead rest against mine. "You think he'll still try to use it?"

"I don't know. Maybe."

"Then we'll tell the others. But tonight—for the rest of it—I don't want to think about anything but the two of us."

"I just have one question."

"Anything," he murmured.

"Will this make it harder for you? Your past? I would hate to be a part of that."

"No." Noah shook his head. "I don't think it will. Those memories are something I'll always struggle with. But being able to do good? Helping the animals we rescued and stopping things like guns and drugs from entering communities? Or making sure more people don't end up like Brandon? That only helps me.

"And even if it did make it worse," he said. "It wouldn't be your fault. Nothing would have stopped me from coming for you."

He kissed me again, and this wasn't easy or lazy. It was leading somewhere. We stumbled out of the shower together, barely slowing to dry off before we collapsed on the bed. It felt like so much longer than a day since he'd touched me like this. Since I'd been able to touch him.

JOSIE JADE & JANIE CROUCH

And I loved him. Now I could say it. Now I could *think* it.

Noah looked down at me, remnants of water dripping from his hair. This, yet again, felt different. Whatever we'd gone through before, we'd come through this together. And the simple act of breathing each other's air was more intimate now.

There wasn't time for slowness. I needed Noah inside me as much as I needed oxygen. He got a condom on, and we surged together. I wrapped my legs around his hips and he pushed in. Our groans were identical.

Everything felt like more. Fuller. More sensitive. The echoes of that first thrust rippled through my body, and I arched into his touch.

Noah dragged his lips over my collarbone. Over my chest. Tasting me wherever he could while I was busy pulling him closer. I needed to feel all of him, as much as humanly possible.

Every breath was in sync. Every movement. The frenzy that had brought us together rose under my skin. I poured all of that fear and desperation into him, the terror that had wrapped around me like claws when I'd thought he was about to die. I gave it all up and let myself fall into pleasure.

There was no making it last. No drawing it out. We went over the edge together, sharing breaths and moans and everything else.

And we didn't stop. One orgasm ended and we barreled toward a second. Noah drove himself into me, face buried in my neck. He whispered my name into my skin, and I found my voice.

It echoed off the walls. The second orgasm was deeper than the first. It cut me open and left nothing but the love I had for him. It was one of those moments—the kind that changed your world.

I didn't want to turn back.

Noah came with a groan, burying himself deep, the aftermath of pleasure echoing through me.

My heart pounded in my chest, sudden nerves in my stomach. I was sure that I already knew his answer, but it was still nerve-wracking saying it out loud. "Can I tell you something?"

The way we were still connected made everything that much more intense. "You can tell me anything," Noah said with a smile. "I want you to just so I can listen to the sound of your voice."

I swallowed, and when I spoke, it came out as a whisper. "I don't want to go back to Missoula." Aside from Brandon, that city no longer felt like home. Noah felt like home now. When Brandon recovered, I would do whatever it took to help him and support him. But Resting Warrior —and this man holding me—was where I wanted to be.

For a second his face froze in shock, and then he was pulling closer, rolling us so I was sprawled over his chest, smiling so wide that it had to hurt.

"I love you," he said, lips brushing mine. "I don't want you to leave. Ever. I want this to be our home. I want to wake up tangled with you every day, covered in kittens. I want to take you riding and make love to you under the open sky. I want everything with you, Kate."

Tears blurred my vision. This was everything.

Everything.

The way the world had brought us together would always be painful. The memories of today, and that fear of losing each other, wouldn't go away either. Now that I understood the possibility of being without him, I never wanted to feel it again.

Every moment spent with Noah was precious. "You couldn't get rid of me if you tried."

Running his hands up my spine, they ended up tangled in my damp hair. The smiles on our faces were mirrors of one another. "Welcome home."

We forgot about sleep entirely.

Epilogue

Kate

Christmas Morning

Salem dove beneath a piece of wrapping paper, all but disappearing into the sound of crinkles, and I laughed. Garfield was somewhere halfway up the Christmas tree. If I squinted, I could see green eyes peeking out from in-between the branches.

We'd tried to keep him from climbing up there, but it was no use. Luckily, Noah had now rigged the tree to the wall so we wouldn't wake up in the middle of the night to the sound of crashing again, hearts pounding out of our chests because we thought someone was breaking in.

Velcro—the newest addition to the family, since there was no way we could get rid of the kittens—sat beside me with his head in my lap. The sweet Jack Russell had bounced back beautifully. He remembered Noah from his time spent on the ranch and once again had made himself inseparable.

I felt lucky that he'd also fallen in love with me.

Noah appeared from the kitchen in nothing but black sweatpants, carrying matching cups of coffee, since I was pinned by the puppy. "Thank you."

"You're welcome."

The paper that Salem was playing with crinkled again, and black paws stabbed out from beneath it before retreating. It was the piece of paper that had wrapped a box with a necklace. Tanzanite—the deep violet color Noah claimed matched my eyes. The kiss I'd given him had almost ended up with us back upstairs and not down here with the animals.

Later, we would go to the lodge to exchange gifts with the rest of the Resting Warrior family, but I was happy to have a quiet day before then. I was happy the last few weeks had been quiet in general.

Everyone who'd escaped from the raid had disappeared, just like the first time we'd lost them. Those that had been caught had been cooperative, and the network that ran everything from drugs to guns was mostly dismantled. Not entirely, but it was at a severe disadvantage now.

We'd never said it was completely over, because there had been no sign of Simon. He wasn't a man who gave up. Until we knew what happened to him or where he'd gone, everyone at Resting Warrior would have it in the backs of their minds.

Especially me.

I'd told the man about my company. And now that one of my busy seasons was on the horizon, I was half expecting a call at any time saying that the cops had found him or his people in a client's home. But people were looking for him now, starting to check empty homes, whether or not they were a part of my business.

Now that we'd opened our presents to each other, there was nothing to do but relax, and that was nice.

Noah sat down on the other side of Velcro and took my hand along the back of the couch. It was a perfect chance to drink in his body, the long, lean muscles that I still couldn't get enough of, and I wasn't sure I ever would.

"Did you sleep okay?" I asked him.

I knew part of the answer. Rescuing me had made his nightmares resurface. And changed them. Now it wasn't Jude or the other captives screaming in the caves. It was me. I'd woken up to him outside with Al Pacacino more than once, face gray and haggard because of what his own mind was putting him through.

"Better than some nights."

That was true. I had my own nightmares now. And the really bad nights were the ones where we both ended up awake. More than anything, I was glad that neither of us had to face it alone.

At the same time, those experiences had helped his PTSD in other ways. Dr. Rayne was working with him, and now, she was working with me too. Resting Warrior was the perfect place to recover. Just like it was known for. At the very least, Noah slept more than when we'd first met.

Brandon was here too, and this time around he was taking on the program with determination—not planning to skip out for an easy fix to his problems. Noah working with him to take care of the animals, hoping that working with them would help my brother the same way that they helped him.

"Yeah," I said. "Me too."

"We have time to take a nap," he said with a wink. "Before we have to go over to the lodge."

"I like that idea."

"Maybe I can see how fast your gift will go."

I laughed, holding up my hand. It had been a whim. When I'd seen it, I'd known it was right. "Are you sure you like it?"

"I love it."

The black band around his wrist looked like a watch, but it wasn't. It was linked to the silver band that now rested on mine. If you tapped the faces of the watch, a light pulsed—synced to the other's heartbeat. The bands picked up the wearer's pulse and transmitted it to the other.

Both of us now needed that reassurance when we were apart. With the exception of the most isolated and desolate places in the world, they would work.

"Really?"

Noah tapped the face and watched the light pulse, a smile he wasn't even aware of on his face. "Yes."

Gently, he picked up Velcro and set him aside before pulling me over to straddle his lap. "I love being able to carry your heart with me," he said, pulling me in for a kiss.

"Me too."

I sank into him, letting him push my robe off my shoulders and kiss the pulse point at my throat. "It's like I'm doing this all the time."

"You can't say that," I breathed. "I'll be turned on every time I see your pulse."

He laughed, sucking on my skin. "You don't think that's my plan?"

My robe ended up on the floor, his fingers sliding under the hem of my camisole and up my ribs. "What's your plan for right now?"

"Christmas seduction."

"It's working."

He smiled, pulling me tight to his chest. "I love you. So much."

"I love you t—" I didn't get the words all the way out before he was off the couch and carrying me to our bedroom to show me how fast he could make my pulse race.

Acknowledgments

A very special thanks to the Calamittie Jane Publishing editing and proofreading team:

Denise Hendrickson
Susan Greenbank
Chasidy Brooks
Tesh Elborne
Marilize Roos
Lisa at Silently Correcting Your Grammar
Elizabeth at Razor Sharp Editing

Thank you for your ongoing dedication for making these romantic suspense books the best they can be.

And to the creative minds at Deranged Doctor Designs who fashioned all the covers for this series and made the books so beautiful—thank you!

About the Author (Josie Jade)

Josie Jade is the pen name of an avid romantic suspense reader who had so many stories bubbling up inside her she had to write them!

Her passion is protective heroes and books about healing…broken men and women who find love—and themselves—again.

Two truths and a lie:
- Josie lives in the mountains of Montana with her husband and three dogs, and is out skiing as much as possible
- Josie loves chocolate of all kinds—from deep & dark to painfully sweet
- Josie worked for years as an elementary school teacher before finally becoming a full time author

Josie's books will always be about fighting danger and standing shoulder-to-shoulder with the family you've chosen and the people you love.

Heroes exist. Let a Josie Jade book prove it to you.

About the Author (Janie Crouch)

"Passion that leaps right off the page." - Romantic Times Book Reviews

USA Today and Publishers Weekly bestselling author Janie Crouch writes what she loves to read: passionate romantic suspense featuring protective heroes. Her books have won multiple awards, including the Romance Writers of America's coveted Vivian® Award, the National Readers Choice Award, and the Booksellers' Best.

After a lifetime on the East Coast, and a six-year stint in Germany due to her husband's job as support for the U.S. Military, Janie has settled into her dream home in Front Range of the Colorado Rockies.

When she's not listening to the voices in her head—and even when she is—she enjoys engaging in all sorts of crazy adventures (200-mile relay races; Ironman Triathlons, treks to Mt. Everest Base Camp...), traveling, and hanging out with her four kids.

Her favorite quote: "Life is a daring adventure or nothing." ~ Helen Keller.

facebook.com/janiecrouch

amazon.com/author/janiecrouch

instagram.com/janiecrouch

bookbub.com/authors/janie-crouch

Printed in the USA
CPSIA information can be obtained
at www.ICGtesting.com
CBHW031346030824
12612CB00014B/461